Kate by the Book
and
The Mailboat

by Susan Page Davis

Mainely Romance, Book 4

Kate by the Book

Chapter 1

Kate Pierce carefully entered the due date on the computer then ran the hand-held scanner over the spine of each book as the eager children waited.

"There you are, Mrs. Sloan." She smiled as she tore off a printout for the woman who was waiting. "Those are due the twenty-eighth."

"Thank you. See you next week."

As the patrons left the children's room, librarian Marilyn Jordan approached Kate at the desk. "Two officers will be here to set up for the fingerprinting at one, and I'd like to take my lunch hour before that starts."

"Sure, go ahead," Kate said.

Marilyn went to the back room and returned with her sweater and purse. She tied a scarf over her graying dark hair. "Oh, we need to confirm with Officer Abbot that he'll be in Thursday for the toddler story hour."

Kate nodded. "I'll mention it to him."

"He's been very faithful." Marilyn headed for the door that opened onto a side street. "But I like to remind our readers. Occasionally they forget, and we end up having to fill in at the last minute."

She went out, and Kate was left in charge of the children's room of the public library. It was actually three large rooms thrown together. In the preschool area, a mother was helping her little girl choose picture books. A home schooling mother and her three elementary-age children browsed books on the Middle Ages in the nonfiction area.

Kate moved about the main room, where the desk was, returning stuffed animals to their resting places and straightening a display of books with autumn themes. The side door opened, and a woman in uniform came in carrying a briefcase. She held one side of the double door open, and a second officer entered, a soft carryall hanging from his shoulder and a cardboard box in his arms.

He smiled at Kate. "Hello. I'm Charlie Abbot, and this is Roxanne Dufour. Where should we set up for the fingerprinting?"

"Oh, well, it's a little early." Kate threw a worried glance at the clock.

"It takes us a while to set up." Officer Abbot set the box down on the nearest table. His pleasant, friendly demeanor would put the children at ease, Kate thought.

"Mrs. Jordan told me you'd be setting up over there." Kate pointed toward the nonfiction area.

"That will be fine," Officer Dufour said. Her red ponytail swung as she strode across the main room carrying the briefcase.

Charlie Abbot smiled again. "Is Marilyn Jordan in today?"

"She went to lunch," Kate said. "She asked me to confirm that you'll be reading during the toddler story hour on Thursday."

"Wouldn't miss it." He eyed her for a moment, and Kate felt her cheeks warm. She was still getting used to her new job, and having law enforcement officers hanging around was a new experience that set her nerves a little on edge.

"You new here?" he asked.

"Yes, two weeks now. My name is Kate."

"Charlie, I need you over here." Officer Dufour's peremptory tone brought a wince from Charlie, but he kept his cheerful gaze on Kate.

"Duty calls." He brushed the dark hair back from his forehead and picked up the carton.

During the next half hour, Kate waited on patrons and shelved books as the officers set up their table.

"How's it going?" she asked once as she passed them with an armful of books.

"Fine," Charlie replied with a grin. "Would you have a trashcan we could use here?"

Kate took the wastebasket from behind the desk over to him.

"Watch it," Roxanne said gruffly as Kate brushed the edge of the table where she had set out her materials.

"Sorry," Kate murmured.

She glanced at Charlie, who rolled his eyes a little.

At ten minutes to one, Roxanne approached Kate's desk. "We're all set up. Charlie says we might as well start." Her pale eyebrows were lowered, as though she disapproved of his decision to begin a few minutes early.

Kate hoped Roxanne would smile when the children had their fingerprints taken. She might be pretty if she smiled, and she would certainly be less intimidating.

Half a dozen mothers were already waiting with their kids in tow. They formed a crooked line with their children. Roxanne took each child's name, birth date, and other information from the parent, then sent them on to Charlie. He greeted each child cheerfully, sitting so that his eyes were near the level of the children's. The mothers were charmed by his friendly demeanor, and most of the little ones were excited.

Carefully, Charlie inked the fingers on each child's right hand and rolled them on a card. Then he wiped them with a paper towel and repeated the process with the left hand. He gave the mothers moist towels with which to perform a more thorough cleaning job, handed the children lollipops, and gave the cards to their moms. The process seemed to be going smoothly.

7

Kate helped the children who were finished choose a few books to take home.

Marilyn returned just after one o'clock.

"Officer Abbot says he'll be here on Thursday," Kate told her.

"Oh, good. He seems to enjoy it, and his son is in the group. Charlie makes a very exciting reader for the children. His uniform and all, you know."

"He brings his son?"

"Oh, Mrs. Abbot brings him in," Marilyn said. "Charlie gets an hour off from work to come in and read." She chuckled. "Chief Townshend did it for about six months, but I think he got tired of it, and Charlie volunteered. The children relate to him much better than they did to the chief, but I would never say that to anyone in the police department. Charlie puts so much feeling into his reading!"

When the officers closed shop an hour later, Kate was at the checkout desk. Charlie paused on his way to the door. "We fingerprinted fifty-six children," he said. "That's pretty good."

"Great." Kate looked up into his rich brown eyes. "Thanks for doing this."

Roxanne scowled at her and headed for the door with the briefcase. "Come on, Charlie. We've got paperwork to do."

Charlie grinned at Kate. "Duty calls."

She watched them go with a sudden anticipation for Thursday's toddler story hour.

***

When Kate arrived in the children's room on Thursday, Marilyn greeted her with worry etched on her face.

"Kate, I don't want to upset you," she said quietly, "but I have a feeling something odd is going on here."

Kate glanced around to be sure the early bird patrons were out of earshot. "What happened?"

"When I came in this morning, the cushions from the park bench were on the floor over in the picture book area," Marilyn said.

Kate's eyes went automatically to the child-sized park bench where two little girls sat comfortably browsing storybooks. The wooden bench had bright flowered seat and back cushions, held in place by fabric ties.

"Really?"

"Yes. I'm sure they weren't that way when I locked up at six last night," Marilyn said. "And another thing ... my candy jar in the back room was empty this morning."

"Your Tootsie Rolls?" Kate was incredulous. "It was half full yesterday. I had one on my break."

"That's what I thought," Marilyn said. "They're gone."

"Well, we don't lock the back room," Kate mused. "I suppose a child could have gone in there during the afternoon and taken them."

Marilyn frowned. "It's possible. But those cushions. Someone had to untie them to move them into the toddler room, and I'm sure they were on the bench last night. I always straighten up before I leave."

A woman was approaching the desk with her son and a stack of books, and Marilyn turned to check them out. Kate thought about the mystery as she put her jacket and purse in the cupboard and locked it. She picked up Marilyn's candy jar and looked inside. It was empty, all right.

When there was a lull in their work, she asked Marilyn, "Do you think someone was still inside when you locked up last night?"

"I can't say, but there was no one here when I came in this morning."

"Who else has keys to the children's room?"

"Just you and me and Mr. Carter, as far as I know."

"Maybe you should ask him if anyone else has a key."

"I think I will," Marilyn said. "He and I and his assistant have keys to the outside doors, but we lock the entrance to the children's area every evening so no one can come down here during the evening hours upstairs."

"Maybe you should talk to the police," Kate suggested timidly.

Marilyn nodded, as though she'd reached a decision. "I'm going up and see Mr. Carter. Can you handle things for ten minutes or so? If he thinks it's serious, I'll mention it to Charlie Abbot when he comes to read."

"Good idea." Kate smiled as a mom with two toddlers came to the desk.

When Marilyn returned, parents were bringing their toddlers in for the ten o'clock story hour. Kate estimated Charlie would have at least a dozen in his audience.

He arrived ten minutes early, and Marilyn drew him into the back room and closed the door. Kate helped the mothers and children find books to enjoy at home and kept an eye on the closed door. Five minutes later, Charlie and Marilyn came back into the main room. Marilyn handed Charlie a stack of picture books she had chosen, and he sat down in a corner of the preschool area. He glanced through the books, picking the ones that appealed to him most.

By starting time, fourteen youngsters sat eagerly in a circle on the rug around him, their mothers sitting behind them in low chairs or on the floor. As Kate shelved biographies near the side door, a woman of about fifty came in, holding the hand of a dark-haired boy of four.

"Hello, Betty. Hello, Alexander," Marilyn called. "The story hour is about to begin."

Alexander pulled away from his companion and ran for the nonfiction area.

"Alex, don't run," the woman called after him. She watched him go straight to Officer Abbot, who scooped him up in his arms.

10

So that was Charlie's son. Kate watched with interest as he spoke quietly to the little boy then set him down on the rug near his feet. The older woman waved and then went back out the door.

It grew very quiet, and Kate could hear Charlie's deep voice rising and falling as he read the first story. She chose several returned books about geographical locations and went to the shelves near the opening to the next room, where she could hear the story and glance in at the rapt youngsters while she reshelved them. The children's attention was riveted on the police officer.

Charlie's boy was now seated comfortably on his dad's lap, leaning back against Charlie's chest, where his gold badge was pinned. Kate paused, struck by the resemblance between Alexander and his father.

Brown eyes, large and lively, a few freckles across the bridge of a straight nose, and straight, dark hair. Charlie's was parted on the left, and cropped short around his ears, but Alexander's was a little longer. On top, it threatened to rebel and stick up in the back, and the part was only a memory. Adorable little guy!

Charlie glanced up as he turned a page and she looked away, aware of heat suffusing her cheeks.

Chapter 2

The rooms were so quiet during story hour that Kate finished shelving all the returned books. Marilyn came back from her talk with the head librarian and found her in the picture book section.

"Mr. Carter says no one else has a key to this area but you, me, and him. I told Charlie about it, and he says to keep an eye on things and tell him if we notice anything else odd."

Kate nodded soberly. "You be careful, Marilyn. You ought to have someone with you when you unlock in the morning and lock up at night."

"It never once occurred to me to worry," she said. "I always check to make sure everyone's out before I lock up. You don't think someone could have hidden in here all night?"

"You said there was no one here when you came in this morning, right?" Kate asked.

"I don't think so."

Kate shook her head. "I don't understand it."

"You may as well take your break now," Marilyn said. "It will be pretty quiet until the story time is over."

Kate sat at the desk and opened a newspaper she had brought with her that morning. In the local section was the weekly religion page. The bottom half was a listing of area churches. Kate perused it thoughtfully and circled two possibilities. Soon the story time was over, and she pushed the newspaper aside in preparation for an onslaught of checkouts.

When the crowd had thinned somewhat, she looked up to find Charlie and Alexander Abbot confronting her with two picture books in hand.

Kate dropped her gaze to Alexander's. "I see you like horse stories."

Alexander nodded and shrank against his father's leg.

Charlie smiled. "Kate, isn't it?"

"Yes, Kate Pierce." She took the picture books from his hand and scanned them.

"I'm afraid Betty ran off with the library card," Charlie said.

"Oh, dear, I know there's a way to circumvent that problem, so long as we know the patron." Kate punched a couple of buttons, then gave up and called for Marilyn. "Sorry," she said to Charlie as he waited.

"Not a problem."

Marilyn came to stand beside Kate. "You search by last name. Go ahead, you won't forget if you do it yourself."

Kate punched the function key for "search," then tapped in the name "Abbot."

"One T or two?" she asked nervously, aware that Charlie and Alexander were watching every stroke.

"One."

"There it is," she said with relief.

"See?" said Marilyn. "It's easy. Thanks for coming in today, Charlie." She moved back to the table where she had been working.

Kate carefully set up the due date for the books.

"You're looking at churches?" Charlie asked.

Startled, Kate looked up and saw that his eyes were on the newspaper she had left open at the side of the desk.

"Sorry," he said. "None of my business."

"Well, I am, actually," Kate said. "I've just moved here, and I've been to three different churches in the past three weeks, but I haven't found one that feels quite right yet."

"If I'm not being rude, I'd like to suggest this one," Charlie said, tapping the newspaper with his finger where she had circled a church of the denomination she was raised in.

Kate smiled. "Thanks for the recommendation. Is it your church?"

"Yes. I've been a member for ten years." He leaned over the desk and read the fine print of the newspaper notice. "That's Pastor Wilson's phone number. If you call, he or his wife would be happy to talk to you, I'm sure. If you have any questions, I mean." He smiled at her.

"Thanks. I think I'll try it. I was getting a little discouraged."

The side door opened, and the woman who had brought Alexander to the story hour came in.

"I'm sorry I'm late getting back, Charlie," she said, stepping quickly toward the officer and his son.

He glanced at his watch. "It's okay, Aunt Betty, but I do need to get back to the station."

Kate handed him the two picture books, and he gave them to his aunt. He bent low and scooped Alexander up in his arms.

"I'll see you later, buddy."

Alexander hugged his father fiercely around the neck. "Can I go with you, Daddy?"

"No, not this time." Charlie kissed him without embarrassment and put him down again on the floor. "I'll read the books with you when I get home." He turned to Kate. "Have you met my aunt, Miss Pierce?"

"No," Kate said hesitantly.

"Aunt Betty, this is Marilyn's new helper, Kate Pierce. My aunt, Betty Abbot."

"Hello," Kate said.

Betty smiled at her and nodded. "Glad to meet you. Alex and I come in often."

"I'll look for you," Kate said. "Are you coming to the puppet show Saturday? I'm working the dragon."

"That sounds like something Alex and I could do together," Charlie said. "Well, I've really got to run. See you two later." He ruffled Alex's hair, smiled at his aunt, and walked quickly out the side door.

***

Kate followed Officer Abbot's recommendation on Sunday and attended the church he'd told her about. The people were friendly, and she felt almost at home.

In the Sunday school class, she met Jill Palmer and her husband Mike. They invited Kate to sit with them during the worship service, and Kate soon found that, although Jill was eight years her senior and the mom of three lively children, they had a lot in common. After the class, when she learned Kate was a library assistant, Jill peppered her with questions.

Pastor Wilson's sermon focused on Romans 11:33, a passage Kate loved. *Oh, the depth of the riches both of the wisdom and knowledge of God! How unsearchable are his judgments, and his ways past finding out!*

She took encouragement from the words, realizing that although God's plan for her had veered sharply away from her self-generated goals, He was still in control of her life.

When the worship service ended, she said goodbye to Jill.

"We'll look for you at the library," Jill promised. "I'll bring Amy in one day this week."

As she headed for the doorway, Kate caught a glimpse of a tall man and a graying woman. Charlie Abbot went out through the double door, and she thought she saw little Alex holding on to his hand. She had forgotten the Abbots and sent up a quick prayer of thanks for Charlie's recommendation. The church might be the place God had for her now. She resolved then to return that evening.

In the entry, Sarah Wilson clasped her hand eagerly. "You're Kate, I know it," she cried.

16

"Yes, and you must be Sarah."

"I am." Sarah presented her husband, Pastor Mark Wilson, and Kate told him she appreciated his sermon that morning. The pastor was about forty, with brown hair and eyes, and glasses that gave him a studious look.

"Could you eat lunch with us?" Sarah asked. "I'd like a chance to get to know you. It will be just us and the children."

Kate accepted, and soon was in the parsonage kitchen helping Sarah and her two daughters, Heather and Deborah, prepare lunch.

"Our oldest boy, Mark Junior, is away at college," Sarah said. "He's a freshman."

She told Kate more about the family and the church as they worked. Sixteen-year-old Heather prepared the salad, while her little sister Deborah set the table.

The pastor and thirteen-year-old Jonathan came to the table when lunch was ready. Pastor Wilson asked the blessing, and they passed dishes of chicken casserole, mashed potatoes, salad, rolls and pickles.

"So you work at the library," the pastor said. "You don't have any extra time you could spend at the school library, do you?"

Kate had learned that morning that the church had a Christian day school in a nearby building. "Well, I—"

"Because we have a very small library, but we don't have a librarian right now," he went on. "One of our teachers stays after school to put books away, and I try to get all of the staff to check out books for their students, but it's too much. We need someone who could just come in for a couple of hours a day, even."

"I might be able to do that," Kate said. "I only work thirty hours weekly at the public library, and I've been looking for another part-time job." She hesitated, wondering suddenly if the pastor was seeking a volunteer.

"That would be terrific! What are your hours?"

By the time lunch had ended, Kate was engaged to appear at the school each weekday from seven to nine a.m., at minimum wage. The pastor apologized for the meager stipend, but Kate assured him she would be willing to do it for that. Finding another job that dovetailed with her library schedule would be difficult, and she would enjoy being part of the church's ministry.

"Great," Pastor Wilson said. "I'll speak to some of the school board members this evening, but I'm certain the board will approve."

"How did you hear about this church?" Sarah asked Kate.

"Well, I saw your notice in the newspaper," she said, "and one of the patrons at the library recommended it. Charlie Abbot."

"Oh, Charlie," Sarah said with a smile. "He's very nice. He's had a rough go of it, but he's a fine man."

"I was hoping to meet Mrs. Abbot at church," Kate said.

Pastor Wilson refilled his water glass. "Betty was here this morning."

"Betty?" Kate said. "Isn't she his aunt?"

"Yes, that's right. She lives with Charlie and takes care of Alexander for him while he's on duty."

"But I thought—" Kate stopped in confusion.

"Charlie's wife is deceased," Sarah said gently. "It was an auto accident, about three years ago."

"Oh, I'm so sorry. I didn't know." Kate flushed, thankful she hadn't made a thoughtless remark to Alex at the library about his mother.

***

That evening, Kate returned to the church, and was again blessed by the message. The pastor introduced her to two school board members after the service, and Jill Palmer brought her mother-in-law, Dorothy Palmer, to meet Kate.

Dorothy's warmth impressed Kate, and she felt a pang for her own mother, who had died ten years before.

"Where do you live, dear?" Dorothy asked.

"I have an apartment down in the south end of town."

Dorothy frowned. "Do you have a roommate?"

"No, it's just me."

"Well, you be careful. And if you get lonesome, you come visit me."

"That's so kind."

As she turned to make her exit, Kate came face to face with Charlie Abbot. "Hello, Kate," he said. "I'm glad you decided to visit our church."

"So am I. Thanks so much for steering me here."

He shrugged. "You probably would have tried it anyway. You had it circled. So, what did you think?"

"I like it very much," she said. "I feel as though I could get some real spiritual teaching here." She met his warm brown eyes, and suddenly felt awkward as she recalled Sarah's words. Talking to Charlie Abbot had been easy and natural before, when he was just a library reader, the father of a little boy who came there for books. Now he was a widower whose wife had died tragically, and she felt she had to choose her words carefully.

"That's great." Charlie stooped and stood up again with Alex in his arms. "Alex, do you remember Miss Pierce from the library?" he asked the boy.

Alex nodded gravely, then buried his face in his father's collar.

Kate smiled. "I hope you've enjoyed your books, Alex."

"He loves them," Charlie said. "He'll be in to get some more soon."

Chapter 3

The next morning, Kate went early to the school and was shown to the disorderly library. The small, square room had no windows. The card catalog was inadequate. Pine shelves lined all four walls, about half filled with books of all kinds. Books in boxes or piled on the floor waited to be shelved. Those in the bookcases were roughly divided into fiction, biography, literature, sports, history, science, and religion, but Kate could see that classification had been sketchy. She set eagerly to work.

At seven thirty, students began arriving at the school, and Heather Wilson poked her head inside the library.

"Good morning, Miss Pierce," she said. "I have twenty minutes before class. Could I help you?"

"You certainly could," Kate replied, thankful the pastor's daughter had offered. "I've sorted this stack of books alphabetically by authors' last names. Could you shelve them over there with the other fiction?"

Heather smiled and carried an armful to the fiction side of the room. The two worked in silence for several minutes, until two junior high girls looked in at the doorway.

"Hi," one said uncertainly.

Kate looked up. "Hello, girls. I'm Miss Pierce, and I'll be here in the library until nine every morning, if you want to check out books."

"Great," said the blonde, with a big smile.

"That's Ashley and Tracy," Heather said.

During the homeroom period, Kate had several more visitors in the library, and three teachers came by to thank her for taking on the job. At ten minutes to nine, she stopped by the office to tell the secretary she was leaving and hurried to the public library. When Marilyn was free, Kate told her about her new part-time job at the academy.

"Good for you," Marilyn said. "I'd have liked to have you here full time, but the city budget is tight. Full-time employees are so much more expensive than part-time ones."

Kate said, "I understand."

"When they make up the budget for next year, I'm going to request that your position be made full time," Marilyn said. "They probably won't give it to us, but I'm going to ask. You ought to have insurance."

"Thanks. The ten hours a week at the school will give me a little extra."

***

The next morning, when Kate arrived after her stint at the academy, Charlie Abbot was in the children's room, deep in discussion with Marilyn. Kate was immediately sidetracked to help a mother locate books on lions for her son. As they left with their finds, Kate greeted a daycare provider bringing six four-year-olds in through the side door.

Marilyn soon joined them, and Charlie left quietly by the stairs. Kate went on about her work, her curiosity piqued.

There was no opportunity to talk with Marilyn until almost noon. For a few minutes, they were the only two in the rooms, and Marilyn opened the subject.

"You saw Charlie this morning?"

"Yes," Kate admitted. "I wondered if he was here on business."

"He was. Mr. Carter called him. When I unlocked this morning, there was a damp stain on the carpet over there near the poetry shelves." She pointed, but Kate couldn't see anything unusual from where she stood.

"Also, I've been emptying the trash in both restrooms at night since the last episode. Charlie told me that might be a clue. As soon as I saw that stain, I checked, and there were dirty paper towels, a soda can, and Tootsie Roll wrappers in one of the wastebaskets."

"Sounds like our prowler isn't much for nutrition," Kate said.

"Yes. Charlie's convinced someone is coming in here at night."

"Do you think it's during the evening hours? They're open upstairs until nine, aren't they?"

"Well, the stain was still wet this morning," Marilyn said. "Charlie thought someone had spilled a soda and used some paper towels to mop it up. The towels were damp too. He thought they would have dried out overnight."

Kate frowned. "So, someone comes in here and snacks at night?"

"Maybe. And maybe sleeps on the rug."

"That's scary."

"I had some change in the desk drawer, too, from overdue fines I collected yesterday. Not much, but it's gone," Marilyn said. "Charlie took all the trash away in a bag. He'll tell us if he can make anything of it."

***

As September went on, Kate adjusted to her new routine. Her two jobs filled her days, and she began to know more and more patrons at the public library and students and staff at the school.

On Thursdays, guest readers came to the library for the story hour, and Alex and Betty Abbot were nearly always present. Jill Palmer and Amy became regulars as well, and Jill always had a word of encouragement for Kate. Marilyn continued to monitor the trash in the rest rooms and watch carefully for signs of an intruder, but no more evidence turned up.

Kate did errands and shopping on Saturdays, cleaned her apartment, and paid bills. There was never much money left over, but she was managing. On Sundays, she was at the church morning and evening, becoming acquainted with a wider circle of the members, and beginning to feel at home. Occasionally she saw the Abbots at close range before or after church, and they exchanged cheerful greetings.

The last Saturday in September, her brother came to visit her, a big boost to Kate's morale.

"I'm sorry I don't have a bed for you," she told Chad when he arrived.

"That's okay. I don't mind sleeping on the couch." The sofa had been in their parents' home, and this wouldn't be the first time Chad had stretched out on it.

Her brother had light hair and blue eyes like Kate, their mother's legacy. He was two years older than Kate. She realized how much she had missed her big brother since they'd moved out of the family home, and her grief for the loss of their parents swept over her afresh.

"How's it going financially?" she asked him, as they ate grilled cheese sandwiches in the kitchen. Rain beat on the window, keeping them from the hike they had planned that afternoon.

"Well, I pulled enough cash together to buy gas to get down here on," he said with a strained smile.

"Any special needs?" she asked.

Chad eyed her cautiously. "I don't like to ask you."

"Well, I don't have much, but if you need something ..."

"There's a fee for one of my classes. I didn't expect it. I guess I just miscalculated. I'm sorry, Kate."

"It's okay." She gave him fifty dollars and knew she'd have to get by on the groceries she had in the apartment until the following Friday, but she didn't tell him that.

"Stay over tonight and go to church with me in the morning?" she asked, handing him the cash with a smile.

"I really need to get back to school and work on my term paper."

"It's a really nice church." Disappointment shot through her. "You'd like it. You'd like Pastor Wilson too, Chad. You really ought to go to church, you know." When their parents were living, they would never miss a Sunday. She and her brother had grown up immersed in their church family.

"I know, and I want to," Chad said, "but this paper is really important."

Kate fought back the urge to argue. "All right. But come again soon, and go to church with me then."

"I'll try."

"Promise."

"All right. Two weeks from today. I can't next weekend, but I'll come in two weeks, and I'll stay over until Sunday afternoon."

She hugged him and tousled the blond locks that fell down over his forehead. "Thanks. I've really missed you."

He let out a sigh. "I wish you could go back to school."

"Maybe next year," she said, but she didn't feel optimistic. She was barely supporting herself.

"If I land a good job after graduation, I'll be paying your tuition next year," he said fiercely.

Kate smiled but knew she couldn't hold him to it. "We'll see." She had no doubt Chad loved her, and that he'd help her financially when he could. But there were no guarantees. She wouldn't stop trying to find ways to make extra money and squirrel away small amounts when she could.

Chapter 4

Children's book artist Alice Tilley was the guest reader the first week in October. The children loved her books but were a bit overwhelmed by her outlandish clothes and personality. Her loud voice startled them. She read two of her own stories, then left early.

Marilyn Jordan stepped in and read a gentle tale of a boy and his teddy bear in her soft grandmother's voice. The children settled down in their mothers' arms, some sucking their thumbs, and listened quietly.

"Well," Marilyn said to Kate when the group was gone, "I don't think we'll ask Mrs. Tilley to read to the preschoolers again."

Kate nodded. "A bit much for the little ones."

Betty and Alex approached the desk, and Betty laid three picture books down in front of Kate.

"Hello, Miss Pierce." Betty wore a black crocheted hat and carried a gold jacket. "The air's a bit nippy today."

Kate was getting to know Betty, and she appreciated the older woman's wry humor and patience with Alex. Her blue eyes always held a glint of amusement.

"Well, Alex, I see you're getting some new stories today," Kate said. "This one is brand new. You're the first boy to take it home."

Alex's eyes widened.

"His father will bring him next week," Betty said.

Kate nodded. "That's right, next week is Mr. Abbot's week to read."

"Yes, and I'll be away," Betty told her.

"Oh, having a vacation?" Marilyn asked, opening a desk drawer in search of a pen.

"Of sorts," Betty replied. "The garden club is having a tour of Longwood Gardens in Pennsylvania. We're taking a bus on Thursday and coming back Sunday."

"That sounds exciting," Kate said. She knew Betty's passion was growing irises, and her perennial gardens were said to be gorgeous from late spring to early fall. "Who's taking care of Alex?"

"Charlie is taking two days off from work so he can be home with him."

"That's nice," Kate said. "Father and son."

"Yes. He's doing it for me. Charlie's such a thoughtful boy. He knew I wanted to go, but I didn't like to ask him to let me."

"So he just offered?" Marilyn asked.

"Yes. Edna Jasper was at the house, and she asked me in front of Charlie if I was going. Well, as soon as he heard about the trip, he said, 'Of course you've got to go, Aunt Betty.' He knows I'm crazy over these things."

"That's so nice," Marilyn said. "You have a good time."

"I will, but I worry about my boys."

"You don't need to," Marilyn assured her.

"Oh, I don't know. That Roxy girl. Have you seen her? The patrol officer?"

"The redhead?" Marilyn asked. "Yes, I've seen her."

Kate said nothing, but she remembered the female officer who'd assisted Charlie in the fingerprinting. She turned away and began sorting the books on the return cart.

"She's been after him since they took her on last year as a rookie," Betty said in a confidential tone. "I didn't think

28

Charlie would be fool enough to look at her, but she keeps putting herself in his path, if you catch my drift."

"I get you," Marilyn said. "Charlie's levelheaded, though. And he'll be spending the whole weekend with Alex. I don't think you need to fret."

Kate smiled at Alex, who stood somberly waiting for his aunt. She took an armful of books to the science area, at the far end of the non-fiction room, where she could no longer hear the conversation.

***

Kate began attending a church membership class during the Sunday school hour, with Pastor Wilson leading it. The class met in the pastor's study. Bill and Felicia Wishart had recently moved to the area. Bill taught wood shop at the public high school, and Felicia was seeking part-time work. Their daughter, Tara, was a high school junior, and the Wisharts had enrolled her at the academy. The three of them joined Kate in the membership class.

When the first session was over, she went into the auditorium to find it three-quarters full. She hesitated in the aisle, looking for a seat. There was one halfway back, next to Betty Abbot—but, no, Alex and Charlie were sitting beside Betty. She wouldn't want anyone at church to think she was placing herself in Charlie's path. She found another spot farther back.

***

On Thursday, Kate hurried from the school to the library to help Marilyn set up for the preschool story hour. Charlie and Alex were coming down the steps from the main reading room when she entered the children's room by the side door.

"Hello, Kate," Charlie called with a smile. He was wearing jeans and had a checked shirt under his black jacket.

"Good morning. Hello, Alex." Kate hurried to the back room to leave her things, then arranged the chairs while Marilyn talked to Charlie, pointing out several books he might want to read from.

Alex approached her, walking slowly and shooting shy glances her way.

"Would you like to help me, Alex?" Kate asked.

The little boy nodded solemnly.

"Here, why don't you push this chair over there, so one of the moms can use it?"

Alex grasped the back of the sturdy oak chair and pulled it ponderously across the rug.

"Did Aunt Betty go on the bus today?" Kate asked.

He stood up straight and nodded.

Kate smiled at him. Slowly, he smiled back, a sweet, sincere smile. Kate felt that he didn't give them to just anyone.

"Are you and Daddy having fun today?"

He nodded, still smiling, then said in a very grownup voice, "Daddy isn't working today. We're going to the park."

"Really?" It was the first time he had spoken since entering the room, and Kate felt she had accomplished something fine. "That sounds like fun. What will you do there?"

"Swing and slide and crawl."

"Crawl?"

"There's a tunnel he likes to crawl through," Charlie said behind her.

Kate turned around quickly.

"Didn't mean to startle you," he said.

"It's all right. I just—Alex was telling me you are going to the park."

"That's good," Charlie said. "He's doesn't talk to a lot of people."

He stood looking at her for a moment, and Kate cast about for something to say, feeling embarrassed as he continued to watch her.

"What are you reading today?" she asked, stammering just a little.

"Dog stories," Charlie said. "Really simple ones, with nice pictures."

She bent down to Alex's level and said, "Do you like dogs, Alex?"

He nodded. "We don't have one."

"Aunt Betty's not a dog person," Charlie explained.

"I like dogs," Kate told Alex, "but I'm not allowed to have one in my apartment."

"Too bad," Alex said sincerely.

"Yes. When I was little I had a collie."

"What was his name?" Alex asked.

"Betsy. She was a girl. I named her for a character in a book I liked."

Kate stood up. A mother with two toddlers was coming slowly down the stairs for story hour. "Have fun at the park today," she said.

"Thanks," said Charlie, and Alex smiled. Charlie sat down, placing the pile of books on the floor beside him, and unzipped Alex's jacket.

Kate went back to shelving and checking out books, but she went close to the reading area when she got a chance, so she could hear Charlie's animated reading and the children's delighted laughter.

As usual, the checkout desk was busy when the story hour was over. Charlie lingered with Alex, acting out a story with the stuffed animals Marilyn kept in plentiful supply. When Kate glanced toward them, she wondered if it was a happy story. Father and son looked very grave as they made the animals talk, and Alex seemed to take even his play time seriously.

31

When most of the others had gone, the two came to the desk with the books they had selected. Kate took them with a smile and began the now routine process of checking them out.

"Kate," Charlie said, "I was wondering if—are you ever free in the afternoon?"

Kate caught her breath. She hadn't allowed herself to think in that direction. "Sometimes. Today I'm leaving early, because I need to come in for a couple of hours on Saturday for the puppet show."

"Oh, yes, the puppets," said Charlie. "The dragon was excellent last time we were here. Not *too* fierce."

"That's very kind of you," she said. "I'm being promoted to squirrel this time. I'll actually have lines."

"We've got to come see it." Charlie looked down at Alex. "Don't you think so, buddy?"

"Yes," said Alex soberly.

"So ... would you like to go to the park with us today?" Charlie asked.

Kate looked from him to Alex. She wanted to accept, but she wondered how Alex would feel about it.

Alex's head went up and down slowly. "Please," he said.

Kate smiled. "That's such a nice invitation. When are you going?"

"We're flexible," Charlie said grandly. "You name the time."

"Well, I'll be done here at two," Kate said cautiously.

"Great. We'll come back and get you at two."

She started to object but smiled instead. "All right."

* * *

For the next three hours, Kate was on edge. Instead of eating when Marilyn released her for a half hour's lunch, she raced to her apartment and changed from her dress into a sweater and nice pants, then drove straight back to the library. She ate a granola bar as she walked across the parking lot and called it lunch.

She waited on mothers and helped a daycare owner pick out a stack of Halloween-themed books, then checked them all out. She located a biography of John Adams for a home-schooled boy, found books on Columbus for his mother, and Richard Scarry stories for his younger sister. Always, Kate's eye returned to the wall clock.

At two o'clock, Charlie and Alex came in the side door.

"Well, Charlie," Marilyn said cheerfully, looking up from where she was putting Mylar covers on new books. "Are you and Alex back for more books already?"

"No," said Charlie, "actually, we're back for Miss Pierce. If you can spare her, that is."

"Oh, well, yes, it is time for her to go." Marilyn looked a little unsettled as Kate went for her jacket and purse.

When she returned to the main room, Charlie was telling Marilyn, "She's determined to win the best of show next time, and she's already planning her iris entry. She's adamant Milton will never beat her again."

Marilyn laughed. "Betty usually gets what she wants."

"Well, she wanted that ribbon, and I'm not sure she'll forgive Milton, but she admits his iris were superb this year." He turned and smiled at Kate. "All set?"

"Yes, thank you."

Charlie turned back to Marilyn for a moment. "No more problems here?" he asked quietly.

"No, nothing I've detected."

"And you're sure there's not an extra key to the door at the top of the stairs?"

"The key I gave to Kate last month was the extra. Mr. Carter assures me there are no others, and the lock on the side door was changed last summer. We've accounted for all of those keys too."

"Where was the extra key before you gave it to Kate?" he asked.

"In the top desk drawer. It stayed there for months."

"And no one can get in here without a key, once you lock up."

"That's right."

Charlie nodded. "I checked the ceiling and the ventilation system. I couldn't find any way someone could get in, other than that side door, the door at the top of the stairs, and the door in the back room that comes out in the parking lot."

"And we always keep the back door locked," Marilyn said. "It's more of an emergency exit."

"Well, stay alert. I hope there's no more to it."

"Thanks, Charlie." Marilyn smiled at Kate. "I'll see you tomorrow."

Charlie grasped Alex's hand, and they went out the side door into bright sunlight.

"Another beautiful day." Charlie nodded toward the Concourse. "My truck's over here."

They crossed the street and walked a few steps to the lot where his green pickup was parked between a minivan and a silver Camaro. He took his key fob from his jacket pocket and unlocked the truck's doors.

"Your chariot awaits." He held the door open.

Kate climbed in, and Charlie carried Alex around to the driver's side. He placed the boy on the seat between them and fastened the seat belt around Alex.

"Now the park?" Alex asked him solemnly.

"Now the park," said Charlie.

Alex smiled.

Charlie drove to the park on North Street, and Kate's mild nerves began to fade, until she felt carefree. They got out and approached the playground with Alex holding tightly to his father's hand, his eyes wide. Two women were pushing toddlers in baby swings, and three little girls were climbing on the wooden apparatus and scooting down the big slide. The foliage had peaked, and crumpled oak and maple leaves rustled along the ground and under the climbing platforms.

Alex stopped, and Charlie stopped, too, standing motionless while Alex looked at all the playground equipment. Kate tried to imagine the excitement the little boy must feel. The park she'd lived nearest when she was a child hadn't had a playground this extensive, just a few swings, a slide, and a metal jungle gym. Here there were ladders and decks and rings, swings and seesaws. A hundred children might easily use the equipment at once.

Alex pulled at Charlie's hand and led him to the tunnel, which snaked under some of the platforms. Charlie threw an apologetic glance over his shoulder at Kate.

She found a place to sit on the edge of one of the wooden platforms and watched Alex crawl into the plastic tunnel and come out the far end, joy written on his face. Charlie was waiting for him, and he swung Alex up into his arms and held him close for a moment.

"Again?" he asked, and Alex nodded vigorously. Charlie put the boy down, and Alex dived into the tunnel. Charlie jogged the few steps to the other end and met him as he scrambled out at Kate's feet. Alex and Charlie shared a laugh, and Kate laughed too. She had never seen the two of them look so happy. Alex's expression of joy was a treasure to hold in her memory, so different from the solemn face he usually wore.

Chapter 5

Alex turned and looked thoughtfully at the smaller slide. There were no other children on it. He walked slowly toward the steps, looking back toward his father. Charlie nodded and positioned himself at the bottom of the slide. Alex came tumbling down, giving a happy little squeal as he landed in the sand and dry leaves at Charlie's feet.

Before Charlie could help him up, he was on his feet and running around to the steps again. Charlie walked slowly over to Kate and sat down beside her. Alex waved to them from the top of the junior slide, and they waved back, then Alex pushed himself forward and went down.

"We don't come here often enough," Charlie said. "It's mobbed in the summertime, too busy for Alex. Aunt Betty brought him a couple of weeks ago, but she said he was too scared. Wouldn't ever let go of her." He shook his head. "I really should bring him more."

"He's a wonderful boy," Kate said.

"New things are hard for him, but he really loves this." Charlie glanced at her, then turned back to watch Alex whoosh down the slide again. "I took him to that indoor playground once, but it was even worse."

"Crowded?"

"Yeah, kids everywhere—and noisy." He sighed. "I can't imagine him being ready for kindergarten next year. It's hard to know what to do." He glanced at her then back at his son.

"Betty thinks he should go to kindergarten so he'll get used to being around other kids."

"What do you think?"

"I don't know. It seems like it would be too painful, throwing him into a group like that. He's doing pretty well at Sunday school now, but he's been in the same class over a year, and there are only half a dozen kids." He frowned a little, watching Alex climb the steps to the slide again.

"There's a preschool and kindergarten room at the academy," Kate suggested timidly.

"Yes, but there must be twenty children in there. Alex really freezes up in a situation like that. Too many people, too much noise."

She looked up at his somber face. "If you could do anything with Alex, what would you choose?"

He smiled sadly. "Stay home with him all the time and do things with him. Like this. He doesn't remember his mother. Aunt Betty fills a lot of the gaps, but…" He sighed and was quiet.

"I'm sorry, Charlie," Kate said softly.

He shrugged and then stood up and walked toward the slide.

An hour later they were drinking hot chocolate at a restaurant in the Concourse. Alex stirred his and blew on it a lot, then spooned out the marshmallow and ate it. Kate sat across from him and Charlie, thinking what a carbon copy the boy was of his father.

"So, what brought you to the Waterville Public Library?" Charlie asked.

Kate chuckled. "It was not premeditated. In fact, it wasn't at all what I planned to do this fall."

"What did you plan to do?" he asked.

"Go back to school."

"Where?"

"Eastport College."

"That's a good school," he said.

"I was studying journalism." Kate picked up her cup and sipped the hot chocolate, then set it down carefully.

"Why did you quit?"

"I haven't quit," she said. "I've just been interrupted. I hope to go back someday."

He nodded. "So, what happened?"

She hesitated. "No money."

"Oh. I understand that."

"Well, actually, there's more to it. My father died in June. He was supporting me at school, and—well, the money just wasn't there. I'm on my own now."

"I'm sorry." His tone told her that he understood her grief.

"Well, I'm hoping that I'll be able to finish my degree someday." She tried to inject confidence into her voice.

He nodded. "I considered Eastport once myself."

"Did you?" She turned to face him.

"Yes. The seminary was recommended to me."

"Seminary?" Kate stared at him, astounded.

He laughed shortly. "Is it so farfetched?"

"No, I suppose not, but—unexpected, at least." He was a cop. She would never have imagined him in the ministry, his uniform and career seemed such a part of him.

"Yes, well, things didn't work out for me, either." He picked up the bill and stood, reaching for his wallet. Kate zipped Alex's jacket, and they were ready when Charlie returned to the table.

***

"Where to now?" Charlie asked as they walked out of the restaurant.

"Well, my car's parked just around the corner," Kate said. They were close to the library.

"Seems like we should do something else," Charlie said. "Unless—well, maybe you had plans for this afternoon."

"Lots of plans," Kate said. "Laundry, shopping, vacuuming …"

He laughed.

"I really should do all those things."

"Well, Alex and I are going to play some more. Come with us," he coaxed.

"Oh, I don't think—"

"Charlie!" came a strident voice.

Kate glanced across the parking lot. Roxanne Dufour strode rapidly toward them. They stood still as she approached. Kate thought her eyebrows were darker than they had been the first time she'd seen Roxanne, and she was definitely wearing a heavy coat of mascara and bright lip gloss. The makeup seemed a bit overpowering with her red hair and uniform.

"Hello, Roxy," Charlie said easily when she was close. "You've met Miss Pierce, I believe."

"Oh, the girl from the library," Roxanne said in dismissal and turned her attention toward him. "Charlie, are you coming in tomorrow?"

"No, I'm off until Monday."

"Too bad. There was a burglary on West Street this morning, and Chief Townshend took it away from Jerry and me and gave it to the detectives. If you'd been there, he wouldn't have done that."

"Well, that's the breaks, Roxy."

"Aw, come on. Maybe you could call the chief and just ask him to—"

"No, I don't have any influence on those things. You know that."

"Well, you're going to make detective soon," Roxanne persisted.

"Oh, I don't know, nothing's certain about that." Charlie shook his head.

"You'll make it. Jerry said you'd have made it three years ago, but you wouldn't take the test."

Charlie glanced toward Kate. "I don't really want to discuss it now, Roxy. I'll talk to you later."

"Call me," Roxanne said, looking intently into Charlie's eyes. She turned on her heel and walked away toward the used bookstore on the other side of the parking lot.

Charlie stood looking after her then turned slowly toward Kate. "Where were we?"

"I was about to get in my car and head for home. You and Alex are headed for a wonderful evening together."

"I think I missed something," Charlie said with a hint of confusion, but he walked with her toward her car.

"Do you think there's anything to this library intruder thing?" she asked.

"I think someone was in there, unauthorized, at least twice," he said. "You and Marilyn should take it seriously. He could be going in there more often than we know."

"Do you think so?" Kate glanced at Alex. He was watching her gravely, and she regretted raising the subject in his hearing. He already had enough fears.

"Well, it's impossible to prove he *wasn't* in there on any given night." Charlie looked up at the clouds. "We only know for sure he's been there when he messes up and leaves some evidence behind. Be careful."

They had reached her car, and Kate unlocked the driver's door and opened it.

"Thanks for going with us, Kate. I know Alex enjoyed it."

Charlie's smile tugged at her, almost the way Alex's did. She wished she could banish his sorrows too.

"Thanks for taking me."

Alex's eyes were large and trusting. Kate smiled, and the boy smiled back. "Come see me again at the library soon, Alex," she said, and he nodded. She wanted to pull him into her arms, but she held back. Looking briefly at Charlie, she gave him a half smile. His expression was plaintive as she got in the car and carefully backed out. She waved and headed for her apartment, wishing badly that she was headed for more adventures with the two of them.

***

All day Friday, Kate thought about Charlie and Alex. Over and over, she replayed the afternoon in her head. She had enjoyed being with them and had felt her heart opening to the serious little boy and his melancholy father. But the memory always ended with Roxanne saying, "Call me," in a proprietary manner.

At the library, Marilyn asked her if she had enjoyed the afternoon, and she truthfully said yes, but she frowned when she said it.

"I don't think Charlie has much of a social life," Marilyn said.

Kate declined to comment and busied herself sorting books on the return cart.

"Betty has tried to match him up with all sorts of girls," Marilyn continued.

"Really?" The remark startled Kate, and she couldn't help responding. "She wants him to get married again? I thought she loved being with him and Alex."

"Oh, she does, but Charlie is lonely," Marilyn said. "She wants him to find a companion. And Betty wants a life of her own. She loves her boys, but she has other interests too."

"The garden club," Kate suggested.

"That's one. She does genealogy too. She's a member of the D.A.R., and she reads a lot. She has a lot friends. Betty would like to see Charlie find a nice girl. A new mother for Alex, you know. She's afraid he likes that policewoman."

"Do you think he does?" Kate felt disloyal to Charlie as she said it. She wished she hadn't let Marilyn draw her into the discussion.

"Oh, please," Marilyn said, "not that one! She's hard as nails. I hope Charlie wouldn't be so foolish. But still, he sees her at work every day."

Kate couldn't picture Alex sitting on Roxanne's lap with a book. She gave Marilyn a weak smile and pushed the book cart toward the fiction shelves. She wondered if Roxanne would give up her career to mother a sensitive little boy.

Chapter 6

Kate rose early Saturday and thoroughly cleaned her small apartment. She wondered what Charlie and Alex were doing, and if Aunt Betty was having fun, and if Charlie had called Roxanne. She hoped he hadn't.

When she arrived at the library at nine thirty, one of the volunteers was there preparing for the puppet show.

"Hi," Lisa called, her dark braid swinging over her shoulder as she turned toward Kate. "Jocelyn's late. Guess we'd better set up the puppet stage."

Kate put her things in the cupboard and took one end of the folded stage, and the two of them carried it into the nonfiction room. As they carefully set it up, Jocelyn, the other girl who helped with the puppets, came puffing in.

"Sorry I'm late! My mom made me vacuum this morning, and it took forever."

They lined up a row of chairs, laid out their puppets and props, and quickly went over the cues. A buzz of talk grew in the main room as children gathered in expectation of the show. There was no time to review the script of *Raccoon Finds a Treasure*.

"Curtain time!" Lisa signaled them to take their places as parents and toddlers appeared in the opening to the nonfiction room.

As they ducked behind the puppet stage, Kate caught a glimpse of Charlie sitting down on the rug and pulling Alex onto his lap. She determined to make Squirrel give an outstanding performance. She made him speak cheerfully and playfully as he encouraged the other puppet animals.

When the show was over, she put the puppets away and pulled on her jacket in the back room. Marilyn had started a Halloween cartoon, and Kate slipped out through the darkened nonfiction area to the main part of the children's room. Marilyn was sitting behind the checkout desk, entering data into the computer.

"Good performance, Kate," she called. "See you Monday."

"Thanks." Kate headed for the side door and stopped before she reached it. Charlie was sitting in a chair near the toy box with Alex on his knees, and Alex was holding a stuffed elephant to his chest. Kate thought a tear clung to the boy's long eyelashes.

"Hi," she said tentatively.

"Hello," Charlie said, looking up at her over Alex's head. "The puppet show was great, but Alex doesn't care for the movie today. It's a bit scary."

She nodded and took a step closer. "I'm sorry, Alex."

He struggled to get down from his father's lap and walked toward Kate. Looking up at her, he stood still for a moment, then said, "I liked the squirrel."

She dropped to her knees, smiling. "Thank you so much."

Alex let the elephant fall and put his arms around her neck. The rush of emotion surprised Kate, and she blinked back tears as she held the little boy. Looking past him, she met Charlie's eyes, and she couldn't read the expression on his face. He stood up slowly and came toward them.

He said quietly, "We all need to eat lunch. Come with us, Kate. Please don't say no."

Kate couldn't think of an excuse that would sound logical, but she felt she would end up hurting somehow if she went. Every time she saw Alex her heart melted, and every time she saw his father across the church auditorium her heart pounded, but she couldn't tell Charlie that.

"Come on," he said again.

Alex released his hold on her and stepped back, looking gravely into her eyes. "You come with us."

She capitulated and walked with them out into the chilly morning. The wind blew cold across the parking lot, and a few brown oak leaves tumbled past them. They went to Charlie's truck, and he drove without speaking to a fast food restaurant in the north end of town. Kate couldn't think of anything to say, but Charlie and Alex didn't seem to mind. How much time did Alex spend in silence?

***

"How's your weekend going?" Kate asked when they were seated with their food.

"Fine, but ..." Charlie shook his head. Glancing at Alex, who was absorbed in unwrapping his sandwich, he said softly, "I've been taking him places, trying to let him have some new experiences. I don't want him to be like me."

Kate thought she knew what he meant. Charlie was lonely, but he didn't want to change his life in order to remedy that. Alex was lonely, too, unable to reach out, paralyzed sometimes by anxiety.

"Halloween is such a frightening time for young children," she ventured. "I don't blame him for not liking the film. It had some very scary images."

Alex's eyes flickered toward her, then back to his cheeseburger.

"It's not just that," Charlie said. "I can screen things like TV and films, but sometimes it seems like he's scared of everything. New people, new places, any experience that's different from what he knows. There are swimming classes for kids his age at the Boys and Girls Club, but when I told him I couldn't be in the water with him, he cried, so I didn't sign him up. Maybe Betty's right about the preschool."

"She thinks you should send him to school now? Not wait for kindergarten?"

"Yes, force him into a new situation where he has to learn to cope."

Kate frowned. "You can't do that to him." She blushed as she realized it was none of her business. "Sorry. I shouldn't have said that."

"No, it's okay. Actually, it helps that you don't think I'm nuts and overprotective." Charlie unwrapped his sandwich but didn't take a bite. "What would you do?"

"Me? I'm not the right person to ask," Kate said.

"Well, I'm asking anyway."

She thought for a moment. "Try to take him places like you have been, I guess, and introduce him to new people while you're there to make him feel more secure with it."

"I've been doing that some, but it's hard to get time, and, well, to be honest, I'm not so comfortable with change myself. It's a whole lot easier to stick to our routine." He shook his head, watching the boy take the paper wrapper from his straw. "I never was much good with crowds myself."

"You do great with the story hour."

Charlie shrugged. "Kids."

"How about at work? You must have to deal with strangers every day, in difficult situations."

"It's different when I'm in uniform," he admitted. "I guess the badge gives me some confidence. I know I have the right and the obligation to get in the middle of things when I'm wearing it. It's different in social situations, don't you think?"

"I guess so. I don't seem to have any problem talking to the people who come into the library, but it's really hard to just introduce myself to someone, say at church."

Charlie nodded. "It's a hundred times worse for Alex."

"He does well one-on-one."

"Yes, he does better, anyway," Charlie agreed.

"Is there a boy in his Sunday school class …?" she stopped.

"Tyler Blake," Charlie said.

Alex looked up, and Kate wondered if he minded them discussing him, and how much he understood.

"You like Tyler, don't you, Alex?" Charlie asked.

Alex nodded.

"Talk to his mother," Kate suggested.

"Yes, I could."

"Maybe she'd take Tyler to your house some morning for a short visit, and they could play. It wouldn't be threatening for Alex if it was at his house, with his toys."

"Would you like to have Tyler come and play?" Charlie asked Alex.

The boy nodded slowly as he drank, moving the paper cup and the straw up and down so he could keep sipping.

Charlie bit his lip. "It sounds reasonable. I'll speak to Angie at church."

They ate slowly, and Alex took a long time drinking his milkshake.

"About the swimming thing," Kate said, and Charlie looked at her expectantly. "Maybe next summer you could find a place where you can teach him privately. Then, when he's confident in his skill, he might be willing to go and swim with other kids."

"That might be good." Charlie chewed the last bite of his sandwich and swallowed. "I hope Aunt Betty's having a good time."

"Isn't it a bit late in the year for garden tours?" Kate asked.

"Well, the season is longer in Pennsylvania. I think they're getting some workshops on fall planting and things like that. And Betty has an admirer on the tour."

"Really?"

"Yes. She'd deny it, but she and Milton Frye really get along."

49

"Why is that name familiar?" Kate asked.

"Frye Landscaping."

"Oh, right. I see his trucks everywhere."

"He's got a successful business."

"So he and your aunt…"

"She'd say they're friends," Charlie replied. "I don't push it."

Kate smiled.

"They have this intense rivalry ever year at the flower shows. At the Skowhegan Fair last month, I was afraid she was going to try to sabotage Milton's exhibit."

Kate laughed. "She wouldn't really."

"No, I guess not. But having Milton to compete against has made her really outdo herself with the iris. And she's already decided she'll be the first one to win Yard of the Month next spring, when the garden club starts giving the award out again."

"What's the prize?" Kate asked.

"Nothing."

"Nothing? You're kidding."

"Well, we get to have a little sign that says *Waterville Garden Club's Yard of the Month* on our front lawn for a month. Then they give it to someone else for the next month." Charlie sipped his soft drink and chuckled. "Last year, Aunt Betty got it in May, and Milton didn't get it until July. He kept making smart remarks to her about it all summer."

"So, do people come from miles around to look at your yard?" Kate asked.

"Not usually. But once a year the garden club organizes a tour, where they all spend the day driving from one member's house to the next so they can all see each other's gardens. Betty is a nervous wreck for about two weeks before that little event. Everything has to be perfect. She's not finicky about other things, but her flower beds are—well, I won't say it's an obsession, but she finds it very absorbing."

SUSAN PAGE DAVIS

"Do you like gardening?" Kate asked.

"We have pumpkins," Alex said, and Kate turned to him, surprised.

"You grow pumpkins?" she said with admiration.

Alex nodded vigorously. "And carrots."

"Alex and I grew a few vegetables this year," Charlie said. "That's the extent of my gardening skills. I don't do flowers. Aunt Betty handles that."

51

Chapter 7

In the pickup, Alex leaned against Kate, and she put her arm around his shoulders. "I'm glad you invited me, Alex," she said. "I enjoyed lunch. It's a lot better than eating alone at my apartment."

"You're welcome," he said soberly.

Charlie drove down the street toward the library, and Kate told him where her car was parked. He found an open space next to it and pulled up.

"Alex is asleep," he observed, putting the gearshift into park.

"Poor little guy," Kate said. "You've tuckered him out."

"For the past couple of days, I've been trying to do all the things with him that I don't usually have time to do. Guess we should stay home tonight and relax." Charlie unbuckled his seat belt and turned toward her. "How've you been doing?"

"Fine."

"I've been praying about your situation," he said.

"You have?"

"Yes, that if the Lord wants you to, you'll be able to finish school."

"Thanks. I don't know if it will happen. I've prayed about it a lot, and I'm not sure what God has in mind for me. But if it's not possible for me to go back to school, I know He's got *something* planned."

Charlie nodded. "I'm having a bit of trouble determining God's will myself lately."

"You mean, for Alex?"

"For Alex, for me, for Aunt Betty." He sighed and gripped the steering wheel with both hands. "If I could just *know* I was doing the right thing."

"Sometimes we don't know until after, not for sure," Kate said.

"Well, I'm pretty sure I did the wrong thing the last time I faced a decision like this." He looked at her speculatively, then out across the parking lot toward the little garden at the back entrance of the bank, where Kate could make out a small *Frye Landscaping* sign.

She wasn't sure whether to pursue the subject, or if he would think she was prying. She sat, Alex's head against the side of her jacket, thinking she ought to excuse herself and get out of the truck, but then Charlie and Alex would be gone.

"The seminary," she said at last, and it hung there between them.

Charlie nodded slowly. "I was going. It was all set. Alex and Joy and me." He pressed his lips firmly together. "He was only a year old, just starting to walk."

Kate instinctively tightened her hold around Alex. He seemed so vulnerable, so wounded, and she was glad he slept peacefully.

Charlie looked away from them, out the side window, and was silent. The wind gusted, and a cloud of spent leaves swirled across the parking lot.

"I feel like I'm living the worst part of my life all over again," he said at last.

Kate felt the pain radiating from him. She took a deep breath and asked softly, "How?"

His eyes met hers cautiously, as if he was taking a great risk. "First, this detective thing came up. The same thing happened before. I wanted it. Badly."

"But you passed it up." Kate tried to remember what Roxanne had said.

"The timing was wrong." Regret filled his voice. "I was going to seminary. Joy and I had prayed about it for months. I felt the Lord was calling me into the ministry. At least ... I thought so. So I gave my notice to the police department, and I was happy about it. Mostly."

Kate waited, sensing his regret and doubt.

He reached up and adjusted the visor at the top of the windshield. "When my wife died, I couldn't go. I—I just couldn't. Alex was so little. I'd have had to put him in daycare or something when I was in class. I didn't know what to do. But I called the school and told them I wasn't coming."

"And you'd already given up the promotion," Kate said softly.

"Yes. Another guy got it. A friend of mine, Bob Sorenson. He's a good cop. But I felt like the Lord had knocked me flat on my back. They kept me on at the department, but I'd lost the job I'd been dreaming of, and the place at seminary, and—I'd lost Joy. She was—" He shook his head and didn't finish.

His anguish was so evident, Kate wished desperately that she could do something to ease it. "But you've hung in there for three years. That takes strength."

He shook his head. "In some ways, I feel like I've just been marking time. Oh, Alex is terrific. He's brought me a lot of comfort. But I'm still a patrolman. I really felt God wanted me to preach for a while there, but I'm no closer to that now."

"Do you still think He wants you to?" Kate asked timidly.

"I don't know. Sometimes, when Pastor Wilson preaches about giving your talents to God and following His will no matter what, I feel like I've failed. I get really depressed. Sometimes lately I've wondered, if God does want me to be a minister, did I have to go through all of that to be ready? Other times ..."

After a moment, she said softly, "Other times, what?"

He huffed out a breath. "I think I had it wrong back then, and God wanted me to stay where I am. But ..."

Kate clenched her teeth. She could imagine his thoughts. *But did Joy have to die to make that happen? To keep me here?* She didn't know what to say.

Charlie looked up. "But then I think, how could I do that now? Alex is bigger, but—" He looked her in the eye. Kate waited for him to on. "He needs special care."

She frowned. "How do you mean? He's very bright, and yes, he's sensitive, but surely there's nothing wrong with him."

"No, nothing at all. And I don't want to ruin that."

"Then how do you mean, he needs special care?"

Charlie sighed. "I can't leave him with just anyone. I don't think I could take him to daycare. It would crush him."

Inwardly, Kate agreed, but she thought it would crush Charlie too. And Alex needed to learn to handle himself in the world. "Maybe he's tougher than you think. You can prepare him carefully."

"That's what I'm trying to do, but maybe not soon enough."

"God says He won't give us more than we can bear," Kate ventured.

Charlie was quiet for a moment, then said, "I know you're right."

"You got through that awful time somehow."

"I couldn't have done it without Betty. I couldn't have kept Alex, I mean, and kept my job. At first I tried babysitters, but Alex would cry and scream when I left him. I was at my wit's end after the first month. I'd be up all night with him, and exhausted when I was out on patrol. I felt like my job performance was slipping, but I couldn't help it. I tried three or four different sitters, but none of them was right, and every time I switched to a new one, Alex got worse."

"It must have been a very difficult time."

"Lousy." He took a deep breath and nodded. "Really rotten. I was hurting so bad myself, and I felt like I couldn't help Alex. Then Aunt Betty offered to come. She's been such a help! It took Alex a while to get used to her, but she told me she was staying, and in time he would adjust, and she was right. She was always gentle with him."

"She's very good with him," Kate said.

"I think he screamed half the day at first, and she would just hold him for hours. But gradually he'd quit earlier. Now he's comfortable with her. Betty and I are all he's got."

Kate nodded.

"But he's got to get used to people," Charlie insisted.

"He's fine at the library, and at church."

"As long as one of us is there. I never could leave him in the nursery at church. I always had to keep him with me or Betty."

Kate wondered if more time and patience would have made a difference, or if Charlie gave up on trying, but she didn't ask.

He stared off toward the library. "I used to think about what he would be like if … Joy … had lived. How happy he'd be, how different."

"You can't do that," Kate said.

"No, it doesn't help to think about that. I just wish I could see how this will all end." He gripped the steering wheel. "This last year, Aunt Betty's been hinting that I ought to think about getting married again. But Alex …" He shook his head. "She'd have to be special. Someone Alex could trust."

Kate felt very inadequate. "Maybe you'll find someone like that."

"Pray for me," he said simply. "If God wants me to go to the seminary, well … I know Betty would support me in my decision, but I don't think she wants to leave Maine, so I wouldn't have anyone to take care of Alex. And now there's another detective's slot that's opening in the department. I'm wondering if I should go for it this time."

"How would that change things?" Kate asked.

He shrugged. "Better pay, hours a little shorter." He smiled. "No uniforms."

Kate laughed.

"Maybe I'd enjoy work more," he added. "It would be more challenging mentally. No more traffic duty. And Alex and I would stay here with Aunt Betty, and Alex would feel safe, at least for a while."

Kate said cautiously, "But you've felt lately that God is calling you again?"

"Not really. I've thought about it, but ... I'm not sure if God really wants me to pursue it, or if it's just guilt feelings for not going before. And I keep thinking Aunt Betty wants a life of her own." Charlie's face scrunched up.

"I'll pray for you." She wished she knew him better, could offer him more. She felt his confusion and the ache of his loneliness as he struggled with important decisions.

"Sometimes I think it's just too hard to make changes, you know?" Charlie gave a helpless shrug. "I was all ready before. We'd sold our house to pay for seminary. We were going to sign the papers the next day. I backed out of the sale when Joy died. I felt like Alex needed the security of our home, but maybe it was really me who needed it."

"Children are resilient," she said, but she wondered how true it was for Alex. He stirred a little and turned around so that he was facing his father and nestled into her side. His hair had rebelled in the absence of Aunt Betty and was now completely disheveled.

Charlie put his hand out and touched the boy's chin. "If I could find the right mother for him, someone who could put up with me too. Not one of these girls Betty meets in the produce department at the store, but someone with some substance, you know?"

"You're not serious? She brings women home from the grocery store for you?"

"Well, no, she hasn't actually gone that far. But she did get a phone number from a young woman she met there. Nice girl, Betty said. Teaches aerobics and likes to sky dive."

"Ouch." Kate winced.

"I didn't call her." Charlie looked at her for a moment, then out the side window. "There's someone..." He let it peter out.

Kate's heart plummeted. There was someone, after all, whom Charlie was seriously considering. She waited, but he didn't say anything.

At last she said, "Someone who would go with you to the seminary?"

"I don't know if she would or not. Frankly, I'm more concerned about Alex right now. I won't sacrifice him. I've struggled with that, and I really feel, deep down, that he's my first responsibility. I don't think God would be honored if I threw Alex to the lions so I could study the Bible."

"So ... you're going to stay and try for the promotion?" Kate asked, unsure of the ground beneath her feet.

Charlie leaned back against the headrest. "I just don't know."

Chapter 8

On Sunday, Kate went to the auditorium after the membership class and looked for Jill Palmer. The Palmers welcomed her into their row, and she made herself focus on the sermon. She didn't see Charlie until the service was over, and then she only caught a glimpse of him lifting Alex into the pickup truck in the parking lot.

Jill insisted that Kate join the Palmer family for lunch, and she went, glad to have the company of someone who would keep her mind off Charlie and Alex. Helping Jill prepare the meal and playing Memory with Joey and Rachel afterward kept her from brooding.

Mike sat at the kitchen table, addressing a manila envelope. A computer disk in a cardboard holder lay on the table.

"What are you doing?" Kate asked as she helped Rachel put the game's pieces in the box.

"Sending the sermon to my brother and his wife," Mike replied.

"They live way up in Aroostook County, on the Quebec border," Jill said. "There's not an English-speaking Protestant church within a hundred miles of them, so we send them a video disk of the pastor's sermon every week."

"Can't they watch it online?"

"Their Internet reception's spotty," Mike said. "This way, they don't have to worry about interruptions if the weather's bad or the signal fails for some other reason."

Kate nodded. Modern technology hadn't solved every problem. "Do they like it up there?"

"Yes, they love it," Jill said. "Nick's a game warden, and they're living out his childhood fantasy." She brought Mike a return address label.

"They're coming down next weekend," Mike said, popping the disk into the envelope. "It'll be great to see them. They come down once a month or so. They probably won't be able to come much in the winter, though."

"Nick will be tied up for the whole month of November, too, with hunting season," Jill said.

"Do they have kids?"

"Not yet." Mike smiled. "They got married last Christmas. Libby was Joey's teacher." He sealed the envelope.

"Yes, we're very happy about that match." Jill grinned as she picked up the game box. "And Mike still has one single brother, for what it's worth."

Kate smiled weakly. "Don't look at me."

"Steve's in the Navy," Jill persisted.

Kate shook her head. "No, thanks. I'm hoping to go back to school next year."

***

She called Chad on his cell phone that afternoon, feeling an intense need for sibling fellowship.

"Hey, I got an A on my paper," he said happily. "Well, an A minus, but that's an A, right?"

"Right," Kate said with a laugh. "I'm proud of you. You're coming down next weekend, right?"

"Yes!"

"Do you have gas money?"

"I think I'm okay for the moment. I'll come Saturday morning."

"Meet me at Piper's on Main Street," Kate said on a whim. "We'll have breakfast out to celebrate."

"Can we do that?" he asked doubtfully.

"Hey, if we were solvent, it would be dinner, but we've got to celebrate, Chad. If you quit marking great occasions, it's a sign of giving up."

"All right. How will I know you? Will you be wearing a red carnation?"

She laughed. "It's not that big a place. "They sell gourmet coffee and jellybeans. They have about five tables. I'll be the one in patched jeans and an old Eastport sweatshirt. And besides, I'm your sister."

"Hmm, guess I'll be able to spot you."

***

That evening, Charlie and Betty arrived at church late, during the second hymn. Betty came into the pew and sat beside Kate, and Charlie took the aisle seat, with Alex in his arms.

When the pastor allowed a time for greetings, Kate turned to Betty and shook her hand.

"How was your trip?"

"Lots of fun!" Betty's grin was contagious. "It was kind of like going to an away game on the high school bus."

"Wild garden club outing?" Kate asked.

"Well, about as wild as people my age get when they're sober." Betty laughed. "We sang on the bus and had a midnight feast at the hotel. There are some really nice people in the club."

"Sounds like you had a great time."

Alex extended his hand, and Kate shook it formally.

"Pleased to see you," the boy said earnestly.

"I'm pleased to see you too," said Kate.

Charlie leaned over and shook her hand, too, and gave her a fleeting smile.

***

All week, Kate worked frantically in the school library. The school had an open house scheduled, and she wanted to have the library in order when the parents saw it. Heather Wilson and Tara Wishart came to help her during their home room period each morning.

Marilyn gave her some colorful posters that had come with book shipments. The public library got so many they couldn't hang them all. Kate hung them at eye level on both sides of the school library door.

When all the books were shelved, she began visiting the classrooms during home room period, to show the children some of the books that would appeal to them most. In the early hours, before school began, she worked on the card catalog and classifying the books.

At the public library, she was becoming proficient with the computer system. Marilyn had taught her how to make minor book repairs and encouraged her to set up a display of circus themed books when a circus was advertised to be in the area soon. Kate was given the job of lining up all the guest readers. She tapped city councilors, firemen, and an Air Force recruiter, filling out the story hour schedule for the month of November.

Thursday's story time brought out Jill Palmer and little Amy. Kate helped Jill locate a book on electricity for a school project of Joey's before the reading began. Betty and Alex came through the side door, and he ran joyfully to Kate as soon as he spotted her.

"Miss Pierce!"

She bent down and embraced him, and he put a crayon drawing of a squirrel in her hand.

"Thank you Alex." She gazed at his picture, gladness brimming up in her. "This is a nice surprise."

Aunt Betty followed him at a leisurely pace, pulling off the soft gray gloves that matched her fleece jacket. "Alex has taken a shine to you," she observed with a smile.

"We're friends," Alex declared with pride.

"Yes," Kate agreed. "Have fun today, Alex. A fireman is going to read to you. He has a story about a firehouse dog." She led Jill to the checkout desk.

As she set the due date for Jill's book, she heard Betty tell Marilyn, "Charlie had a rough night last night."

"Oh?" Marilyn looked up expectantly from her work.

"Had to respond to a suicide." Betty's face was grim now.

Kate glanced apprehensively at Alex, wondering how it affected him, hearing about the stark reality of his father's job. She reached toward Jill for the book.

"Comes with the job, but I can tell these things wear on him." Betty was resigned to Charlie's choice of careers, it seemed. She shook her head. "I worry about him sometimes. Law enforcement is a very demanding occupation."

Kate frowned as she ran the scanner over the bar code on Jill's book.

"Betty's cheerful today," Jill whispered wryly.

Kate nodded.

"Charlie ought to get married," Marilyn said.

"He won't listen to me anymore," Betty replied. "I think he'd rather brood. Although, I've been wondering lately if there isn't a girl who could interest him." She chuckled and said, "Don't tell him I said that. He'd kill me if he knew I was discussing his social life with you." She took Alex's hand and walked toward the nonfiction room, where the firefighter was ready to read to the children.

Kate handed Jill the book with a tight smile. "There you go. Enjoy the story time."

"Are you okay?" Jill asked.

"Yes."

Jill stood still, watching her.

"I'm sorry," Kate said. "I'm just not sure people should talk about Charlie like that, especially in front of Alex."

Jill nodded soberly. "I'm sure Betty doesn't realize how it sounds," she said quietly. "She loves him very much."

Kate managed a little smile. "Thanks, I know you're right."

Jill smiled back and led Amy to the story corner.

When Marilyn excused her for her break, Kate skipped up the stairs and into the main reading room, where she pulled the day's paper from its rack. She had learned in Journalism 101 that newspapers seldom reported on suicides, unless the person involved was a public figure. She laid the paper out on one of the oak reading tables and turned quickly to the obituary page.

Cancer, accident, long illness. Ah, that must be it. *Angela Dumont, 29, died suddenly at her home in Waterville.* "Died suddenly" was the standard euphemism. Kate sat down and scanned the family information. *She is survived by two children, Alicia, 11, and Martin, 4.* No husband was mentioned.

She prayed silently for the Dumont children, and for Charlie Abbot. Seeing a boy Alex's age bereft of his mother must have been especially grueling for him.

***

Entering Piper's in her comfortable jeans on Saturday morning, Kate wished she had described a more stylish outfit to her brother. She fixed herself a cup of vanilla-flavored coffee and went to the only empty table. As she took her quilted blue jacket off and hung it over the back of the chair, she noticed Roxanne Dufour sitting at another table, wearing her uniform. Another uniformed woman was with her.

Kate nodded slightly when Roxanne looked her way. Roxanne lifted an eyebrow and turned to say something to her companion. Kate's cheeks burned, and she wondered what was being said. The second officer glanced her way and leaned toward Roxanne, smiling as she said something. Keeping one eye on the door to the shop, Kate slowly sipped her coffee.

It was a long ten minutes before Chad arrived. She had watched Roxanne and the other officer drink their coffee and eat Danish. They were standing up and putting on their winter uniform jackets when she spotted Chad through the plate glass window.

He came through the door, and Kate stood. He looked around, spotted her, and grinned.

"Chad!" Seeing him again made her even happier than she'd expected. She took a step and met him in the tiny space between tables. He threw his arms around her and kissed her on the cheek.

"How you doing?" he asked.

"Not bad. Your hands are freezing, though! Get some coffee."

Chad went to get himself a drink and muffins for both of them. Kate sat down and saw Roxanne looking her way as she waited for her change at the cash register. Her heavily-lined green eyes were calculating slits. When Kate met her gaze, she tossed her red ponytail and turned away.

They lingered over breakfast, and Chad described to Kate the courses and professors he would have in the following semester at his school, the University of Maine.

"I think I'm really going to enjoy the spring semester. All my classes sound interesting, and the load won't be too heavy. They'll help us find jobs before graduation, too. There's this big career day in January, and scouts from all the big engineering firms will be there. Kate, I've got a good chance of landing something decent. Really."

"Of course you do." Chad had never lacked confidence before their father's death had reduced them to penury. "Your grades are terrific. Those scouts are going to try to lure you to work for them."

His smile spread across his handsome face. "I hope so. So, you're doing all right?"

"I'm working forty hours a week, between my two jobs. My pay isn't princely, but it's meeting the rent and assorted other bills. If neither of us gets sick, we may make it through until you land that fantastic job."

"Kate, you're going back to college next fall. I mean it. Are you able to put anything aside?"

"Not yet," she admitted. "I had a couple of hundred stashed away, but then the car insurance bill came. I'm wondering if I should sell my car. I can walk to the library, but the school is really too far."

"Keep the car," Chad decreed.

"Well, I guess I will, for now."

They emptied their pockets to pay for breakfast and climbed into Chad's car for the ride to her apartment. Later that morning, they walked around the Colby College campus, lingering near Johnson Pond. The foliage was peaking, with the brilliant colors foretelling winter. Students rambled past them, seemingly carefree, and Kate wondered if she could slip back into the academic life.

"We can go skating here this winter," she told Chad. "Bring your skates down after it freezes."

"All right. Maybe we can catch a hockey game too. Their team is supposed to be great this year. Too bad you couldn't take a couple of classes here."

"No way," Kate said. "Tuition is astronomical, but I do come up here a lot for art shows and concerts, and they let us use the library for free. I walk up here just to soak up the atmosphere. It has that upper crust campus feeling."

They spent the afternoon lazily, companionably. Chad had brought his A-earning term paper for Kate to read, and they went through old photo albums together, remembering times when the family was intact and they'd been carefree.

"I think you should put in an application for Eastport now," Chad said. "Reserve your spot in the dorm for next fall, you know?"

"I'm not sure," Kate mused. "If for some reason I wasn't able to go, we'd lose the deposit. That's assuming we could come up with a deposit in the first place." She laughed and shook her head.

"But once you have your degree, you'll get a job that pays twice as much."

She shrugged. "Maybe. I'm not so sure I want to be a journalist anymore, Chad."

"Really? I thought that was your one goal in life."

Kate considered. "I'm starting to like library work pretty well."

"So, you want to study library science?"

"Maybe. But I don't think Eastport offers it."

"Maybe you could work in the college library while you finish your degree in something else," he suggested.

"I'm really praying about it, because I just don't know anymore what God has in mind for me." Saying it to Chad made her realize suddenly how uncertain she was about her future. "I never used to think it would be up to me to support myself for the rest of my life, you know? It's a little scary, and I'm asking the Lord to give me some direction."

"I guess I haven't been praying much lately," her brother conceded.

"Oh, Chad, don't stop. We need the Lord now, more than ever."

He nodded sheepishly.

"I've been praying for you," she said. "I'd like to know you're praying for me, too."

"All right. We can pray right now, if you want."

Chapter 9

The next morning, Kate rode to church with Chad in his car. He had come prepared to attend services, and he looked quite dashing in a navy blue blazer and gray slacks. She'd forewarned him that hardly anyone wore a tie at their church.

In the car, the close, spicy smell of his aftershave brought back a vivid memory to Kate of their father. It had been months since she had smelled it, and the onslaught of grief jolted her.

"I miss Dad," she choked, fighting tears as her brother drove down College Avenue.

"Me too." Chad turned toward her. "What made you say that?"

"Don't laugh."

"Okay."

"You smell like him."

"Sorry. Too much aftershave?"

"No, it's not overpowering. It was just … unexpected."

"Don't know why I use it. Maybe it reminds *me* of him too. Like driving his car."

"I'm glad you kept it."

He parked outside the church, and they entered together.

"I need to go to my membership class," Kate told him at the back of the auditorium. "The general adult class meets here."

"That's fine. I'll be okay." Chad settled into a seat near the back, and Kate headed down the hallway. Looking back, she saw one of the deacons stop beside her brother to welcome him.

When she came back at the end of the lesson, Chad stood up and let her pass him to sit in the pew beside him.

"How was it?" she whispered.

"Pretty good, actually. I really ought to find a place to go Sundays in Orono, near campus, or Bangor even."

"Yes, you should. Of course, any weekend you want to drive down here and go with me, I won't object." The drive took an hour or so each way, and she knew he couldn't do it every week.

Kate thought Pastor Wilson's sermon was especially fine that morning. She jotted a few notes, and Chad sat attentively beside her. She found herself glancing about as they stood for the final hymn, her eyes settling on Charlie, two rows forward on the other side of the church. She had been praying often that the Lord would guide him in his decisions about his future, and that Alex would find adjustments easier as he grew older and encountered more and more changes.

She wished she could talk to Charlie again, easily, the way they had in the truck the week before, and get an update on the family. But he hadn't been to the library, and Kate couldn't bring herself to seek him out.

From where she stood, she could see him almost in profile. His dejected air stirred her. If only she could do something that would bring back his dashing smile. She wanted badly to know whether he had applied for the detective's position or had thought more about the question of seminary. *It's none of my business,* she thought. But she wished it were.

When the service was over, Jill Palmer crossed the aisle eagerly. "Kate! Don't tell me. This is your brother."

"Yes, it is." Kate laughed with surprise. "Chad, this is my friend, Jill. How did you know?"

"Your eyes are identical, and that blond hair. You two aren't twins, are you?"

"No, Chad's two years older than me."

"Well, the resemblance is striking. Mike thought you had a boyfriend, but I knew he was related. Had to be." Jill put her hand to her mouth. "Oops, that wasn't very tactful. Sorry."

Kate chuckled. "I knew what you meant."

"Look, why don't you and Chad have lunch with us?" Jill asked. "Nick and Libby are here, and you'd like them, I know. They've got some wonderful stories about life in the far north."

Kate looked at Chad, and he shrugged. She accepted.

"It will be a good meal, and good company," Kate promised her brother in a whisper.

As they went out of the church, she looked around for Charlie's green truck, realizing with a pang that they hadn't exchanged so much as a nod. The truck was pulling out of the far end of the parking lot. Kate watched it go then hurried along with Chad to his car, giving him directions to the Palmers' house.

***

All week, Kate tried to keep Charlie's sad brown eyes out of her mind. She got out her old Eastport Christian College catalog and pored over it in the evenings. She ordered a new one online, then called the University of Maine and asked for one of theirs. She even picked up one at the business college on the outskirts of Waterville.

Still, she wasn't sure the classroom was the right place for her. As she explored options, she prayed earnestly for direction in what to do.

She prayed sincerely for Chad every day, and for Charlie and Alex. She prayed for Betty Abbot too. At fifty, Betty was not too old to begin a new life, Kate realized.

The school library was so improved that parents donated more than two hundred dollars for new books during the open house. Kate borrowed book catalogs from Marilyn and had the happy task of choosing new books for the children at the academy.

On Thursday, she was at the desk in the children's room when Alex and Betty brought their choice of picture books to check out.

Alex gave her a huge smile, and Kate went out from behind the desk, crouching down so she could speak to him at eye level.

"I'm so glad to see you," she said.

"Me too." He put the books up on the edge of the desk and held out his arms. Kate hugged him close.

"I'd better check your books out," she whispered. "There are lots of people here today, and we don't want to make them wait."

He nodded.

She stood up smiling.

Betty said, "Charlie's taking the test today."

"Test?" Kate asked, scanning the spines of the books.

"For detective grade. It's a pretty sure thing he'll get it if he does well on the test."

"Really?" *He's made a decision.* Kate remembered him saying, "There's someone..." That someone must be someone who wanted to stay in Maine and marry a detective.

She handed Alex the books and said tremulously, "I'll see you soon, Alex."

"Can you eat lunch with us again?" he asked wistfully.

"Not today, my friend. Maybe another time."

Betty was watching her. Perhaps she expected a comment about Charlie. Kate couldn't trust herself to say anything just then. Alex took Betty's hand and pulled her toward the street door.

***

As October waned, the Halloween frenzy escalated. Marilyn was planning a Saturday Halloween party and a special puppet show. Kate asked to be excused from the program. Her heart wasn't in it, and she knew the show would be too scary for Alex. She asked once if Marilyn didn't think the cutouts of ghosts and an especially garish witch would frighten the toddlers, but Marilyn didn't agree.

"They're not like ghoulish monsters," she said.

Kate let it drop, but the morning of November first she quietly began removing the Halloween decorations. Marilyn said nothing, but late in the morning she went to the back room and returned with a box of Thanksgiving cutouts.

"Perhaps you'd like to put these up."

Kate looked in the box and nodded. "I'd be happy to."

Soon the children's room walls were covered with plump turkeys and apple-cheeked Pilgrims, cornstalks and Indian children. Marilyn brought in two pumpkins after her lunch hour and let Kate draw pleasant faces on them with a permanent marker.

That night, Kate sat alone at her kitchen table, eating soup she had heated in the microwave. She took her notebook and began writing a list of things she was thankful for. Her jobs, her apartment, her church, Chad, her friends...

She realized she hadn't seen Charlie up close for more than two weeks. He'd waved across the church the day before with a curt smile, and Alex had visited the library with Aunt Betty, but Charlie had stayed away.

Chapter 10

On Tuesday morning when she arrived at the library, Kate was greeted by a white-faced Marilyn at the bottom of the stairs in the children's room.

"I've had Charlie here this morning," the librarian said in a low voice. "Our visitor was here again last night."

Kate arched her eyebrows, glancing quickly around to gauge the proximity of the patrons.

"Anything missing?"

"Candy again, and the cushions were untied. Paper towels in the trash. I emptied it right before I left last night."

"What did Charlie say?"

"He thought maybe it was because it was so cold last night. This person maybe needed a warm place to sleep."

"There's a homeless shelter on Ticonic Street," Kate said.

"Yes, but if he had the opportunity to have his own private place ... And just the ability to get in here when he isn't supposed to might be appealing, especially to a young person. The excitement of knowing he might be caught."

"Did Charlie do anything?"

"Yes, he looked around some more to see if there was anywhere a man or a teenager could hide, and then he went up to talk to Mr. Carter about the keys and maybe changing the locks. We really ought to. That old door at the top of the stairs should have a safety bar. I'm surprised they never replaced it with a fire door."

Kate nodded. She hoped Charlie and the head librarian could come up with some solutions.

***

The week dragged, and on Thursday Kate almost dreaded seeing Alex as the story hour approached. Seeing Alex would make her think of Charlie, and thinking of Charlie would remind her that he seemed to be avoiding her at church, and he never came to the library when she was there anymore.

She tried all week with moderate success to keep her thoughts in check. When Alex came in with Betty, his smile lifted her spirits. He wore denim overalls over a red-striped jersey, and his grin was so genuine, Kate couldn't help but return it. She stooped to hug him, and he gladly embraced her.

During the story hour, Kate shelved books. A city councilor was reading, and her voice droned on in the next room. As Kate knelt to replace a picture book on the bottom shelf, a little hand touched her shoulder.

"Miss Pierce," Alex whispered.

She turned around, still on her knees.

"Alex! Is everything all right?"

"Yes, but the story is kind of boring, and I think Aunt Betty's asleep."

Kate smiled. "Would you like to look at this?" She took a picture book off her stack. "It's about a mouse."

"I can tell," he said. "*Mouse House*."

She eyed him in surprise. "Have you had this book home before?"

"No."

"Then, how did you know it said *Mouse House*?"

Alex shrugged.

"Would you like me to read it to you?"

Alex nodded.

Kate sat down on the rug and smoothed her khaki skirt. Alex wriggled onto her lap.

"A little mouse lived in a house," Kate began. She turned the page. "I wonder what this says?" she whispered conspiratorially.

"It was a little green house," Alex said distinctly.

Kate sat very still. "That's right. Alex, are you sure you haven't checked this book out before?"

"No."

Kate turned another page. Maybe Charlie had read it during story time.

"Can you tell me what this says?" she asked.

He said slowly, "He had a little blue bed and a little red chair."

"Great." They went through the short book, and when they'd finished, she reached behind her to the shelf of picture books and pulled one out at random.

"What's this one called?" she asked.

Alex was quiet for a moment.

"That's okay," Kate said. "I can tell you."

"It's *Frog Finds a Friend*," said Alex.

Kate squeezed him and planted a kiss on his cheek. "That's right, Alex! I'm proud of you! I had no idea you were so grown up."

"Alex?" Betty Abbot called softly.

Kate and Alex scrambled to their feet.

"He's over here," Kate said.

"Oh, there you are." Betty's jaunty blue beret sported a fabric rose.

"I'm sorry," Kate said. "He told me the story hour was—" she glanced around quickly, then leaned close to Betty and whispered, "boring!"

"It's banal today," Betty said. "I can't blame him for escaping."

"Do you read to Alex a lot at home?" Kate asked.

"Yes, quite a bit, and Charlie reads to him almost every night. Alex is big on bedtime stories, aren't you, Alex?"

The boy nodded seriously. He held up *Frog Finds a Friend*. "May I take this one, Aunt Betty?" he asked.

Betty peered at it through her spectacles. "I don't see why not. Do you want to find a couple more?"

Alex turned to a low table where several books were laid out on display.

"So, how did Charlie's test go?" Kate asked.

Betty let out a little sigh. "He hasn't heard yet."

"I guess he wants this promotion pretty badly?" Kate ventured.

"Oh, I don't know. He doesn't seem very enthusiastic about it, really. I think maybe he's trying a doorknob."

Kate looked at her blankly.

"You know, to see if the door will open. He's really struggling right now, trying to find the Lord's will for him."

Kate nodded. "He told me a little bit about that. Said there were some options he was considering."

"Yes, well, I don't think he knows what he wants." Betty's mouth skewed. "I had hopes. He seemed to care about—" She stopped and shook her head.

"I've been praying for him," Kate said hesitantly.

Betty looked at her sharply.

"He asked me to," Kate said quickly, as a blush heated her face. She wished she hadn't said anything. "But I haven't seen him for a while, and I didn't know if he'd made any decisions."

Betty glanced toward Alex, who was several feet away, slowly turning the pages of a book. She leaned toward Kate and said in a low tone, "When my nephew was younger, he had a lot more confidence. Charlie was always quiet, but when he knew what he wanted, he just went after it. Now—well, since Joy died—it's like he can't make a decision. He puts them off until the last possible moment."

Kate frowned. "I'm sorry Mrs. Abbot. I'm not sure you should be discussing this with me, though."

"Perhaps you're right, but—" Betty shook her head. "I did have hopes, but he seems to have lost his initiative again."

Kate said in a small voice, "Doesn't taking the test show initiative?"

"I'm not so sure," Betty said. "If you care, Miss Pierce, then I would suggest you keep on praying for him." She looked toward the boy. "Come, Alex, are you ready?"

Kate walked ahead of them to the checkout desk, trying not to read more into Betty's words than was warranted.

***

At Sunday services, Kate sat behind the Abbots. She didn't plan it, but the church was filling fast. She sank into the nearest empty seat, then realized Charlie's straight back was right in front of her. She thought about moving, but where to? The song leader stood up, and she gave up the idea.

She channeled her thoughts into a narrow lane that led to worship. Time after time, she jerked her eyes from the back of Charlie's navy blue jacket and the lighter blue collar of his dress shirt, with a fine navy stripe, where it showed above the collar of the jacket, just below the soft, dark hair that tapered at the back of his neck.

It bothered her that she could tell he'd had a haircut that week, and she shifted in her seat so that she looked along the edge of the center aisle toward the pulpit, not between Charlie and Betty, over Alex's head.

She began making notes on the back of her church bulletin, to focus her thoughts on the message, instead of on Charlie's ears. She caught his profile as he turned to settle Alex once, and a powerful sadness went through her.

When the service ended, she stood up and gathered her things, but not quickly enough.

"Miss Pierce," Alex cried joyfully.

She smiled and sat back down, unable to take a deep breath. Alex peered at her over the back of his pew.

"Hello, Alex. It's nice to see you again." She didn't look up but kept her eyes on the boy. She could sense Charlie standing over her, looking down at the top of her head. She hoped her part was straight.

Alex held out his arms. Kate hesitated only an instant, then leaned forward and hugged him tight as tears welled up in her eyes. She glanced toward Betty and was relieved to see that she was talking with Dorothy Palmer, facing away from them. Kate rubbed the back of Alex's manly little vest gently. "Have you read those books yet, Alex?"

He nodded vigorously, against her shoulder, and Kate laid her cheek against his head for a moment.

Charlie cleared his throat, and she had to look up. She blinked furiously, but one tear escaped and landed in Alex's hair.

"So how have you been?" Charlie asked quietly.

Kate didn't think she could speak. She nodded diffidently and released Alex. Slowly she stood, her heart hammering. She took a deep breath. "Have you heard anything about the test yet?"

"No, but we should hear this week." Charlie held his Bible in one hand, and the other rested on the back of the pew. He leaned on it. "I, uh, decided I should take it and see what happened." He looked at Alex, then at Kate's face.

Alex stood up on the pew, his little hand on Kate's sleeve. She set her purse down on the seat and held his hand. She wondered if Charlie knew Alex's secret. Maybe it wasn't a secret at all. She looked into Alex's brown eyes that were too large for his face and decided it was too personal to discuss in the aisle after church.

"I've been praying for you all," she faltered.

"Thanks," Charlie said. The sad look still hovered in his eyes. "Angie Blake brought Tyler over to play once."

"How did it go?"

"Betty said it went well, and she took Alex to meet them at the park after that. It was cold and they didn't stay long, but the boys got along all right."

Kate nodded. She was staring. She made herself look away from his face, stooping down to Alex again. "Did you have fun with Tyler?"

"Yes. He has a cowboy hat."

Kate smiled. "Did you like the hat?"

He shrugged. "Tyler likes it," he said noncommittally.

Charlie said, "Look, I—" he stopped, and an unspoken question hung in the air.

Kate returned his look helplessly, feeling sick or giddy, impossible to tell which.

"Charlie, can I see you for a minute?" Howard Banks was standing beside him.

"Sure," said Charlie. He turned to Kate. "Could I leave Alex with you for just a minute?"

"Of course." She sat down again.

Alex held out his arms, and Kate embraced him and pulled him over the back of the pew into her row. He settled contentedly on her lap.

"Daddy read me the frog book last night," he said.

"Did you read it for yourself, too?"

"Yes. And the dog book."

"Was it hard?" Kate asked.

"No, that one was baby."

She smiled. "Does your daddy know that you read the books yourself?"

He shook his head emphatically and looked up at her through his long black lashes.

"Is it a secret?" Kate asked.

He nodded slowly.

"I don't think Daddy would mind," she said. "He might even be happy if he knew."

Alex sat, thoughtful for a moment, then looked up at her. He put his arm up around her neck and pulled her head down close. In her ear, he whispered, "He might not read to me anymore."

Kate swallowed hard, trying to gauge this latest fear that had surfaced for Alex. If his father knew he could read for himself, would he still bother to read out loud to him? She knew Charlie went home tired every night, but she also thought she knew something of the intensity of his love for Alex.

Before she could tell the boy that, Charlie was back, gazing quizzically at the two of them. The congregation had thinned, and Kate suddenly felt they must look odd, her holding Alex on her lap, her eyes brimming with tears, and the little boy clinging to her.

"I'm sorry," she said, standing up carefully. She passed Alex into his father's arms.

"For what?"

She had no answer. She wasn't sorry she loved Alex, or that she had let Alex feel it. Perhaps it was for the tears. She fumbled in her bag for a tissue and turned away from Charlie to wipe her eyes. When she turned back, he was still there, his dark eyes troubled.

"Everything all right?" he asked.

She nodded. "We just—he touches me somehow. He's so great." Her voice broke, and she gave up, picking up her jacket, Bible, and purse and stepping out into the aisle with a little wave. Alex waved, and Charlie nodded solemnly.

Chapter 11

Kate called her brother that afternoon.

"Chad, you've got to come down again. I can't stand it."

"Can't stand what, Katie? Is something wrong?"

"No, not really. I miss you. I miss Dad. I—I'm just weepy today, I guess."

"Come up here next weekend."

"No, I'm not coming to your dorm room."

"I'll meet you someplace."

"Come down here, Chad. Please?"

"Katie, I have a date."

A moment of silence stretched out, while Kate adjusted to the idea.

"You've met someone," she said at last.

"Yes. Her name is Ellen. You'd like her. Come on up, and I'll introduce you."

"No, that's—that's okay. I just needed someone to talk to."

"Look, I'll come a week from Friday," Chad said. "It's just that I made this date with Ellen, and it's kind of a big deal at the church."

"Church? You're going to church?"

"That's where I met her," Chad said. "I started going after I was at your place. This morning was the third time. And Ellen—well, she's great, Katie. I met her at the church, and they're having this harvest supper, and I really want to take her."

"Go with her," Kate said. "I'm happy for you, Chad. Really. It sounds nice, and I want to meet her sometime."

"All right. I'll come down next week. Are you sure you're okay?" There was a pause. "Kate, is there a man?"

"No," she choked. "Well, there is a guy. He's four years old."

"You're kidding, right?"

"No, I'm not kidding. He's an adorable little boy who is far more intelligent than his family suspects. He reads, Chad, and nobody knows it."

"Nobody but you?"

"I think so. He read me a book at the library the other day."

"Must have had it memorized."

"No, I tested him a little. He was reading, Chad."

"Did you tell the parents?"

"No. He wants to keep it a secret."

"Why on earth?"

"He's afraid," said Kate.

"Afraid of what?"

"It's a long story. He's afraid of lots of things. Strangers and water and being left alone. In this particular case, he's afraid that once they know he can read, they'll quit reading to him. It's one of the things he loves most, and he doesn't want it to end."

"Do they beat him?"

"No, they love him very much."

"Sounds like a weird kid," Chad said.

"No, no, he's wonderful."

"Katie, you need a life."

***

"Miss Pierce!"

86

Kate stopped on her way down the school corridor and turned back toward the library. Heather Wilson, the pastor's daughter, came hurrying to catch up with her, an armful of notebooks and textbooks threatening to spew from her grasp.

"Miss Pierce, are you coming to the program tomorrow night?"

"I hadn't really thought much about it," Kate said. "Are you performing?"

"Yes, the high school is doing a Mayflower pageant, and I'm singing with the chorus. Please come. Tara and I are Pilgrim women, and we really need some supporters in the audience."

"I'm sure everyone will be supporting you," Kate said with a smile. "You and Tara will be the beauties of the Mayflower."

Heather giggled. "Tara is Priscilla Mullins, and she gets to have a really great part. But I'm Ellen Billington, and she's known as a gossip! I get put in the stocks."

"Really?" Kate cried.

"Yes, and the governor, the one who makes me be put in the stocks, is Jeremy Poirier."

"Oh, I've got to see it." Kate knew Jeremy was the subject of much whispering between Heather and Tara while they worked in the school library mornings. He was considered the best-looking senior boy, but he was bashful around the girls. She had seen him glance at Heather over the top of his encyclopedia a few days before, as he sat doing research at a library table during home room period. Every time one of the girls looked his way, however, he lowered his gaze and appeared to be engrossed in his work.

"So you'll come?" Heather pressed her.

"I'll be there."

***

Kate was a few minutes late leaving the school building. She drove to the public library by the most direct route, but at the junction of College Avenue and Main Street, she had to wait precious minutes while a long ladder truck made a three-point turn in the intersection and backed ponderously into the fire station.

Roxanne Dufour stood under the light. Clad in her uniform, she authoritatively waved on the drivers from Upper Main Street first, then those from Elm Street, and finally Kate and the others from College Avenue.

She must have seen me sitting here, late for work, and deliberately made us go last, Kate thought, then laughed at herself.

Charlie Abbot was already in conference with Marilyn when she walked into the library's children's room. Alex ran to Kate from the stuffed animal bin. She dropped to her knees and folded him in her arms.

"Alex, honey, you're making me cry," she said with a little laugh, as he burrowed against her neck.

"Don't cry," he said, all concern. "Are you sad?"

She reached for the tote bag she had let fall to the floor and pawed through it for a tissue. "I'm not sad, Alex. I'm glad to see you. I'm always happy deep inside when I see you."

"I'm happy inside too," he said.

Kate wiped her eyes and stood up. "I need to put my things away," she told him. "Do you want to come with me and help get ready for story time?"

He nodded.

"Go ask your daddy."

He ran to Charlie and tugged at his sleeve. "Daddy, can I help Miss Pierce?"

Charlie turned around and looked at Kate, who was picking up her things. "Sure. Just be good." He ruffled Alex's hair and gave his attention back to Marilyn.

Kate smiled at the boy and led him to the closed door of the back room.

"This is a secret room," she said. "No one goes in here except people who work at the library."

Alex's eyes were round.

"But today, you can come in here, because you are going to work here and help me with the chairs."

She opened the door and they went inside. Alex stopped and stared at the collapsed puppet theater, folded on itself and leaning against one wall.

"Is that the puppet stage?" he asked.

"Yes. We keep it in here between shows." Kate took out her keyring. "We also keep our coats and things in here, in this secret cupboard."

He watched with big eyes as Kate put her purse, jacket, and tote bag inside, then closed the cupboard and locked it again. Kate smiled, and Alex smiled.

"Sometimes we workers come in here and drink coffee," she said confidentially.

"Coffee?" Alex asked, his eyes bigger.

"Well, little people who work here don't drink coffee. But they might eat Tootsie Rolls." She reached for the jar Marilyn kept stocked. There were a dozen candies in the bottom, and she took one out for Alex. He held it in his hand, looking at it for a moment, then slowly unwrapped it and put it in his mouth. He chewed with great effort, then smiled endearingly up at Kate.

"Come on, fella," she said with a grin. "Let's go get the chairs ready. It's almost story time."

People were beginning to arrive as they quickly arranged the chairs for Charlie and the mothers.

Charlie came over, saying, "Hey, Alex, you sitting with me today?"

"If Miss Pierce doesn't need me," Alex said in his most serious tone.

"I can spare you for a little while," she said. "Thanks for helping."

"Kate."

She turned back and looked expectantly at Charlie. He shot a glance past her at the approaching mothers and preschoolers. "I appreciate your attitude with Alex." He looked as though he would have said more, but a mother was waiting to greet him. Kate nodded and walked away.

Chapter 12

Kate worked in the main room during the story hour, checking out books for the smattering of patrons who needed it, shelving returned books, and straightening the toys for the preschoolers who would rush for them when Charlie finished. All the time, she thought about Alex, reading silently when he thought no one would know. She wondered how proficient he was, and why he had been willing to let her in on his secret.

Betty came in a few minutes before the story hour was over. When Charlie brought Alex out, he handed the boy over to his aunt for help in choosing the week's reading material. Kate was helping a mother whose child was clamoring for a particular picture book, and Marilyn had stepped behind the desk. When Kate placed the special book in the little girl's hand, the mother thanked her and took her little girl to the checkout desk. Charlie stepped over near Kate.

"Charlie, I had a question for you," she said, before he could speak.

"Oh? I had a question for you too. Go ahead." He smiled with even, white teeth.

Her heart was racing again, and she took a step backward. "Well, I was wondering if I could read with Alex sometimes. I mean, maybe go to your house after I'm done work some days, if you and Betty wouldn't mind. Go be with him when you can't be there, I mean." She felt she was expressing herself badly, and she came to a stop, eyeing him uncertainly.

"Give him more reading time?" Charlie asked. "He loves to be read to."

"Oh, I know, and I like spending time with him. He seems to be comfortable with me. I could give Betty a break if she wanted to run errands or something. I mean, if you don't think that's—pushy—or—counterproductive or something," she said lamely. Would that other woman, the someone whom Alex might trust, read to him?

Charlie's smile was heartier than it had been in weeks. "I think that would be great. Alex likes you a lot."

She nodded. "I like him. I—" She almost said, I love him, but she thought better of it.

Charlie swallowed and looked around the room. A few family groups were still perusing the bookshelves, and two mothers and their children stood before the desk where Marilyn was at work.

"I'm trying to figure out a way we can catch this library prowler," he said.

"Do you think he comes in here a lot?"

"Marilyn thinks he was here last night. There's nothing definite, but she thought some things were out of place this morning."

"Have you thought about having an officer stay in here one night to see if anyone shows up?"

"Yes, I've considered it. But the prowler doesn't seem to come every night. We could spend an awful lot of time and money for nothing."

"Well, he hasn't hurt anyone."

"Yes, that's one consolation." Charlie glanced toward the checkout desk. "Look, am I keeping you from your work?"

"Probably." Kate gave a nervous little laugh.

"Well, I wanted to ask you—would you consider doing something with—with Alex and me tomorrow night?"

Kate opened her mouth then closed it. She had thought Charlie's interests lay elsewhere and had given up hope of his extending another invitation. But the academy was presenting its Thanksgiving program Friday night. What timing! She never had evening plans, never. Except this one time.

She shook her head slightly. "I'm sorry, I—I can't tomorrow." She would have tried to explain, but Charlie gave a resigned shrug and a tight smile.

"Okay," he said. "Well, feel free to go by the house and read to Alex anytime. I'm sure he'd enjoy it." He put his hat on and walked toward Alex and Betty.

Kate started to follow him, wanting intensely to explain about the Thanksgiving program.

She heard a muted trill. Charlie stopped walking and took his cell phone from his pocket.

Opportunity lost. Kate grabbed an armful of books off the return cart and walked toward the biography shelves, breathing shakily. *All right, Lord, I can see the timing isn't right here,* she prayed. *I don't want to push something that's not part of Your plan.*

"Okay, I'll be right there," Charlie said into his phone. He put it away and went over to Alex and Betty.

Kate watched bleakly as he bent to kiss Alex good-bye and walked toward the side door without looking her way.

I should have done something, she berated herself, then pulled up short. *No, Lord, You are in control here, not me. I want things Your way, even if it hurts.*

When Charlie was out the door, Betty said to Marilyn, "That was Roxanne phoning him. I could hear her." She scowled. "She knew it was his day for the story hour. Guess she thought he was a little slow getting back to the station."

"Does she call him often?" Marilyn asked.

"She called him at home last night." Betty's voice was tinged with disgust. "He ought to be able to relax with his family when he's off duty."

She zipped Alex's jacket and gathered up his books.

"Good-bye, Miss Pierce," Alex said plaintively, as he passed her on his way out.

Kate smiled and waved, but she felt like crying.

***

The next day, Kate left the library at three o'clock and drove to the Abbot house. The yard was trim and neat, the perennial gardens ready for winter. A toy wagon on the lawn near the path was the only thing she saw out of place.

The old house had white clapboard siding and black wooden shutters. There was no doorbell. She knocked a medium-loud knock, and Betty opened the door.

"Miss Pierce! Come right in. Charlie said you might come by."

"Thank you. It's Kate." She stepped inside and set her tote bag down on a bench near the door.

Betty took her coat and called, "Alex! You have company. Come see who's here."

Alex peeked shyly around the doorjamb between the kitchen and the dining room. "Miss Pierce!" He ran to her gleefully.

Kate scooped him up and kissed him. "Alex! Hello. Is it all right if I visit you at home?"

"Yes! Yes!"

"Would you show me your house?" she asked, smiling.

He took her hand and gave her a tour. "This is my kitchen, and this is my Aunt Betty."

Betty had gone to the ironing board that was set up between the kitchen table and the sink. She had one of Charlie's blue uniform shirts spread out and was pressing the sleeve with the police department insignia.

"These shirts are supposed to be permanent press, but they aren't," she said.

Kate flashed her a smile as Alex tugged her into the next room. "This is my dining room."

Kate looked quickly around at the maple table and chairs, the sideboard, and deep, lace-curtained windows as Alex pulled her through to the next doorway.

"This is my living room." He stopped before the fireplace and looked up at an eight-by-ten framed photograph on the mantel. "That's my mommy." He stared at it for a few seconds.

"She was very pretty," Kate said. In the picture, Joy stood on a wharf holding a canoe paddle. She wore khaki shorts, a navy blue sweatshirt, and hiking boots. Her light brown hair waved back from her smooth forehead. Her smile was natural, as though the photographer had just made a witty remark.

Alex pulled gently at her hand and led her to a doorway, through which she could see a toy bulldozer and a Duplo block set on the rug. "This is my toy room." They moved to another doorway. "This is my bathroom."

He headed for the stairs with wide pine treads and a square, green balustrade and banister.

"You don't need to show me the upstairs, honey," Kate said. "May we sit down here and look at some books?"

Alex looked up at her questioningly, then smiled broadly. Fifteen minutes later, Betty brought in a tray with two glasses of milk and a plate holding four peanut butter cookies. She found Kate and Alex on the couch. Alex had taken his shoes off and was nestled up against Kate. They each held one side of a large story book. Betty set the tray down and went back to the kitchen, then came through again and went up the stairs with a basket full of clean laundry.

Kate read a story, and Alex read a story, very quietly, glancing often toward the stairway, on the alert for Aunt Betty. Kate helped him with an odd name, but his reading was nearly flawless.

Betty returned to the kitchen, and after a while Kate smelled meat cooking. She finished up the story they were reading, *My Brother and Me,* and said, "Alex, I have to go now. Your Daddy will be home soon, though."

"I wish I had a brother," Alex said wistfully, gazing at the book cover. "Do you have a brother?"

"Yes, I do. His name is Chad." She put the books she had brought into her bag.

"Really? A real brother?" His eyes were enormous.

Kate nodded thoughtfully. Chad had always been there, and she had taken him for granted. "He's coming here next weekend," she said.

"Here?"

"Well, not to this house," Kate explained. "He's coming to Waterville to visit me."

"Can I see him?" Alex asked.

"Well, maybe, if he goes to church with me Sunday. If he stays for church, I'll introduce him to you."

"Is he little?" Alex asked.

"No, he's big, like me, or like your Daddy. He's grown up."

"Tyler's going to get a brother," Alex confided.

"Really? That's exciting," Kate said.

"I told him I'm getting a brother too."

Kate tried to think of the right thing to say, but nothing seemed quite appropriate. "Maybe you should talk to Daddy about that."

He nodded.

"Talk to him tonight," Kate said firmly.

Again he nodded.

She put her arms around him. "I'll see you soon," she whispered.

Chapter 13

After a solitary supper in her apartment, Kate drove to the church for the Thanksgiving program. The Wilsons welcomed her enthusiastically in the entry and persuaded her to join them as they watched their children perform.

The elementary school children gave their presentations first. Joey Palmer stole the show as a plump turkey who shed tail feathers all over the stage, running from the zealous Pilgrim boy who chased him with a blunderbuss.

The high school pageant stirred Kate's heart as the boys portrayed the Pilgrim men, gathered in the tiny cabin of the Mayflower to sign the Mayflower Compact. Tara blushed through her scene with Philip Banks, who played a lovestruck John Alden.

Heather and Jonathan Wilson carried their parts well, and Heather drew laughs as Ellen Billington, going from goodwife to goodwife, carrying a tale about one of the elders. Her shrill protests were convincing, as Jeremy ordered her clapped in the stocks. Jonathan played her son Francis, and he stood by his mother in her moment of humiliation.

The audience rewarded them with prolonged applause and cheering.

"Come to the house for a while," Sarah coaxed Kate when the program was over. "We're having ice cream."

Kate yielded and was glad for the diversion. She was determined to stay busy so that she wouldn't brood over what she should have said to Charlie Abbot.

***

Saturday dragged endlessly. Kate cleaned her apartment and took a load of laundry to the basement utility room, then she went to the grocery store. No puppet show was scheduled that weekend, and for the first time in months, Kate was bored. When she had put away her groceries, she went to the laundry room to put her clothes in the dryer.

"Miss Pierce," her downstairs neighbor greeted her on the stairs.

"Hello, Mr. Epson," Kate said.

The middle-aged accountant lived alone in the apartment below Kate's, and she rarely saw him, but his parking space was next to hers outside the building, and they occasionally exchanged greetings as they left for work mornings. She went on down and shifted her laundry to the dryer, then trudged back up the stairs and sat down with a book, trying to divert her mind from Charlie.

She put her hand on the telephone receiver once, with the idea of calling Betty to see if she could go over and read to Alex again, but the thought that Charlie would be spending his day off with his son held her back. She didn't want to intrude on their time together or cause Betty to think she was chasing Charlie.

Finally she pulled on a thick sweater and her parka and walked half a mile to the hospital. The lobby held an art display area, and a local artist's watercolors were on exhibit for the month of November. Kate took her time examining the vibrant florals and still lifes, then bought a cup of tea in the coffee shop before heading home again.

She was glad to know she had a busy week ahead. Marilyn was scheduled to attend a librarians' seminar on Thursday and Friday, and Kate would spend those entire days in charge of the children's room, opening at nine in the morning and locking up at six. Jocelyn was coming in to help her from three to six both days. Other than that, Kate would be alone on duty in the children's area, and she expected to be scrambling to keep up with the checkouts and returns.

"May we sit with you?" Jill Palmer asked cheerfully on Sunday, just before their class was to start.

"Of course." Kate smiled and moved over a little so Jill and Kate would have plenty of room. She was for the company.

They stay with her between the services, and Jill's bright conversation kept her occupied. Kate told herself with satisfaction when the worship hour began that she had no idea whether or not Charlie Abbot was within ten miles of the church. She'd deliberately chosen a seat near the front of the auditorium to keep herself from gazing around for the Abbots.

She left the building congratulating herself on doing so well at uprooting the obsession. Every time Alex or Charlie had come to mind during church, she had firmly relegated the thoughts to oblivion.

She went down the steps and turned purposefully to the right, where she had left her car and walked quickly across the parking lot, looking only toward her hatchback.

She stopped in her tracks. Alex was standing by the door of her car, looking anxiously toward her. His eyes were wide below the cuff of his blue knit hat. She moved forward again, quickening her steps, and stooped down when she reached him.

"Alex, what are you doing here?"

"Daddy wouldn't let me come sit with you at church, and I missed you. I thought your brother was coming."

Tears sprang into Kate's eyes. "Oh, honey, that's next week. I'm sorry."

Alex swallowed hard, and she patted his shoulder. "I should have made it clear. You'd better go back to your daddy. Where is he?" She looked around surreptitiously. In the next row of cars, Charlie was deep in conversation with Don Blake. Tyler hung on to his father's arm, tugging impatiently at Don's sleeve.

"Alex, you'd better go," Kate said.

He looked up at her sadly, then held up his arms. Kate hesitated. She didn't want to be flooded again with the love and grief that Alex brought her.

"Are you happy inside to see me?" he asked wistfully.

"Oh, yes, honey!" She picked him up and stood leaning against her car, holding Alex tightly, her eyes closed.

"Will you come to my house again?" he asked.

"If you want me to."

"Come today," Alex said.

"No, I can't."

"Why not?" Alex asked, with just the suggestion of a pout.

Kate looked into his eyes. "Alex, you may not understand this, but I can only come when your daddy isn't there."

He looked at her gravely. Tears spilled over and coursed down her cheeks as she looked into the eyes that were too much like Charlie's.

"Miss Pierce, are you sad again?" Alex crooned.

"A little bit."

"Kate, I'm sorry."

She jumped and turned toward Charlie. He was standing beside her, holding out his hands to his son.

"Come on Alex, don't bother Miss Pierce."

Alex went into his father's arms, and Charlie set him down on the pavement.

"He's not bothering me," Kate said, turning away and hoping Charlie had not seen her tears.

Charlie stood silent for a moment, then said regretfully, "I'm sorry, Kate. Whatever it is … I'm sorry."

She wondered what would happen if she told him that she loved him, and that his son pulled at her heart in a way that made her feel desperate. Even if she had dared, she couldn't have spoken at that moment, but she couldn't just stand there with tears dripping onto the tar.

She opened her purse and rummaged frantically for a tissue. Catching movement from the corner of her eye, she glanced up. Charlie and Alex were walking away hand in hand. Charlie's shoulders were slumped, and Alex was looking back at her, his eyes troubled.

***

"Are you sure you'll be all right tomorrow and Friday?" Marilyn asked on Wednesday afternoon.

"Yes, I'll be fine," Kate said. "You go and have a super time."

Marilyn held out the checklist she had made. "Don't forget about the story time."

"I called the reader today," Kate assured her.

"Good, and if the new book order comes in, just leave the cartons in the back room. I'll open them Monday."

"Got it."

"If you have any problems, call on Mr. Carter."

"I will."

"Oh, and here! I almost forgot. This is a gift for you and your brother." Marilyn held out an envelope, and Kate took it.

"What is it?"

"Richard was able to get you two tickets for the hockey game Saturday. I thought you and your brother would enjoy it."

"Oh, Marilyn, thank you! Chad will love it. Please thank your husband for me too. I never have any way to entertain Chad when he's here. This is great!"

***

Kate dressed slowly for prayer meeting that evening. She dreaded the chance of meeting Charlie again. She put on the red plaid skirt and black sweater that usually made her feel snug and confident, but she felt vulnerable and helpless.

At the church, she slipped into the back pew and kept her eyes down during the Bible study, but when prayer requests were given, she found herself looking at Betty Abbot. Betty was sitting with Alex beside her on the other side of the aisle, and Charlie was nowhere to be seen.

When the congregation broke into small groups for prayer, Kate prayed silently for guidance, and walked slowly toward Betty.

"Hello, Kate," Betty said pleasantly, and Alex's eyes lit up.

"Miss Pierce!" He flung himself at her, and Kate scooped him up into her arms, laughing.

"I guess you'll have to join us," Betty said with a smile. "Alex won't let you get away."

"If you don't mind," Kate said.

"Of course not. Sit down here." Betty slid over to make room for her. Jill Palmer came with little Amy and sat in the pew in front of them, turning halfway around toward them.

"Hello, Jill," said Betty.

"Where's Charlie tonight?" Jill asked.

"He's working a new shift this week. Goes in at four in the afternoon and works until midnight. I hope it's just for this week."

Kate took a deep breath and tried not to analyze the wave of emotion that washed over her. Relief, yes, but longing too. She held Alex, glad for the chance to be with him without fear of encountering his father.

When the women had prayed, Betty asked, "When are you coming over again, Kate? Alex has been pestering me every day to ask you to come again."

"I'd like to," she said. "I'm working longer hours this week because Marilyn will be away for a couple of days, but I could come tomorrow night, if you're sure you wouldn't mind."

"That would be great," Betty said. "Charlie always reads Alex a bedtime story or two, and Alex doesn't like this new schedule. I read to him from *Mrs. Pigglewiggle* last night, but I could tell he missed his father."

Kate looked into Alex's face. "But Daddy must be home more during the day now," she said. "Haven't you had time to do things together?"

"Yes, but we didn't read today," Alex said plaintively.

"I will come tomorrow night," Kate declared. "It will be about six thirty, but I will come, and I'll stay until your bedtime, and we'll read lots of stories."

"Goodie!" Alex hugged her fiercely around the neck. "And you don't have to worry about Daddy. He's gone until way late in the night."

Betty laughed. "Why would she worry about Daddy, silly boy?"

Kate said nothing, but Jill was watching her keenly.

Chapter 14

Thursday flew, and Kate had no time to think about Charlie. She had told the academy staff that she would be unable to go to the school library that morning or Friday. Arriving early at the public library, she put her things away and made sure everything was ready for patrons. Promptly at nine, she opened the children's room. She spent the first two hours waiting on patrons and shelving. The story hour was well attended, and she was kept busy until noon with mothers and young children.

Jill and Amy Palmer were part of the story hour audience that week. An EMT read picture books, but Jill didn't stay afterward. She pulled Kate aside just long enough to whisper, "You look so harried that I think Amy and I will come back another day for our books. I'm praying for you."

"Thanks," Kate murmured, and went back to her work.

At one o'clock, she dashed to the back room for a minute to eat her sandwich. She heard people coming down the stairs and went back to her post, shoving a candy bar into the desk drawer in case there was a lull later when she could eat it.

By the end of the day, she felt as if the nightmares from her early days at the library were coming true: load after load of books were waiting to be shelved. Jocelyn came as quickly as she could after her classes and worked with her from three o'clock on. Theoretically, Kate could go then, but there was too much to do, and she didn't want to leave the college student alone. She even stayed fifteen minutes late, after Jocelyn left.

Her promise to Alex lay heavy on her mind, and at six fifteen, she went through the rooms, picking up stuffed animals, straightening displays, and turning off the lights. She remembered to check the rest rooms and empty the trash cans, then went up the stairs into the library's main lobby. She closed the door to the children's room, turned the key in the lock, and tried the knob, just to be sure.

"Goodnight," she called to the evening assistant at the main desk.

"'Bye."

Kate went out the front door and hurried to her car.

***

"You came!" Alex was jubilant.

"Of course I came. And I brought lots of books." Kate hung her jacket on a hook and picked up her bulging totebag.

"Would you mind if I went out for an hour or so?" Betty asked.

"No, that's fine," Kate said. "Alex and I will do some reading, and I'll tuck him in at eight if you're not back."

"Thanks. I left you some cookies and milk on the table."

Kate and Alex curled up on the couch and read and laughed and ate together, reveling in each other's company. Kate had a book of silly riddles, which Alex found hilarious. Then they sailed through several picture books, taking turns reading the text. As his bedtime approached, Kate chose a quiet story with a happy, satisfying ending. Alex sat on her lap, with his head pillowed on her shoulder. He was yawning when she finished reading.

"Come on," Kate whispered. "Let's get you into bed."

He led her sleepily up the stairs, and Kate found that Betty had laid out his clean sleeper. Alex took her through his bedtime routine: bathroom, toothbrush, pajamas, prayers.

She sat on the edge of his bed, stroking his fine hair.

"Good night, Alex. I love you."

"I love you, too. I wish you lived with us."

"That's not possible, honey."

"Why not?"

She struggled for a childproof explanation. "I just don't think God wants it that way."

"Why? God wants good things."

She smiled. "Yes, Alex. I don't know why things are the way they are, but God knows best. If He wanted us to be in the same family, we would be."

"Can I still meet your brother?"

"Yes. If he stays over for church on Sunday, you'll meet him."

His eyes were troubled. "Daddy says I can't get a brother like Tyler."

"Oh," Kate said sympathetically. "Sometimes, that just can't happen."

"Daddy said God doesn't want us to have a brother." His little face was full of woe.

"I'm sorry Alex." Kate put her arms around him and hugged him. "Sleep tight. I'll be right downstairs until Aunt Betty gets home."

***

Kate went quietly down the stairs, stacked the books, and put their dishes in the kitchen sink. As she rinsed the milk glasses, the telephone on the kitchen wall rang shrilly. She hesitated, then picked up the receiver.

"Abbot house."

"Oh, hello. Is that you, Kate?"

Apprehension and joy struggled within her. "Yes, Charlie. I came to read to Alex, and Betty stepped out for a moment."

"I just wanted to check on things and see if Alex went to bed all right tonight. Betty told me he's been a little fussy about it this week."

"He was fine," Kate said. "I just tucked him in."

"He really likes you, Kate."

Unsure of what to say, Kate hated the lump that closed her throat every time Charlie spoke to her.

"I think he's going to grow up just fine, Charlie," she said at last. "He feels things deeply, but he's very wise for his age."

Charlie was quiet.

"He does miss you, but I think he understands it's your job," she said.

"Thanks. I've been trying to be there for him during the day, but it's just—well, it's a change. That doesn't make it any worse, but change is scary for Alex."

"For us all."

"Well, yes, I suppose so."

There was another pause, and Kate wondered if she ought to end the conversation, but she didn't want to. It seemed a little easier, somehow, to talk to him without seeing him, without those penetrating brown eyes searching her face.

"Kate, I'm still praying for you," he said softly.

"Thanks."

"I don't know what you're dealing with right now, but I got the feeling Sunday there was something really big. If there's anything I can do to help you ..."

It's you! her brain screamed.

"I didn't want Alex to upset you," Charlie persisted.

"He didn't upset me."

"Well, it just seemed like you wanted to be alone, and he got away from me there, when Don was talking to me –"

"Charlie, it's okay. Alex is never a bother."

"All right." He took a deep breath. "Well, thanks for going over tonight. I didn't know you were going to be there."

"You don't mind, do you?"

"No, of course not. I told you that."

"Thank you."

There was another silence.

"Well, I'd better get back to work," Charlie said at last.

***

Friday was even more hectic at the library than Thursday had been. Jill and Amy Palmer came in during the lunchtime lull.

"Hi! How you doing?" Jill asked.

"Well, it's been really busy, but I'm surviving," Kate said. "There's a daycare class of fifteen coming in at two o'clock, though."

"I'm glad we came early," Jill said.

She helped Amy choose four new books and brought them to the desk, where Kate was quickly downing her sandwich. "We're interrupting your lunch."

"That's okay. Thought I'd grab a bite while not many people were in here. I'm never sorry to see you." Kate punched in Jill's code on the computer and scanned the spines of the books.

"Is everything okay with you, Kate? Not work, I mean. Personally."

"Everything's fine."

Jill said nothing, and when Kate handed her the books, she found her friend's gaze was skeptical.

"Don't try to carry the load by yourself," Jill said quietly. "If you don't want to talk about it, at least remember Jesus is there."

"Thanks." Kate felt dangerously close to tears again. "He knows about it. But I'd appreciate it if you'd keep praying for me."

The side door opened, and two young mothers came in with strollers and toddlers.

Jill nodded. "We'll talk sometime, when you're ready, but I'll be praying for you. You can be sure of that."

Kate smiled at her and put the sandwich bag in the desk drawer. If she had time later, she would eat the candy bar she had left there the day before. She glanced at the contents of the drawer, then opened it wider. The candy bar was gone.

Chapter 15

When Jocelyn came in at three o'clock, Kate was checking out a tall stack of science books for a teacher. Jocelyn waved, on her way to the back room, and Kate looked meaningfully at the two laden book carts. The girl nodded, and when she had put her coat away, she plunged into the task of shelving.

Kate joined her whenever she could, but when it was time to close three hours later, there were still dozens of volumes on one of the carts.

"Time to go, Jocelyn," she said. "Thanks for your help."

"I was hoping I could finish up, but they just kept bringing back more and more books." Jocelyn shrugged. "Oh, well, I guess Marilyn will have something to do tomorrow morning."

Kate frowned at the book cart and went to check the restrooms and the back room. When she returned to the main room carrying her jacket and purse, she stopped by the cart. Although she was worn out, she imagined Marilyn coming in on Saturday morning and seeing the unshelved books. Marilyn always made sure everything was in place before she left for the night. Every toy, every tape, every cushion, and most of all, every book.

Sighing, Kate laid her jacket and purse on the desk. With Marilyn's key, she locked the side door to the street and then began sorting the books that were left by category and number. Picture books, juvenile fiction, biographies, social studies, science, arts, sports. When she had the divisions roughed out, she pushed the cart into the toddler room and began shelving the picture books.

She worked her way around the edge of the main room next, replacing fiction, then wearily rolled the cart into nonfiction. She dimmed the lights in the main room so no one would look through the glass in the side door and think the children's room was still open. In the farthest corner of the nonfiction room, she knelt in an alcove of science books. Bridges, energy, time … The topics blurred, and only the numbers mattered.

Footsteps sounded on the stairs, and Kate jerked her head around. Had she locked the door to the main lobby at the top of the stairs? She had forgotten. Perhaps the evening librarian was coming down to check and see if she had finished for the night.

As feet in sneakers and legs in ragged jeans came slowly, stealthily into view, Kate held her breath. The person on the stairs was not one of the library employees. Mr. Carter insisted on neat attire.

She shrank back in the alcove, against the shelves, her face low. Should she stand up and confront the intruder?

It was a man. He wore a lined denim jacket, and a long striped scarf trailed over one shoulder. He was turned away from her, dirty blond hair swinging at shoulder level. Pausing at the bottom of the steps, he looked around the dimly lit main room. Kate ducked back into the alcove, her heart pounding. She wondered if the workers and patrons upstairs would hear her if she screamed.

The nonfiction room was the only one where she had left the lights up. Would he find that odd and go back up the stairs? She waited, then she heard the drawers of the desk being opened and closed stealthily.

Kate pulled her knees up and made herself as small as she could in the corner, praying silently, her heart pounding. She was sure he couldn't see her unless he came around the free-standing bookcases in the nonfiction area and approached the alcove. She listened for his footfalls on the carpeted floor and was startled when she heard sounds much closer than expected. He had flipped the light switch in one of the restrooms and closed the door.

Kate waited a moment, then peeked out around the edge of the shelves. The door of the nearest restroom was closed, and water was running.

She stood up shakily and tiptoed to the stairs, going straight up them, and grasped the handle to the heavy door at the top. It was locked.

Standing immobile, Kate tried to swallow her panic and think. He had locked the door behind him when he came down. He must have a key. Marilyn had been wrong, and there was an extra key.

Where were her own keys? She put her hand to the pocket of her skirt, but even as she did it, she knew she had left the keyring on the checkout desk below, beside her purse and jacket.

She tiptoed down half a dozen steps and glanced into the nonfiction room. The restroom door was still closed. Should she dash down to the desk, or go back up and pound on the reading room door, hoping someone would come quickly and release her?

Slowly Kate put one foot down to the next step, then the other. Once she had decided, she couldn't stop. She ran lightly down and across the main room to the desk.

Her purse was open, the contents spilling across the desktop. Where was her cell? Her wallet lay unsnapped, and she picked it up quickly. All of the bills were missing. It hadn't been much, but she felt suddenly very angry and afraid. Her keyring was not there.

She turned back toward the stairway, hearing the restroom door open as she measured the distance to the bottom step with her eye. If the door at the top weren't locked ... But it was.

She thought fleetingly of the side door, but she had locked that. Would it open if she pushed the safety bar? She wasn't sure. If she risked it and it wouldn't open, he would surely hear her, and she would be trapped.

As the possibilities raced through her mind, she moved. Ducking behind the desk, she crouched there on hands and knees, waiting.

The only sounds were very quiet and distant. She slowly raised her head. There was no movement, no figure to see. She was afraid to stand up, knowing he was still somewhere in the rooms.

An orange light glowed on the desk telephone's keypad, and Kate reached across the desk and picked up the receiver. She keyed in the extension for the front desk and got a busy signal. She rose on her knees and pushed down the button that closed the connection, her eyes on the opening to the lighted nonfiction room. She was still alone.

She pushed 911.

"Waterville com center. What is your emergency?" The dispatcher's voice was loud in her ear.

Kate curled up low on the floor and said softly into the receiver, "Yes, there's a prowler here in the library with me. I can't talk loud."

"You say a prowler, ma'am?"

"Yes. He's in the children's room. Officer Abbot has been trying to catch him, and he's here now. I'm locked in, and the phone upstairs is busy. I'm frightened."

"We'll send someone right over, ma'am. Where exactly are you?"

There was a thumping sound, and Kate jumped. *He's in the back room.*

"I'm in the children's room in the basement of the public library. I was working late. A man came down the stairs and locked the door behind him. He doesn't know I'm here. I'm hiding under the desk."

"Can you see him?" the dispatcher asked.

"No, he's in the next room."

"All right, ma'am, stay where you are, and we'll send someone over."

Kate waited, wondering if she was foolish to stay where she was. She might have been out the side door by now, or up the stairs, pounding on the thick door there. She envisioned the man in the back room, rifling Marilyn's candy jar.

"Ma'am, are you still there?" came the dispatcher's voice.

"Yes."

"There's a unit on the way. We're trying to call the library, but the line's busy. If we can get through to them, we'll ask someone to come down where you are. Do you think this prowler is armed?"

"I didn't see anything," Kate whispered. She hadn't thought about weapons, and she wished the dispatcher hadn't suggested the idea. Her hands were trembling now.

"What's he doing now?"

"I think he's in where we leave our coats and things. Sometimes we leave candy in there, and he's taken it before."

"Do you think you can get out now, ma'am?"

"I'm not sure. He took my keyring off the desk, and I can't open the door at the top of the stairs. If someone up there opened it, I could—"

She broke off suddenly, as the door to the back room swung open.

"He's coming," she hissed into the telephone, and lay down with her cheek on the carpet, her heart hammering.

She felt the vibration of his cushioned footsteps on the rug as the man entered the main room. The checkout desk was a counter, and she couldn't see out from under it, but she knew he wasn't far from the other side. Muted sounds, fabric on fabric, reached her, then a sigh, and a soft thud.

He's got the cushions, and he's going to sleep on the floor. She didn't dare to pass the information along to the dispatcher.

The prowler was only feet away, and even the possibility of the dispatcher's voice being heard was a threat.

She willed herself to breathe slowly, silently, and soon she heard the man's breathing. She made the rhythm of her own lungs match his.

"The unit is at the library, ma'am," the dispatcher said clearly, and Kate stiffened.

The prowler stirred, and she held her breath.

"Ma'am?"

She heard the man get up and come closer to the desk. She didn't look up, hoping that if he saw her skirt and sweater in the dimness, he would think it was a coat on the floor. The telephone, she thought. She pressed the receiver hard against her ear.

"What the—" his voice was rough with surprise.

She looked up and saw him leaning over the desk, staring down at her.

"Ma'am?" the dispatcher said again.

Kate saw a quick movement, and the gleam of metal in the light from the next room.

"Help!" She thought she had screamed, but it came out as a hoarse whisper.

"All right, get up," the intruder said. "Don't make any noise. Just get up."

Dropping the receiver, she pulled herself up shakily and stood facing him, the desk between them. His right hand was extended toward her, and in it was a knife.

Chapter 16

The prowler appraised her silently. His faded blue eyes narrowed into slits.

"Come out here."

She stood still, trying not to shake.

"I said, come out here. Doesn't pay to make me mad."

Kate edged slowly along the back of the desk, not taking her eyes off him.

"The police are on the way." The words squeaked out with the bravado of a frightened mouse.

Holding his gaze, she sidestepped to the end of the counter. The light was at his back, and she couldn't read his expression, but she didn't want to leave the desk's shelter.

She cleared her throat. "You should go. You can get out before they get here."

He eyed her as if considering what she said.

"I'm telling the truth."

Before he could respond, the door at the top of the stairs rattled. The man jumped and whirled to face it. Kate leaned toward the wall and flipped the light switch, flooding the main room of the children's department with light.

The prowler clenched his jaw and dashed for the side door. As he threw himself against it, Kate could see the silhouette of an officer on the other side through the glass. Uniformed men rushed down the stairs.

"Over there!" She pointed toward the side door. They ran past her, toward the intruder.

"Hold it right there. Drop the knife."

Hearing Charlie's voice was too much. Kate sank slowly onto the rug, her back against the end of the counter. She sat there, trembling, until an officer leaned over her and said, "Are you all right, miss?"

She looked up into his sober gray eyes.

"I think so."

"I'm Detective Sorenson. Can you tell me what happened?" His hair was graying, his expression kind.

"We've been having this problem for several weeks now, someone coming in here at night, and Charlie Abbot has been trying to catch him. I stayed late tonight to work and … he just came down the stairs."

Sorenson nodded. "Officer Abbot's briefed me on it. Could you come over to the police station with us, and we'll take your statement there?"

She nodded and stood up carefully, reaching for her jacket with shaking hands. "He stole my keys and my money," she said. "My cellphone too, I think."

"Charlie, wait a sec," Sorenson called toward the side door, and Charlie turned toward them.

"Kate! Are you all right?" He released his hold on the handcuffed prisoner, and left him in the charge of another officer, walking swiftly toward them.

"I'm fine," Kate managed.

"She says the subject took her keys, phone, and cash. Want to check his pockets?"

"How much money?" Charlie asked.

"Seven dollars."

Charlie turned abruptly away.

"I'll drive you over to the station, ma'am, and bring you back here after," Sorenson said. "You have a car here?"

"Yes."

Charlie came back, holding out her keyring, phone, and a few crushed bills. "Is that everything?"

"I—I think so. He may have raided May's candy jar again."

"One pocket's full of Tootsie Rolls," Charlie said, with a suggestion of a smile. "This is my friend, Bob Sorenson. He'll take care of you, get your statement. You sure you're okay? He didn't hurt you?"

"No, he never touched me. I was just scared. I was hiding behind the counter with the phone, but he heard the dispatcher and came looking for me. He had a knife."

Charlie nodded. "We got it. All right, you go with Bob, and we'll take the prisoner over and book him."

Bob Sorensen took her jacket and held it for her. Kate slipped her arms into the coat and zipped it up.

This isn't real!

***

It was after ten o'clock when Kate let herself into her apartment. A shadow moved. She jumped and started to scream, but the scream died in her throat as she recognized her brother coming through the living room doorway, into the kitchen.

"Katie, where have you been? I was worried about you!"

"You scared me!" She threw her arms around Chad. "I forgot you were coming tonight. I'm sorry. You are not going to believe what happened to me."

He made toast and made her eat it and drink tea while he heard her story.

"I'm sorry, sis. That is really weird. You're so sensible, I wouldn't have expected you to have an adventure like that."

"An adventure?" she gasped. "Well, I suppose it was one. At the time, it felt more like a nightmare." She stood up. "I'm exhausted. How about you?"

"I sure am," Chad said. "Brought my sleeping bag."

Her phone rang, and Kate jumped.

119

"Want me to get that?" Chad asked.

"No, I'll take it." She swiped the screen and put her phone to her ear, thrilling at the sound of Charlie's voice.

"Kate, how are things going? Are you okay now?"

"Yes, I'm fine. I know I was a little shaky when you saw me last, but I think I'll be all right."

"I'm glad to hear it. Bob should have had an officer escort you home."

"I'm all right."

"Your prowler had a key to the children's room door."

Kate blinked. "Marilyn was so sure there were only three keys."

"Well, his mother worked at the library several years ago, before Mr. Carter even came there. I guess Mrs. Nelson had kept the key, and her son got hold of it. Nobody upstairs remembered it."

"Did he confess?" Kate asked.

"Well, he admits to going down there several times. He said he fights a lot with his girlfriend, and when she throws him out, he needs a place to sleep. He'd wait upstairs until the children's room closed, then when no one else was in the reading room, he'd unlock the door and sneak down there. Said he might have eaten some candy, but he insists he didn't steal anything else or do any damage."

"So, did he commit a crime or not?" Kate asked.

"Several. He held a knife on you, for one thing. And he did steal your things and the candy."

"Hardly grand theft," Kate said, thinking of the embarrassingly small amount of money she'd had for him to steal. "Breaking and entering?"

"Trespass, anyway. He said the door wasn't locked tonight. That should have tipped him off, but I guess he's no Einstein."

"I'd left my things on the desk too. He ought to have known someone was around."

"He didn't threaten you?" Charlie's voice was full of concern.

"Not exactly. Just waved the knife at me and told me to come out from behind the desk. I'm not sure what he had in mind. He did say it wouldn't pay to make him mad. It was kind of scary." She threw a glance at Chad who was listening with his mouth agape.

"That could be construed as criminal threatening," Charlie said.

"Will he go to jail?"

"I don't know. He could be out on bail tomorrow morning. But I don't think he'll come around the library anymore."

"Thank you, Charlie." There was so much more she wanted to say.

"Kate ..."

She waited, her pulse fluttering, trying not to hear anything that wasn't said.

"Kate, I'm sorry this happened to you."

She looked toward her brother. He was unplugging the toaster and tidying the counter. "Thanks," she said quietly. "And thanks for being there. I don't think I was very smart tonight."

"How do you mean? You called us."

"Yes, but if I'd just pounded on the reading room door and screamed—well, the Lord was merciful."

"Nelson would probably have gotten away then. The side door opens from inside."

"That was stupid of me, too. I could have gone out that way, but I wasn't sure, and I didn't dare try it, in case it wouldn't open and he heard me."

"Well, I'm just glad you're safe."

Kate wrapped his words around her like a warm blanket as she hung up the receiver.

"Friend of yours?" Chad asked.

"Yes, sort of. A police officer who goes to our church."

121

"Sounded friendly to me."

She wondered how much she should bare her raw emotions to Chad. "He's Alex's father."

"Alex?"

"The little boy I told you about on the phone."

"Oh, the timid genius?"

She smiled wryly. "He's a fantastic kid, Chad."

"But his parents are weird."

"No, I didn't mean to give that impression. See, his mother's dead and his father—well, his father's a cop."

Chad leaned back against the counter, evaluating what she had said. "Your weepy phone calls are starting to make sense."

Chapter 17

Kate showed her brother a grand weekend on a shoestring.

"How did you get those?" Chad asked the next morning, when she showed him the tickets to the hockey game.

"Marilyn's husband works for the college, and he got them for us. Marilyn thought we'd enjoy the game this afternoon."

"Great! It will give you something to think about besides creepy guys with knives."

She and Chad shouted themselves hoarse at the hockey rink and were rewarded by seeing the White Mules win by a narrow margin.

Kate cooked a frugal stir-fry for their supper, and they went back to the campus for a free faculty recital. The music was excellent, and Kate relaxed. When thoughts of the prowler crept along the fringe of her mind, she prayed and concentrated on the music. Moments later, she was startled to realize she was thinking about Charlie again. *I'm just glad you're safe.* It was something anyone might say to a friend. Had his voice held more than sympathy?

Chad was more relaxed and content than Kate had seen him in months. When she pressed him about it, he admitted Ellen was influencing him.

"She's terrific. I can't think of anything about her that you wouldn't like," he said, as they pulled on their coats and moved slowly out of the auditorium.

"I'm so happy for you. How did you meet her?"

"In the singles class at Sunday school. I know, I know." Chad held his hands up in protest. "It's corny, but it happened. We've been out three times now, besides church, and I've got to say, she is really something."

"Keep me posted."

When they stepped out of the concert hall, campus police were directing traffic, but a city patrol car sat in the parking lot near Chad's car, blue light flashing. One over-eager music lover had backed into another car, and the damage was significant. A harassed Roxanne was directing traffic around the accident and out of the parking lot, while the officer Kate had seen with her at Piper's took statements from the owners of the damaged vehicles.

Kate didn't expect recognition from Roxanne and prepared to walk by her without comment, but when they passed near her to approach Chad's car, Roxanne glanced her way, then said distinctly, "Well, well, the librarian in distress."

"Good evening," Kate said as pleasantly as she could.

"Yeah, right." Roxanne's voice dripped with sarcasm.

"You know that cop?" Chad asked, when they were in the car and he was maneuvering the roadway according to Roxanne's gestures.

"I've met her a couple of times."

Chad let it drop, and she was glad. The last thing she wanted to discuss was Roxanne's disdain for her.

***

Kate's membership class had ended the previous week, and her brother sat beside her in the large adult Sunday school class, near the front of the auditorium. Between the services, the Palmers invited them for lunch again.

"Oh, I've got to run back up to Orono," Chad protested.

"You've got to eat somewhere," Jill said. "We won't insist that you stay all afternoon. Just bring Kate over for a bite."

"You'll get there in time to see Ellen tonight," Kate said.

"Well, I've got to admit I've thought about the last meal I ate at your house quite a bit, Mrs. Palmer." Chad beamed at her. "Maybe you can give my sister some cooking tips."

"It's Jill. And we're having lasagna today."

"You talked me into it!"

When the worship service ended, they chatted easily with Mike and Jill. Mike grabbed several men who passed and introduced them to Chad. One of the teachers from the academy came to speak to Kate about the school library.

As she stood talking to Mrs. Richardson, Kate felt something brush her ankles. She looked down quickly and saw a dark head appear beneath the edge of the pew. She stepped aside lightly, and Alex wiggled out beside her, his little red bow tie askew.

"Well, hello." She bent down and lifted him onto the pew.

"Miss Pierce," Alex cried.

"Well, where did that little fellow come from?" Mrs. Richardson laughed. "I'll see you in the morning, Kate."

Kate put her arm around Alex and said soberly, "Did you come to meet my brother?"

"Yes!"

"I'm glad. I've told him a little about you."

Alex lowered his gaze. "I asked Daddy again about me getting a brother, but he wouldn't talk about it. I don't think he wants one."

"I'm sorry, honey, but your daddy knows best."

Chad had been watching the exchange with silent fascination. Kate turned to him. "Chad, I'd like you to meet my friend, Alex. He's the young man I told you about."

She turned back to Alex, who was standing on the pew. His face was tipped up, and he stared wide-eyed at Chad. "Alex, this is my own brother, Chad Pierce."

Chad extended his hand, and Alex shook it, saying, "Pleased to meet you, sir."

125

Chad laughed. "Delighted."

"Did you have a nice journey?" Alex asked.

"Yes, I did. I'm going back this afternoon, though."

"Do you and Miss Pierce play together?"

"Yes, we do. And we went to see a hockey game yesterday, and a concert."

"Do you like to read?"

"All the time." Chad gave the earnest little boy his most dazzling smile. "How about you?"

Kate looked around and saw Charlie fighting the flow of traffic in the church aisle, trying to approach them. She smiled, and he shrugged back helplessly.

"Alex, I think your daddy's looking for you."

"Okay," Alex said. "Goodbye."

Kate and Chad said goodbye, and Alex had disappeared under the pew. Kate saw him reappear two rows back, near the aisle, and Charlie lifted him high in his arms. Alex turned and waved at them.

Kate smiled, and Chad waved to Alex. Kate grabbed his hand. "Come on. Let's go check out that lasagna."

***

Chad took his leave soon after lunch, impressing on Kate the need for caution.

"You're not exactly living in the safest neighborhood, you know. You ought to get a roommate."

"Thanks for staying over." She embraced him, wishing he didn't have to leave. "I'll admit it was nice to know a man was sleeping on my couch the last couple of nights."

She stayed with Jill and Mike for a while, dreading going home to her empty apartment.

"How's it going at Agway?" she asked Mike, when the dishes were done and they had settled in the living room with coffee.

"Fine. We're getting in snowblowers and rock salt, all the winter stuff now. How's the library business?"

Kate smiled. "Fine, other than the prowler episode Friday night. Did you hear about that?"

"Jill told me about it yesterday, and I saw it in the paper," Mike replied.

"It scared me to death," Jill said. "I called you as soon as I heard about it, Kate, because I knew Marilyn was away. I'm so thankful you didn't get hurt!"

Kate nodded. "God was watching over me. Chad was waiting for me when I got home, but I'd forgotten he was going to be there. I about jumped out of my shoes when I went into the apartment and he was there."

"You shouldn't live alone," Jill told her.

Mike nodded. "Pretty rough neighborhood you're in."

"Well, I live where I can afford to," Kate said ruefully.

Jill brought out a sewing project and her workbox and sat down in the rocking chair.

"What are you working on?" Kate asked.

"The kids are going to have a Christmas program at church, and I'm making Rachel a new dress for it."

"That's beautiful material." Kate reached out to feel the soft blue fabric. "Wish I could sew."

"I don't know if I actually save any money or not, but I enjoy it," Jill said.

"Do the kids like the school here?" Kate asked, thinking of Charlie's turmoil over putting Alex in a classroom.

"Rachel loves it. Joey's a typical boy, I guess," Jill replied.

"He'd rather be anywhere but school," Mike said.

Jill scrunched up her face. "He liked it more last year."

"Yes, but then his teacher married his Uncle Nick and moved to the tundra."

"So why don't you home school?" Kate asked. "If it's not too personal, I mean."

"I don't mind if you ask." Jill tucked pins into the blue fabric as she talked. "We thought about it, but I feel as though I'm able to give Amy more of my time now, when she needs me most, with Rachel and Joey at school. It was the same way when Joey started school and Rachel was little. We had a lot of special times together."

Kate thought about that. "How about an only child? Do you think he'd be better off at home?"

Jill frowned. "I don't know."

"They need to be with other kids," Mike said.

Jill shook her head. "Oh, that's a myth. I mean, they can socialize other places, besides at school."

"True." Mike frowned and sipped his coffee.

"What brought this on?" Jill asked, looking squarely at Kate.

She shrugged.

"Must have been something," Mike said. "Do you know someone who's home schooling?"

"Don and Angie Blake are thinking about it, I know," Jill offered.

"Well, we have a lot of home-schooled kids come into the library," Kate said. "Most of them seem very well behaved and intelligent. And the mothers are so earnest."

"I guess they feel they're giving their kids the best education." Jill snipped the ends of her thread. "Personally, I like the academy. You just have to decide what you think is best for your family, and then do it."

"Nick said he and Libby will home school if they have kids while they're up north," Mike said. "They could send them over the border to the French school, but they don't think they want to do that. But we've got this terrific Christian school practically on our doorstep. It just seems to be the right thing for us."

Kate nodded gravely. "It must be a difficult decision for some parents."

"Well, I suppose so," Jill said. "I'm not going to agonize over it. We've entrusted the children to God, and we feel they're getting a good education. We try to keep an eye on things at the school and talk to their teachers often. Sometimes I help out in the classrooms."

"And they're both on track," said Mike.

"Joey needs a little prodding, but he's definitely progressing, especially since you started doing math flashcards with him every night." Jill reached for her spool of dark blue thread and cut a length for her needle.

"And parents need time too. I want Jill to be able to channel her energy into other things." Mike took another swallow from his mug.

"Still," Kate said thoughtfully, "if a child was introverted to the point of being terrified—"

"Like Alexander Abbot?" Jill eyed Kate closely.

"Well, yes," she conceded, "I was thinking of Alex."

"Maybe he wouldn't be so scared after he got used to things at the school," Mike suggested.

"Maybe. But what if he was? And what if it scared him so badly that he couldn't concentrate on what he was supposed to learn?"

"Is Betty thinking of home schooling Alex?" Jill asked.

"I really don't know," Kate said. "I think Charlie would like it, but I don't know what Betty's feelings are, so I probably shouldn't talk about it."

"Alex seems like a smart little kid," Mike said. "I've never heard him talk much."

"He's very intelligent," Kate confirmed. "I've gotten to know him at the library, and I'm really impressed with that little guy. If Charlie had time, I think he'd teach him himself."

"Well, teaching them to read is the hardest part, I think," Jill mused. "If Charlie and Betty between them could get him reading, then he'd probably take right off."

"Yes, I think he would." Kate wondered how much to say and decided she must keep Alex's secret for now.

"Poor old Charlie's had a tough time." Mike pressed his lips together. "If Joy were still alive, they could do all that. I mean, Joy was very energetic, and she probably would have loved teaching Alex. As it is, if Betty doesn't want to do it, I think Charlie should put him in school next fall."

"That's up to Charlie," Jill said.

Mike watched Jill over the rim of his mug. "I know one thing. All this talk about Charlie …"

"What?" his wife asked.

"It makes me thankful for what I've got."

Jill smiled and bent her head over her hemstitching.

Chapter 18

Kate entered her apartment cautiously that afternoon and checked the closets and bathroom with her pulse tripping rapidly. When she was sure there was no place an intruder could hide, she sighed deeply and laughed at herself. She couldn't live in fear forever. She prayed for confidence and serenity as she straightened up the living room, where Chad had slept.

Already she missed him. Some people were made to be solitary, she thought, but not Kate Pierce. She had never lived alone until she moved to Waterville, and she decided that independence was not all it was cracked up to be. She wished Chad were there in the evenings to talk with.

Maybe I should advertise for a roommate. She doubtfully surveyed the tiny apartment. *Maybe not.*

At suppertime, she wasn't very hungry. She ate a container of peach yogurt, brushed her long hair into a ponytail, then drove alone to the church. She sat on the aisle for the evening service, third pew from the back, and tried not to think about Charlie. The pastor offered the opening prayer, and the first hymn began.

Betty walked past her in the aisle, the fabric rose on her hat bobbing, and slid into a seat next to Dorothy Palmer. Kate wondered if Charlie was still working the evening shift, and where Alex was. She kept singing.

She became aware of someone standing in the aisle beside her. Looking up, she jumped a little. Charlie stood there with

Alex in his arms, looking down at her questioningly. Alex had left his bow tie and vest at home and was wearing brown corduroy pants and a striped jersey. Charlie wore the same suit he had worn that morning, charcoal gray with a faint pinstripe.

Kate stood motionless for a moment, until Charlie raised his eyebrows, then she moved over a little, sliding her Bible and purse along the pew, not looking at him.

He shifted Alex to his other arm and grasped the edge of the hymnbook she held. Kate couldn't look at him again. She knew she was already blushing and felt that all the parishioners around them were staring. The cuff of Charlie's pale blue shirt showed at his wrist as he held the hymnbook. Kate picked up the song's melody and went on singing softly, hoping he couldn't hear the tremor in her voice. He didn't sing.

Between the third and fourth verses of the song, Charlie leaned close and whispered, "Tell me the man who was with you this morning was your brother."

Startled, Kate glanced upward. Charlie's eyes were intense. She looked back at the hymnbook, but she had lost the place.

In her ear, he said, "Because if he's not, Alex told his first lie today."

Furious, she glared at him. "Alex wouldn't lie," she whispered back.

Charlie said no more but joined in the song at the chorus. When they sat down, he was the model of decorum, holding Alex on his lap and listening intently, eyes front.

Kate's feelings ranged from indignation to sadness. Why would Charlie even suggest such a thing?

When the sermon began, Alex wriggled about until he slithered over onto Kate's lap, and Charlie let him go. He hugged Kate fiercely for an instant. She held him lightly, and he sank calmly into a heap.

Kate and Charlie sat in silence through the message, eyes glued to Pastor Wilson's face, but Kate was sure she would never remember a word of the sermon that night. She felt Alex's breathing grow steady, and his body relaxed in her hold.

She cradled the precious little boy tenderly as he slept, fearing what she longed for was something that was not in God's plan for her and Alex and Charlie.

Dear God, if you want him to be a minister, don't let me be the cause of any hesitation on his part. Let him be willing to go where You're leading. Let us both be willing, and let me be able to let him go.

At the end of the hour, people stood up and lingered in the aisle chatting, moving slowly toward the church doors. Charlie turned and sat looking at Kate and the sleeping Alex in silence. The only movement Kate made was to raise her eyebrows.

"We need to talk," Charlie said at last.

"Do we?"

"Oh, yes, we most certainly do."

***

"I'll take Aunt Betty and Alex home and come back here for you," Charlie said. "Will you wait? We can't all fit in my truck."

"Well, I—"

"If they close the church, just wait in the parking lot," he said. "I'll be right back."

"No," Kate said.

"No?"

"No. Have Aunt Betty take my car. She drives, doesn't she?"

Charlie smiled slowly. "She does."

He went off to find Betty, and Kate sat contentedly holding Alex.

"That's quite a bundle you've got," Mike Palmer said.

"Isn't it?" Kate kissed Alex's hair where the cowlick rose defiantly.

Mike and Jill smiled on her benevolently. Three-year-old Amy was also asleep, and Mike held her with her head against his shoulder.

"He seems to be at ease with you," Jill noted.

"Yes. I feel privileged."

Jill leaned close. "How does Charlie feel?"

"I—don't think that matters," Kate said. "How he feels about me, I mean."

Jill's eyes questioned her silently.

"I just don't think Charlie and I are on the same page of God's plan book," Kate whispered, "but I'm still glad I've been able to know Alex."

"Is this a matter for prayer?" Jill asked.

Kate hesitated, but said, "Yes, thanks. I've been praying alone about it. It would be nice to know someone else was praying with me."

Jill squeezed her shoulder. "I guessed part of it. Be patient." She and Mike moved on down the aisle with their children. Mike's parents, Dorothy and Justin Palmer, smiled and greeted her as they passed.

Charlie returned and said, "All set. I'll take Alex out." He stooped and gathered the boy against his chest. Kate felt cold when Alex was gone, and she pulled on her jacket. Betty had made her way to their pew.

"Are you sure you want me to drive your car?" she asked anxiously.

"Well, not if you don't want to," Kate said. "If it makes you nervous …"

"Well, I'd rather drive it than Charlie's truck."

"It will be fine," Kate told her.

She and Betty followed Charlie outside. It was cold, and the wind blew off the river, shaking the last few leaves off the maple trees. Kate unlocked her car and handed the keys to Betty, indicating the ignition key for her while Charlie buckled Alex into the back seat.

Betty, watching her gaze, said quietly, "Alex was in the car with Joy the day she was killed, you know."

Kate turned to Betty in astonishment. "No, I didn't know."

Betty shook her head. "Terrible thing. Joy went instantly, but Alex was in his car seat, in the back. Not a scratch on him."

"That is strange." Surely Alex was too young to remember that awful day.

"Charlie went to the scene. He was on traffic duty. He's told me about it many times." As Charlie straightened up and closed the rear door, Betty changed her tone to a jollier one. "Well, I'll see you two later."

"Drive carefully," Charlie said.

Betty strapped herself into the front seat and fumbled for the ignition and headlights. She tested the dimmer switch before she backed out.

"They'll be okay," Charlie said, watching the car roll slowly out of the parking lot. "It isn't far."

"I'm sure they will be," Kate said.

They walked slowly to the green truck.

"Where are we going?" she asked.

"I don't know. Anywhere. Maybe nowhere. I just need to talk to you. It's urgent."

She smiled.

"I'm serious. This conversation affects everything."

Kate's smile faded. "What are you saying?"

He opened the door to the truck, and she climbed in. Charlie went to the other side. "I suppose we could sit here or just drive around. Can't go to your house. That wouldn't be proper. Maybe we could talk in the Wilsons' house." He glanced toward the parsonage, but Sarah was leading her three children and the Wishart family inside.

"What's wrong with your house?" Kate asked.

He looked across at her in the half light. "Sure, why not? Betty can chaperone us."

"Chaperone?" Kate asked, her voice cracking a little.

135

"Well, for appearance's sake, I mean." He looked at her in confusion, then started the engine. "I just need a place where we can talk without freezing to death or causing gossip."

"Of course."

He drove slowly, as though still undecided. Kate wondered if she was in for a lecture. Charlie seemed unhappy and nervous.

Chapter 19

When Charlie pulled into his own driveway, Betty was struggling to get the seat belt off Alex. Charlie leaped from the truck and went to help her. Kate climbed down and walked slowly to her car. Charlie sent Betty ahead to open the house, and he carried the inert boy onto the porch and inside.

Kate took the car seat out of her car's back seat and carried it as she followed them into the house. As she closed the door behind her, the welcome warmth of the kitchen greeted her.

Betty turned and saw her with the unwieldy car seat.

"Oh, thank you. Just put it right there." She pointed to an empty spot in the corner.

"I apologize, Betty," Kate said, when Charlie had gone through to the living room and up the stairs with Alex. "It wasn't part of the plan to invade your home tonight."

"That's all right. Charlie says he needs a place to talk to you, and it makes sense. I'll put the coffeepot on."

"Oh, decaf, please," Kate said. "I hope when this is over I'll get to go home and sleep."

Betty bustled about the kitchen, starting the coffeemaker and putting cookies on a plate.

"Make yourself at home," she said, and Kate took off her coat and hung it on a hook near the door they had entered.

When Charlie came back, Betty turned to him. "There, now if you'll excuse me, there's a program I'd like to see tonight." She hesitated, looking at Charlie. "Is that all right?"

"It's perfect. If we need you, I'll holler."

Betty nodded, smiled at Kate, and headed for the living room. Kate heard the television come on and the volume fade lower.

Charlie hung up his coat then pulled out a chair and held the back, gazing mutely at Kate. She went to it and sat down. He walked around the table and sat across from her.

"So." Kate looked nervously toward the gurgling coffeemaker. "Urgent."

"Yes." Charlie seemed to be ordering his thoughts, or mentally outlining an argument. He cleared his throat. "I heard Friday that I did well on the exam. A week from tomorrow morning I am going to be officially promoted to detective. If for any reason I don't want to go through with that, I need to tell the chief."

Kate spread her hands. "I don't understand."

Charlie leaned toward her, over the plate of cookies. "Kate, if I were going to attend seminary—"

She caught her breath and waited. Charlie took a handkerchief from his pocket and wiped his forehead.

"You haven't given up the idea." She couldn't keep her surprise from her voice. "I thought you had decided to stay here."

"I did. But ... I wasn't sure. When I first considered it, after college ... back when Joy was alive, I felt like seminary was the right thing for me. But now, it seems God has opened doors for me in law enforcement. I was getting used to the idea that He wanted me right here."

"Has something changed that?" she asked.

"Your brother was here today…"

"What has this got to do with my brother?" Kate asked helplessly. "Is your future somehow connected to Chad?"

"No. Yes. Well, indirectly." Charlie sighed. "I've been so confused."

"In what way?"

Charlie laughed. "The Lord has been working on me, I guess. See, when I first went into police work, I didn't expect to stay in it forever. But now, the chance came up, and I'd decided to take the test and see if I could make detective. If I'm going to stay here, I'll want to advance in my career."

"But you're not sure you want to stay here?"

He took two breaths and met her gaze. "I do. But ever since I admitted that to myself, I've felt a bit guilty."

"Why?"

"Am I going against what God wants for me?"

"Do you still feel called to the ministry?"

"Not really. And I've been wondering if I wanted that earlier because Joy wanted it. Am I being disloyal to her if I stay in police work?"

Kate leaned toward him. "Charlie, I'm probably not the person to ask about this. Maybe the pastor—"

"No. I need to know what *you* think."

She frowned. If he'd made a career decision once because of what his wife wanted ... She shook her head. "I don't want to influence you on this, Charlie. It's between you and God."

He gave a short laugh. "It's embarrassing to admit, but I can't see myself as a minister now. I wonder if I was simply enamored of the idea of it. Because I'm comfortable here now. I'm a good cop, Kate."

"I know you are."

"But ever since I signed up to take the test, I've been second-guessing myself. Is it my pride? I don't want to do anything because it makes me feel good. I truly want what God wants."

"Do you think you have a gift for the ministry? For preaching and—and counseling, and all that?"

He seemed to consider it for a moment and shook his head. "Talking to people is one of the hardest things in my life."

"I see. But still, God *has* helped some people overcome that to do the work he's planned for them."

"Sure. Moses, for one."

They sat in silence for a moment, and then Charlie said, "I told God if He didn't want me to be a detective, to make me flunk the test. Pretty warped, huh?" He shook his head. "I know you can't dictate to God like that. But that's how unhinged I've been the last few weeks."

Kate got up slowly and went to the counter. She couldn't see how it would be possible for Charlie to fail a test in the field he loved and practiced. She poured two cups of fragrant coffee and brought them back to the table, setting one in front of Charlie.

"I can have the detective's job next week, Kate. But I don't want to take it and regret it. Am I really supposed to stay here, in this job, in this town?"

She shot up a barrage of silent prayer. "What's your gut feeling?"

He picked up his cup and looked down at the coffee. "I think, yes. It's stability for Alex, and it's a place where I can help people. I *do* help people, Kate." He eyed her anxiously, as though he expected her to disagree.

"You certainly do." She sat down again, facing him.

He leaned back in his chair and stared past her to the wall beyond. "I'm sure," he said at last. "God wants me here. And yet, every time I think that, I hesitate. Am I really sure? When Joy died, Alex was my excuse for not going to seminary. I didn't think I should make any big changes because of him."

"You do need to think about Alex," she said. "But, Charlie, changes will come into his life all the time, even if you do stay here."

"Yes." He picked up his mug and blew on the surface of the coffee, then sipped it. "I've thought about that too. I could die. He could lose me, just like he lost his mother."

Kate winced. "I suppose you have to consider that."

SUSAN PAGE DAVIS

"It's the reality. It happened once, it could happen again. If I could guarantee safety and security for Alex ... But if I think that way, I'm leaving God out of the loop."

"Can't you go forward in the way He seems to be leading you and ... well, just keep praying and relying on Him? That's what Chad and I do. Our lives didn't go the way we'd planned, either."

Charlie looked up at her, his eyebrows arching.

"When our parents died, Chad and I were left on our own," she said. "Do I think God wants me to be a children's librarian all my life? Probably not. But for now, I'm doing the best I can at the job He gave me." She threw a glance at him, then looked down at her hands, clasped loosely around the hot mug.

Charlie exhaled and reached for a gingersnap. He dunked it in his coffee.

"If you take the promotion, you need to know you're committed to that," Kate said.

"Yeah. If nothing else, they'll expect me to stay with it for at least a few years. And Alex—I can't tell him we're staying here and then uproot him."

"You're his root system, Charlie."

He nodded. "He's so bright, but so fragile somehow. I don't know how that happened." He met her gaze. "Did I make him that way, or is he just—that way?" He sighed.

"God made him that way, and it's a wonderful thing." Kate weighed carefully the consequences of revealing Alex's secret and decided it was time Charlie knew his son's capabilities. She leaned toward him and met his eyes.

"Charlie, do you know that Alex can read?"

He looked at her blankly. "Aunt Betty's taught him the alphabet song."

"No, I mean reading, whole words, sentences, *books,* Charlie. He reads."

"Come on, he can't." Charlie shook his head in disbelief.

"Yes, he can."

He stared at her for a moment then nodded toward the refrigerator, where bright plastic magnetic letters were scattered over the door. One cluster spelled out *Alex*. "We got those a couple of weeks ago. He's just learning which is which. Betty sings the song with him and points to the letters."

Kate shook her head. "I don't know if he knows the names of the letters or not, but he knows how they work. You've read to him so much, Charlie. He's figured it out for himself. He is reading. He read me three books Thursday night. Three books he'd never seen before."

Charlie cocked his head on one side. "That ... would be amazing. I can't believe it. I mean, I would know. Wouldn't I?" He looked suddenly adrift. "Wouldn't he tell me if he could do something like that?"

"He's afraid to. Afraid you won't read to him if you know. Do you understand what I'm saying?"

Charlie put his head in his hands, then slowly looked up at her. "No, not really."

"Your reading time means so much to him. That's the time when you hold him and share things with him. He feels closest to you then, and safe. But he's afraid that once you know he doesn't need you to read for him, you might quit sharing that time with him, and you might figure he doesn't need you for other things too."

Charlie shook his head. "I wouldn't. I wouldn't do that."

"I know. But he's running on emotion. He hasn't reasoned it all out yet."

"How can I know for sure that it's true, without scaring him?"

"Get me a piece of paper, please," Kate said. When Charlie brought her a tablet and a pen, she thought for a moment and then wrote, "Dear Alex, I came to visit last night, but you were asleep. If you can read this, go to your daddy and give him a big hug. Miss Pierce." She held it out to Charlie.

"Show him this in the morning. Don't say anything. Just show it to him. See what happens."

Charlie put his fist to his lips. "It's true, isn't it?"

She nodded.

"He must think we're really foolish, with the plastic letters and all." He walked to the sink and stood there with his back to her.

Chapter 20

"Kate, I don't want to think I'm being selfish in making this decision," Charlie said after half a minute, swinging around toward her.

"Isn't it as much for Alex as it is for you?"

"At least as much. And if I truly felt I should go to seminary, I would. But so much has changed since I first thought I would do that."

"Alex."

He nodded. "I can't do it to him. I can't take him out there to a strange place and plunk him down in a preschool or something where he doesn't know a soul. And now you're telling me he can read. He would be so bored in a preschool."

"If God wants you to stay here, you should," Kate said.

He gazed off out toward he living room. "I do." His eyes met hers, and he gave her a faint smile. "I don't think I'll regret it. If I went to seminary now, it would destroy Alex. And God gave him to me to look after."

"Charlie," Kate said gently, "Stop beating yourself up. God wants what's best for you and Alex. He knows what's ahead, and He knows better than anyone what Alex needs."

"I have to wonder now if He ever really wanted me to go to seminary. He kept me here. It was brutal, the way it happened, but ... Couldn't He just have shown me in an easier way?"

She had no answer. Silently, she prayed God would give Charlie peace and help him to stop torturing himself over the past.

He pulled off his necktie, draped it over the back of an empty chair, and sat down.

"Kate, I never knew you had a brother."

Puzzled, she said, "We keep coming back to that, but I can't see what Chad has to do with any of this."

"Oh, yes, Chad." Charlie smiled ruefully. "Chad would be the man you introduced to Alex this morning."

"Yes."

"Also the man who was at church with you a month ago."

"Yes."

"Which would be the day after Roxanne saw him kiss you at Piper's."

Kate stared at him. "I suppose she did see that. Roxanne and another policewoman were there when Chad arrived. We hadn't seen each other in weeks. He was meeting me for breakfast, and he kissed me on the cheek. What does it mean?"

"It means I've been a fool. Roxy lost no time telling me your dreamboat was in town, and that she and Pam saw him kiss you in the restaurant. She didn't elaborate, and I ... used my imagination. Which was stupid of me. The next day, there he was beside you in church."

Kate chuckled. "Jill Palmer accosted me that day and asked if Chad and I were twins. She said the family resemblance was quite obvious."

"I guess it wasn't obvious to me," Charlie said. "And this morning ... well, I've already confessed those thoughts and feelings to the Lord. Maybe we'd better not discuss what I thought this morning."

"And Alex came over to meet him," Kate said wonderingly. "Didn't he tell you it was my brother?"

"He tried. I wasn't sure whether to believe him. See, Angie Blake is expecting, and it seems Tyler told Alex he's getting a little brother."

"He told me." Kate smiled, remembering Alex's woeful face.

"Yes, well, he put in his order for a brother of his own last week. I told him it wasn't an option. So then today, when he told me he'd met *your* brother, I thought it was part of this brother fixation, and he just didn't understand who the guy was." Charlie laughed. "I'm such an idiot."

Kate said nothing, but sipped her coffee, trying to suppress the hope that was growing unbidden in her heart.

Charlie ran his hands through his hair, then looked straight into her eyes. "Alex really read to you?"

"Yes."

"He loves being with you, Kate."

She looked toward the living room, where the television still played. "I love ... being with Alex. It's strange, the intensity of feeling I have for him. I hope that doesn't cause any problems."

"How could it?" Charlie asked.

She looked him in the face and saw that his jaw, where stubble was beginning to form, was clenched, and she couldn't hold his gaze. She picked up her mug and lowered her eyes as she took a drink. Her cheeks warmed, and she prayed Charlie couldn't read her mind. What was he thinking, anyway?

***

"Kate, I told you once I'd thought about remarrying."

Her heart lurched at the change of topic. "Yes. You said there was someone you were interested in. Someone Alex could trust." Her throat tightened. The hurt was still there.

"It crossed my mind some time ago that, with a wife, I wouldn't have to worry so much about Alex. I mean, I wouldn't get married just for that reason, but ... well, I think in addition to the other reasons that I might consider it, Alex would benefit from it."

Kate frowned at him. She was happy to weigh in on Alex's situation, but really, this was too personal. She cleared her throat. "Why are you talking to me about this, Charlie?"

"Oh, I—" He definitely looked startled and a little confused. "You're ... a sensible person. I mean—"

"Have you spoken to her?"

His eyebrows shot up. "Not really. I wasn't sure of her feelings."

Kate sighed, wishing she wasn't his practical, sensible friend. "Is she ... does she have a career?"

"Well, yes, sort of. A job, anyway."

"Would she give that up for you?"

"I'm not sure."

"Does she love Alex?"

"Oh, yes, I'm sure she does." His whole face softened.

"Does she love you?" Kate whispered.

He shrugged. "I had thought that maybe she cared about me. No, I'm sure she cares. But love ... Well, I hoped I might win her eventually. But then I got this idea that ... she loved someone else."

"She does?" Kate recalled Roxanne's possessive attitude toward him. "I thought she was after you."

His brown eyes widened. "Who are we talking about?" he asked cautiously.

Newly wary, Kate swallowed hard. "Who were *you* talking about?"

They stared at each other.

"This isn't happening," Charlie said. "I'm going to wake up tomorrow and find it was all a stupid dream ... and I'm still a patrolman ... and Alex can't read." He shook his head. "I was talking about you, Kate. Who were you talking about?"

Kate sat very still. She felt her face go pink, then red, then scarlet. She looked into her empty mug.

"I am humbled," she said softly. "You never once thought of Roxanne as a possibility, did you?"

"Roxy?" Charlie burst out laughing. "Oh, Kate, do you know what one of the big attractions to the detective's job is for me?"

She shook her head.

"It's that I'd spend less time in Roxanne's proximity. This last week, working nights was so peaceful!" He sobered. "To think of her and Alex together—now, that's a real nightmare."

"I'm sorry. It should never have occurred to me. But you did say there was someone, and I thought she liked you. Are you sure you meant—it was weeks ago—" She gave it up and wiped her cheek with the back of her hand, where an errant tear had fallen.

He gazed at her apologetically. "I saw even then that Alex was comfortable with you, and I wondered if, someday, you might be comfortable with me. It was just a remote possibility. I couldn't say anything then, Kate. I wasn't at all sure. I didn't know enough about you." He chuckled ruefully. "I didn't even know you had a brother."

"But you said there was *someone*—"

"Yes." He eyed her pensively. "That day in the truck, I was going to say that there's someone right here beside me who would love Alex. But it was too soon, and I couldn't just say it like that. You would have thought I was deranged. And then I thought—well, there was this man in your life—"

Nervousness seized Kate, and she pushed her chair back. "Have we covered all the ground?"

"Well no, actually, we haven't," Charlie said. "I have to face my chief in the morning and tell him I'm taking the promotion and staying here."

Some of the tension left her. "How does that make you feel, Charlie?"

"I think I'll finally be at rest. It's the right thing. I know God can use me in my new position."

"Yes, He can." Kate stood up. "It's getting late. We both need to be up early. I think I should go."

"But we haven't settled anything," he protested.

"I think we have. You know what God wants you to do."

"But—will you forgive me for my stupid mistake?"

"Of course." She walked to the row of hooks by the door, took down her jacket, and put it on. She picked up her purse. His declaration hadn't sunk in yet. What did this mean to her future—the fact that Charlie Abbot had been thinking of her as a possible wife and a possible mother for Alex? It wasn't a proposal, exactly, but she needed to go home, where she could think about the implications and pour her heart out to God.

"Kate, this isn't over." He shoved his hands in his pants pockets and went with her out the door and down the steps to her car.

She stopped and looked up at the sky, where millions of stars glittered in the frosty night. "Good," she said softly. "Don't forget to show Alex my note." She got in the car.

Chapter 21

All day Monday, Kate thought about Charlie. At the school, she shelved books without thinking about it, mechanically observing the numbers on them and sliding them into place. She greeted the students who came in for books and checked them out like an automaton.

When she got to the public library, Marilyn was already busy. Kate waited on patrons and absentmindedly changed the displays.

"Kate, dear, I asked you to put out Thanksgiving books, not hockey books," Marilyn said, looking critically at the display table.

"Oh, I'm sorry." Kate began gathering the volumes.

"No, that's all right. Leave them." Marilyn frowned. "Perhaps you should take a few days off. Such a terrible thing Friday night … "

"I'm fine," Kate assured her. "I need to work. It gives me something to think about."

After her four-hour shift in the children's room, she went home and made herself a sandwich then began scrubbing the shower. She worked at it for a long time, and when she was done it sparkled, but her mind had been on Charlie the whole time.

He called that evening, about seven o'clock.

"I was hoping I could see you tonight, but it looks like I'll be tied up for a while," he said.

"That's all right. I understand."

"No, we have to finish the discussion we started last night. If I get done at a decent hour—"

"Then you should go home to Alex," she finished.

"Well, yes, I suppose I should, but I want to see you."

She took a deep breath. "There will be time another day, Charlie. He needs you now."

"Kate, I woke him up before I went on duty this morning. Hated to do it, but I couldn't stand to wait any longer. When he was finally awake, I showed him your note."

"And?"

"I went over to stand by his bedroom window. He got out of bed and came over and hugged me." There was a pause. "Kate, how could this happen?"

"I don't know, but it did."

Charlie's voice was strained. "I told him how proud I was and tucked him back in, and he went back to sleep."

"Just keep showing him how much you love him," Kate said with satisfaction. "You should definitely go home as soon as you can tonight. And read to him, if he wants you to."

"When can I see you again?"

She hesitated. "Call me when you have time off and you know I'm not working."

***

"Kate, did you see the paper?" Marilyn's greeting on Wednesday morning sent her anxiety index soaring.

"No. What's happened?"

"There was a big drug bust last night. Charlie is on the front page."

Kate stopped at the desk and took the front section of the *Morning Sentinel* out of Marilyn's hand. Under the banner, the headline of the lead story read, *Seven arrested in cocaine bust.* Beneath was a large photograph. A grim-faced Charlie was leading a man in handcuffs out of a rundown apartment building. She'd expected him to call the evening before, and now she knew why he hadn't.

That evening, he met her in the church parking lot when she arrived for prayer meeting. He walked toward her car and opened her door for her.

"I sent Aunt Betty and Alex inside," he said.

Kate was suddenly nervous. She closed the car door and walked beside him, holding her Bible and purse in her gloved hands.

"Can we talk after prayer meeting?" he asked.

"Of course."

She sat very still beside him in the pew as the pastor led a short Bible study. Betty and Alex sat two rows ahead of them, and Alex kept trying to turn around, staring back at them with large, dark eyes. Each time, Betty turned him gently around toward the front. Kate yearned to open her arms, signaling him to crawl to her under the pews, but she only smiled wistfully at him and tried to refocus her attention on Pastor Wilson.

Several of the parishioners swiveled to looked at her and Charlie. Kate couldn't help thinking they speculated about their relationship, and she almost wished she wasn't sitting next to Charlie tonight. She willed herself not to blush, with so many eyes turned in their direction, but she felt her face reddening anyway.

At the end of the meeting, they stood in the aisle while many of the people greeted Charlie. Word had spread about his promotion, and everyone seemed to have a question. He answered as specifically as he could, but he was rather vague when it came to personal matters.

Finally there was a break, and he leaned toward Kate. "Maybe we can borrow the pastor's study for a minute. I know you need to get home, and I have to take Betty and Alex home, too."

"All right," Kate said, and he left her side for a minute to hold a quick conference with Mark Wilson.

"Come on," Charlie said when he returned. He took her hand and led her into the foyer, then down the hall to the empty study. He flipped the light switched and closed the door softly behind them.

"So." He gazed down at her, looking a bit harried and a trifle at sea.

Kate's blond braid hung over her left shoulder, and she nervously fingered the covered elastic at its end. "You wanted to talk," she said at last.

"Yes." He held the eye contact as he moved her toward a chair. "Sit down?"

Kate glanced around. Two straight chairs sat near the wall, and she perched on the edge of one. Charlie plunked down beside her and stared into her eyes.

"It seemed to take forever to arrange a time to talk to you, but now that we're here, I don't know where to start," he confessed. "I don't think I can do this in two minutes flat, while Betty and Alex are waiting for me. Could we—that is, would you go out with Alex and me tomorrow night?"

Kate smiled with relief that he had asked a question she could answer. "Yes, that would be nice."

"All right. I think so too," Charlie said. "I don't want to say the wrong thing, and Alex is involved in this, too, so he should be there. But there are some things I need to explain to him first. He's intuitive about a lot of things, but then there are others where he just doesn't have a clue."

Kate chuckled, and Charlie looked at her quizzically.

"You really love him, don't you?"

"Oh, yes." She couldn't rein in a big smile.

"Kate, I—I love you." He stopped short and stared down at his hands.

Kate closed her eyes as gratitude and joy ran through her. When she opened them, Charlie was watching her carefully.

She reached toward him, and he grasped her hand. She swallowed, then smiled. "You're right. Alex needs to be in on this."

He squeezed her hand. "Well, let's talk about it tomorrow, then."

***

Her doorbell rang at six thirty. Kate took an apprehensive look at herself in the mirror. Her hair hung smoothly over her shoulders, and her forest green dress with its ivory lace collar suited her, but she still felt unprepared.

When she opened the door, Charlie stood, smiling in his best suit, navy blue with a pale blue, pin-striped shirt and a jaunty red necktie. In his hand was a bouquet of dried flowers. Beside him, very somber, was little Alex. His warm red jacket was unzipped, and Kate could see that he also was wearing his Sunday best. He carried a single pink rose.

Kate laughed, but she felt she was going to cry, too. "You guys are unbelievable." She swung the door open wide. "Come in. Here, let me take those." She took Charlie's bouquet with a smile and examined it closely. "Thank you. These are lovely." She carried it to the counter, pulled a vase from the cupboard, and sank the flower stems in it.

When she turned to Alex, he held up the rose. She knelt down and put her arms around him. "Thank you, Alex." She hugged him, then lifted the rose to her nose. "It smells so good!"

"It means I love you," he said shyly.

Kate hugged him again, exulting that she could show her love for him now without fear of alienating Charlie or toppling their shaky relationship.

When she stood, Charlie said, "I didn't coach him on that."

She smiled and turned to open and close cabinets quickly, positive that somewhere there had to be another vase. She was sure she had brought it when she'd moved to the apartment. It had been her mother's. She spotted it at last on the top shelf and reached for it but couldn't quite reach. Charlie stepped up behind her and reached over her head for it.

"Thank you." Her hand shook as she took it from him and filled it halfway with tap water for the precious rose. She still hadn't let herself be certain that they would be a family, but she knew they would settle the matter before the evening was over.

"So, where are we going?" she asked, setting the pressed glass vase on the table.

"The Clipper Ship," Charlie replied. "If you like seafood, that is. Alex likes their clams a lot, but we can—"

"That's terrific," she said.

"My squirrel!"

Alex had walked toward the refrigerator, and was staring at his drawing, held in place with two small magnets.

"You drew that for Miss Pierce?" Charlie asked with some pride.

"He brought it to me at the library." Kate put on her warm blue parka and zipped it.

"It's her puppet," Alex said soberly.

"I can tell. A very good likeness."

Kate watched them, hoping with growing confidence that this could last. They could be together, and Alex could grow up strong in the security of their home, and she and Charlie … yes, they would be happy.

"I should have borrowed Betty's car," Charlie said as he drove his pickup into the restaurant's parking lot.

Kate hadn't felt it incongruous to be going out to dinner in her best clothes, riding in a truck. She glanced around and spotted two other pickups amid cars of all makes and conditions. "It's okay in Maine."

"Maybe I need to trade vehicles," Charlie said.

Kate wondered if he was thinking of their comfort when the family increased.

Charlie rejected the first table the hostess offered them. Too close to the entrance, he said. He wanted something more private. Then he apologized to Kate for the delay, but she assured him it was all right. They sat on a bench and talked quietly. Alex was full of repressed excitement. After ten minutes, they were shown to a spot in the farthest part of the room, secluded and dim, with a candle burning in a glass globe on the table.

"I can hardly read the menu," Charlie said. "Guess it's my own fault."

"Let Alex read it," Kate suggested.

Alex laid his menu down so the light of the flickering candle shone on it. "Dinner entries," he began.

"Entrées," Charlie said gently. "It's a French word. It means main dishes."

Alex nodded. "Baked scallops, fried clams, shrimp platter…" He went on down the list, finishing with, "All entrées include salad and choice of potato."

He looked up. Kate and Charlie beamed at him, and his grin came out, sure and strong.

When the waitress came they had decided, and Charlie placed their orders, asking for coffee for himself and Kate, and milk for Alex.

"Alex and I have something to ask you," Charlie began, when the waitress had brought their drinks.

Kate looked from one to the other. Both looked nervous.

"Me first," Alex said with decision.

"All right." Charlie nodded and sat back.

Kate turned her attention to Alex. He stared up at her, his big brown eyes hopeful.

"Miss Pierce," he said, "my daddy and I want you to marry us." He got up from his chair and came close to her. Kate couldn't take her eyes from his. "Because we love you," Alex added, reaching up to her.

She hugged him close and kissed his cheek. "I love you, too, Alex." She knew her face was flaming, and she couldn't look at Charlie. There was only one thing that could increase her joy. "Perhaps I should hear what your father has to say."

Charlie cleared his throat. "He knows it's not—I mean, I told him—we talked about it—"

"That's not what you're supposed to say, Dad," Alex scolded.

Charlie nodded and took a deep breath and locked his hands together on the table. He glanced at Kate earnestly, then at his hands. "Kate, I love you. Will you please marry me and be a mother to Alex?"

She swallowed hard. The surge of emotion was startling, and she felt her lower lip tremble as she tried to form a reply.

Alex leaned close to her and whispered, "You're supposed to say yes."

A tiny laugh burst from her mouth, and she squeezed him, making herself meet Charlie's eyes. His anxiety was apparent, and she wouldn't force him to wait any longer.

"Yes," she said simply, and Charlie and Alex both smiled at her, and at each other.

"Hooray!" Alex shouted.

Charlie glanced quickly behind him. "Have to be quiet here, buddy."

Alex shrank into his chair.

"It's okay," Kate assured him, reaching out for his hand.

The waitress came then and put their plates in front of them.

Alex looked up at the young woman and said gravely, "We are getting married."

Chapter 22

Alex slept between them on the seat of the truck, his head against Charlie's right arm, as his father drove back to Kate's apartment building.

"This is Mr. Epson's parking spot," Kate said, as Charlie pulled in beside her car.

"Well, I'm not staying long." Charlie unbuckled his seat belt.

"Oh, don't get out. You'll wake up Alex."

"I'll see you in."

"No, don't leave Alex out here."

Charlie hesitated. "I'll carry him."

Kate sighed. "Nothing's ever simple, is it?"

"Maybe we need to have one outing at some point without Alex," Charlie mused.

"I don't mind him being here."

"Me either, but …" He put his arm along the back of the seat, over Alex's head and bent toward her. Kate unbuckled her safety belt and met him halfway for their first kiss, a sweet promise, full of hope for their future.

"Tomorrow night," Charlie said, as he straightened. "Definitely tomorrow."

"What about a sitter? Will Aunt Betty watch him?"

"I'm sure she will. I'll tell her tonight that you said yes. I know she's been praying about this and rooting for us. But you know, once she hears our news, she might start making plans of her own. Who knows? Maybe she'll end up as a partner in Frye Landscaping."

Kate chuckled. "I can't wait to tell Marilyn tomorrow."

"Will you stay home with Alex after we're married? She'll have to train a new assistant if you do."

"I feel bad about that, but not bad enough to keep working—if you're sure."

"I'm sure. Alex was over the moon when I told him you'd be his new mommy. At the time, of course, that was contingent on your answer to our proposal."

Kate smiled. "I want to be with Alex. But I don't want Betty to feel she's being pushed out."

"I think she'll be relieved, but just in case, I'll tell her she can stay on at the house if she wants to. We have plenty of room."

"That sounds good. Please tell her I'd love it if she stayed with us. And I think I'll call Chad tonight. He'll want to meet you soon."

"I definitely want to meet him."

"It wouldn't surprise me if quite a few people have been praying for us," Kate said. "Mike and Jill Palmer, for instance."

"I know Pastor and Sarah Wilson have been," Charlie agreed. "They've prayed for me for years now, and I gave Pastor a special prayer request several weeks ago." He was quiet for a moment, then said, "Thank you, Kate. I feel as if you've given me a wonderful gift. I love you. But it's more than that. It's Alex too. I can see how you feel about him, and it means so much."

"He stole my heart almost the first time I saw him," Kate admitted.

Charlie chuckled. "I told Alex tonight that you might want to accept him, but not his daddy. He said he wasn't getting married if I didn't. That's when I tried to explain it to him. I *think* he understands."

"He's very bright. I'm sure he does."

"I'll come for you tomorrow about six, if all goes well."

"Call me if anything comes up." She looked out the window toward the apartment building. "You can see my kitchen window from here. Stay with him, Charlie. When you see the light come on, you'll know I'm all right."

"Okay, but it seems unchivalrous." He leaned over the boy and kissed her again, his arms around her and Alex. Kate let her right hand slide up around his neck.

She sighed and opened her eyes to find him smiling at her contentedly. She rested her cheek against his shoulder for a moment, then got out of the truck with her keys ready and went to the door. She looked back and waved. Charlie, sitting in the truck with the parking lights on, waved and smiled, and Kate felt easier about entering the building, knowing he was there.

She let herself into the entry, and as the door closed behind her, looked toward the dimly lit stairs.

A man sat on the fifth stair, leaning back against the wall, watching her with narrowed eyes.

Kate stood not breathing, knowing him immediately. Before he smiled, before he spoke, she recognized the denim jacket and striped scarf, the long, dark blond hair, and the calculating face with several days' stubble.

"Been waiting for you." He pulled himself up by the railing and lounged on the third step.

"How did you get in here?"

He smirked. "No telephone here for you to use."

What would he do if she unzipped her purse and went for her cell phone? His left foot came down to the second step. In that instant, Kate's mind whirled with images of herself vacillating in the library. Confront him or hide? Go for the keys or pound on the reading room door? Try the side door or stay by the desk?

No, she wasn't going to go through that terror again.

She turned and ran for the door, slamming against the safety bar and hearing rapid movement behind her. Kate dropped her purse, but the door gave before her. Stumbling out onto the walkway, she panicked for an instant, until her eyes landed on the green truck.

"Charlie!"

He was out of the truck before she had covered half the ground between them, and she heard the door thud and swing behind her. She fell into Charlie's arms, but he pushed her quickly behind him, his eyes on the door.

"Hold it! Police," he yelled.

Kate turned and looked back, over Charlie's shoulder. Nelson stood looking at Charlie, but was poised for flight, a knife in his right hand. Charlie stood with his hands extended before him in the dimness.

"Drop the weapon and put your hands on your head," Charlie said firmly.

Kate held her breath, wondering if Nelson would make a break for it. Charlie was out of uniform and had no gun. Her heart thudded at twice its normal pace.

Gently, she touched the back of his jacket. "Charlie?"

"Stay back, Kate."

Beyond him, Nelson glanced off to the side, toward the alley between the apartment house and the next building.

"Don't even think about it," said Charlie. "Drop the knife."

Nelson squinted at him, motionless.

"Shoot," the young man said at last. "You ain't even got a gun."

A car turned in at the driveway and rolled slowly toward them.

"Kate, get me some backup," Charlie said quietly. He took a step toward Nelson.

She gulped. She'd dropped her purse, and her cell was in it. Where should she turn?

The car entering the parking lot stopped ten feet away, and she ran toward it.

"Mr. Epson!"

Her neighbor lowered his window and said, "Miss Pierce, do you know whose pickup that is in my spot?"

"It's a policeman. That man near the door has a knife. We need to call 911 and get some backup for Charlie. He's off—"

She turned quickly as she heard scuffling sounds behind her. Charlie and Nelson struggled frenetically on the walk and went down with a thud.

Chapter 23

"Good grief!" Mr. Epson turned wide eyes on her. "What's going on?"

"We need help. That man was going to attack me in the stairway. We need a phone! Please, Mr.—" She broke off as she realized Epson had a cellphone in his hand and was punching buttons.

She turned and ran back toward the walkway, where Charlie seemed to have the upper hand. The knife's blade gleamed from the edge of the paved walk, and Nelson groped toward it, trying to unbalance Charlie so he could lunge for it. Kate sucked in a breath and darted toward it. She kicked it away from the men, then jumped back as they rolled over, panting. Charlie sat on Nelson's back, pulling the scarf from around his neck.

Mr. Epson came timidly forward, his telephone at his ear.

"Miss Pierce, they're sending a squad car. Who are these men?"

"Tell them it's Officer Abbot, and the Nelson man who broke into the library."

She thought she heard a siren several streets over, and she pulled in a deep breath. Charlie was tying Nelson's hands snugly behind him with the scarf.

"Are you all right, Charlie?" Kate dared to ask.

"Yes. Check on Alex." He never looked up but kept his eyes on the man he was subduing.

Kate ran to the pickup and opened the driver's door. Alex was curled up on the seat, his seatbelt still around his middle. She unbuckled it and pulled the boy into her arms, then slid onto the seat, closed the door quietly, and held him, her prayers rushing silently to God.

Alex stirred and whimpered a little.

"It's okay, honey," Kate whispered. She kissed his hair.

"Where's Daddy?"

"He's not far. He'll be here in a minute. Go back to sleep."

Alex cuddled against the front of her jacket and closed his eyes.

As the police car approached, the siren blared louder, and Alex opened his eyes again and sat up quickly.

"It's a cop car."

"Yes, honey. It's all right. It's some of Daddy's friends. They found a bad man, and they're going to take him away."

Alex shivered and stared out the window toward the flashing lights, and Kate held him silently. Charlie didn't stand up until the officers left the car and took control of his prisoner. He stood talking with them for several minutes after Nelson had been put into the patrol car. A second police car arrived in the parking lot. Mr. Epson hovered and was approached by an officer, given his chance to describe his part in the drama.

At last Charlie approached the truck and opened Kate's door.

"Do you feel like giving a statement?" he asked wearily.

Kate and Alex stared up at him. He put out his arms and pulled them both toward him.

"Daddy, the siren scared me," Alex said.

"He slept through most of it," Kate assured Charlie. She slid off the seat and stood beside him, and Charlie took Alex in his arms.

"It's okay now, buddy." He held the boy tight against his shoulder. "It's okay. We'll go home pretty soon and go to bed."

He looked sideways at Kate and asked, "Did I imagine it, or did you give me some help there?"

"Yes, I kicked—" she glanced at Alex, whose eyes were wide as he lay in a heap on Charlie's strong shoulder. "I didn't want him to have that particular item."

"Thought so. Thanks."

Bob Sorenson came toward them, holding out Kate's purse. "Is this yours, ma'am?"

"Yes, thank you!"

Charlie said, "Bob, how about if I bring Miss Pierce to the station in the morning to make her statement? I've got my boy here, and I really don't want to keep him out any later than I need to."

"Sure, Charlie, I guess that's all right. We'll hold this fellow for sure this time."

"Take him to Augusta tonight," Charlie advised. "If he bails out again—"

"He won't. We'll take him right to the county jail." The detective smiled at Kate. "Miss Pierce, I understand congratulations are in order."

"Yes, thank you." She smiled, hoping her blush was not detectable in the light of the streetlamp.

"All right, we'll see you both in the morning." Sorenson turned away.

"Come on, Kate," Charlie said. "I'll take you upstairs, and you pack a bag. You're not staying here tonight."

She started to protest, but realized she didn't want to stay in the apartment alone.

"Thank you."

He nodded and shifted Alex to his other arm. Kate closed the truck door and got her keys out again, and they went together to the door of the building.

"Miss Pierce, are you sure you're all right?" Mr. Epson asked, stepping up behind them. "The officer said that hoodlum attacked you."

"I'm fine. Thank you so much for your help."

"I'll have my truck out of your spot in a couple of minutes," Charlie said.

"No problem, sir. Say, how could he have gotten in here?" Epson asked as they stepped into the entry.

"I wondered that, too," Kate said uneasily. "He couldn't have happened on a key for the apartment building."

"Was this a random thing?" Epson asked.

"No, he was after Kate because she got him arrested in the library Friday night," Charlie said flatly.

"Oh, that was the same fellow?" Epson looked anxiously at Kate. "But I still don't understand how he got in the front door. He couldn't have picked the lock, could he?"

Charlie said, "I doubt it, or he would have opened Kate's door, too, and waited in her apartment upstairs."

Kate shivered and reached for him. Charlie put his arm around her and gave her a little squeeze. "He could have followed someone in," he said, "or just made an excuse—'Hi there, I'm going up to visit my friend Joe.' You'd be surprised how many people would hold the door open for him and say, 'Oh, have a nice visit,' and never give it a second thought."

"Makes you think," said Epson.

"Well, nowadays people like yourself need to look out for their neighbors." Charlie nudged Kate toward the stairs, and Mr. Epson headed for his own apartment door on the first floor.

Kate led the way into her kitchen, and Charlie pulled out a chair at the table. "Just get what you need for tonight," he said, sitting down with Alex on his lap. "We'll come back tomorrow for the rest of your things."

"The rest—?"

"Kate, I don't want you staying here anymore. I know they've got him tonight, but there's no guarantee they'll have him tomorrow. I want you to come and stay with us."

"Charlie, I couldn't. You don't have the space, and Betty might not—"

"Betty will love it, and we have plenty of room."

"But still—"

"I'm not leaving you here. Not tonight, not tomorrow night, or ever again."

Kate bit her bottom lip. He was scared, she could see that. In accepting his proposal, hadn't she given him some rights when it came to protecting her?

"I'll be right back."

In her bedroom, she quickly packed her overnight bag, stopped in the bathroom for her toothbrush and a few toiletries, then went back to the kitchen.

"All set?" Charlie asked. Alex was sitting in another chair, doodling in Charlie's pocket notebook.

"Yes, I think so."

Charlie stood up. "Look, Kate, I didn't mean to be bossy. I just know I'd worry about you all the time if you were living here."

"It's a pretty bad neighborhood," she agreed.

"It scared me pretty bad Friday night," Charlie said, "but tonight—Kate, this was serious. He wasn't here to steal Tootsie Rolls."

***

"I'll make up the bed in the spare room," Betty said immediately after Charlie explained the situation to her. "It will be chilly in there for a while. We've had it closed off."

"Can you put her in Alex's room?" Charlie asked. "This guy's bunking with me tonight."

Alex, clung to his father, his arms tight around Charlie's neck.

"Good idea. I change his bed this afternoon. If you don't mind?" Betty turned to Kate in question.

"I don't mind at all," she said.

169

She slept soundly in Alex's bed that night. Though she'd thought she would lie awake for hours, replaying the seconds in the hallway with Nelson, but she was asleep before she'd finished thanking God for her deliverance.

In the morning, she woke to the smell of coffee and muffled sounds from the lower part of the house. She pulled her clothes on and brushed her long hair. In her haste to pack, she'd forgotten her elastic bands, so she let the strands flow loose over her shoulders and went hesitantly downstairs to find Charlie and Betty in the kitchen.

"Good morning," Betty said cheerfully. "How are you feeling?"

"I'm fine, thanks, but Charlie—oh, man! You've got a black eye!"

He smiled sheepishly as he stood up. "It looks worse than it feels."

"We were just discussing your future." Betty rose and brought the coffeepot back to the table. She poured Kate a mugful and set a plate of muffins near her. "Now that we know you're going to be Mrs. Abbot, Charlie is anxious to get you out of that apartment."

"It's not that bad," Kate said feebly.

Charlie came around the table and pulled her into his arms. "If I'm going to take care of you, I've got to get you someplace safe."

Betty turned away with a smile and busied herself at the stove.

Kate allowed herself the luxury of leaning against his chest for a few seconds. His uniform shirt was crisp against her cheek, and she put her fingertip to his badge, where it gleamed on the pocket. She gently pushed away and sat down. "I'd just feel funny about moving in here. I can't take Alex's bed."

"I've thought about that." Charlie moved his coffee cup across the table and sat down next to her, his left arm across the back of her chair. "We'll fix you a place in the spare room, or we can put a cot in his playroom down here for you. Either way, it will only be for a few weeks."

"I don't know," Kate said.

"My dear, if you're worried about proprieties, I assure you, I'm a very good chaperone," Betty said, coming to the table with a large bowl of scrambled eggs.

Kate smiled. "Thank you. I just ... I think I may need a more gradual adjustment to being with you all the time. Can I think about it?"

"Well, sure." Charlie seemed unsettled. "If you'd rather stay somewhere else ..."

"What about Jill Palmer's?" Betty suggested. "You seem to be good friends."

"Well, yes," Kate said, "but they don't have a lot of space, with three children."

Betty frowned. "Perhaps the Wilsons."

Kate knew the parsonage was full too.

Charlie's brow cleared. "Mike's folks."

"Oh, I couldn't ask them," Kate protested, but she thought about Dorothy Palmer, who reminded her so strongly of her mother.

"I could," Charlie said. "Their kids are all gone, and they have plenty of room. Dorothy would treat you like a daughter."

"You can't just ask somebody a huge favor like that, can you?" Kate asked.

"Yes, dear," said Betty. "When it's another believer, you can. And when they understand what you've been through—"

"I could pay them some rent," Kate said hesitantly.

"Oh, no, they wouldn't want that." Betty shook her head.

"Let me call them." Charlie watched her face anxiously for approval, and Kate felt her reservations crumble.

"If you're sure it's all right..."

***

171

Three hours later, Justin Palmer helped Charlie unload Kate's boxes and suitcases at the farmhouse. His brown eyes twinkled behind his glasses as he hefted a box of books. Dorothy opened the door and held her arms out to Kate.

"Welcome! I'm so glad you and Charlie thought of us. It will be great fun having a girl in the house again."

"Thank you so much," Kate breathed, hugging Dorothy. "I don't want to put you out."

"Nonsense. We'll have a wonderful time together."

"Well, it's just until the wedding," Charlie warned.

"Wedding? How could I not know about a wedding in our church?" Dorothy asked, clearly startled.

Kate smiled. "We settled things last night. It seems so long ago, now, with everything that's happened."

They had been to the police station that morning, and Charlie had hovered protectively while Kate gave her statement to Roxanne. The chief had given Charlie permission afterward to go with her to her apartment, to pack up her meager belongings and move her to a safe haven.

"Well, you've got to tell me all about it," Dorothy cried. "What's the date?"

Kate looked helplessly at Charlie, as he passed through the kitchen with a box of her dishes. "We haven't decided yet. We haven't really had much chance to talk about the details. We're supposed to go out tonight."

"Well, Charlie can come here for supper if you want," Dorothy said.

"Oh, thank you. I'm not sure what he has in mind." Kate looked down the hallway after him. "See, we've never been out together alone, without Alex."

"Ah," said Dorothy, "it's an auspicious occasion. Then I guess supper with Justin and me will be tomorrow night."

Charlie came back in from the living room as Justin entered from outside with two suitcases.

172

Dorothy said, "Charlie, I was just saying to Kate that you and Alex should have supper with us tomorrow night."

"Oh, well—" he glanced at Kate, and she smiled.

"I told her we had plans for this evening," Kate said.

"Yes. I think that sounds fine. Thank you."

"We're going to store your boxes in Steve's old room," Justin told Kate. "That all right?"

"Yes, anywhere. I can't tell you how much I appreciate this."

"They got that guy behind bars this time?" Justin asked.

Charlie nodded. "He's in the county jail. The DA's asking to have him held without bail, but they'll probably arraign him Monday."

You're not working today, are you?" Dorothy asked Kate.

"No, Marilyn insisted I take the day off, but before we left Charlie's this morning, I promised I'd get Alex this afternoon and take him to the library. He missed his usual visit this week."

"Come, dear," said Dorothy. "I'll take you up to your room. It was Peggy's room, and I've always liked it. Very feminine. If you want to lie down you can, or we can start getting you settled."

"I'd better get back to work," Charlie said. "I think we've got everything in now."

"We'll see you later, when you come for Kate this evening," Dorothy told him, and she hustled Justin through the door to the living room.

Charlie smiled and pulled Kate toward him.

"Going to be all right here?"

"Yes, I think it will be wonderful. It will be like having my folks again." She leaned forward shyly and kissed the purple skin beside his eye. "You be careful today."

He grinned and bent to kiss her.

Chapter 24

"I keep looking around for Alex," Charlie confessed that evening.

"I know," Kate said. "I do too."

They had eaten dinner in Waterville's plushest restaurant, and afterward Charlie had driven to Head of Falls. They stood in the middle of the Two Cent Bridge, the old footbridge that spanned the Kennebec River above the dam. On either side were lights from Waterville and Winslow, and downstream was the railroad bridge, dark against the sky. Through its girders they could see the red taillights of cars crossing the Waterville-Winslow Bridge below. The muffled roar of the water rushing over the dam came up to them.

"It's so peaceful here." Kate leaned on the railing, her gloved hands clasped.

"Are you cold?" Charlie put his arm around her.

She wasn't, but she settled back against his arm anyway. They watched the water and the lights.

"Happy?" he murmured.

"Very." She turned her head toward him. "In a few weeks, you'll be a detective."

He nodded. "And you'll be at home with Alex."

"I expect to have great adventures with Alex," Kate said. "He was so cute at the library today. When we went in, Marilyn said, 'Well, Alex, I understand your father's getting married.' Alex gave her this big smile and said, 'Yes, and you can come to our wedding.' Just like that."

Charlie laughed. "Betty mentioned this morning that she's thinking about sharing a place with one of her friends for a while, after the wedding."

"I don't want her to leave on account of me."

"I think she's ready to be unencumbered again."

"What about Mr. Frye?" Kate asked.

"Oh, he's definitely in the picture. In fact, Betty's talking about going to his church with him this week."

They walked slowly along the bridge to the parking lot. In the truck, Charlie put the heater on, and it felt good. Kate took off her knit gloves.

"How much time do you need, Kate? Before the wedding, I mean?" he asked.

"Not long, I guess. We don't need a big wedding."

"It's the first time for you," he said. "We'll have it as big as you like."

She smiled in the darkness. "I don't have a lot of family left. It's just me and Chad. I'll ask the folks from the library and the church, but other than that…"

"My sister and her family will come up from Portland," Charlie said. "Do you mind if I ask the police department?"

"Ask everyone you want to be there."

"So, we ought to look at a calendar."

Kate rummaged in her purse, and he put the dome light on. "Thanksgiving's next week," she said with mild surprise when she had opened her pocket calendar.

"Is Chad coming down?"

"No, he told me last night that he's going to his girlfriend's house. But he's coming down tomorrow, just to meet you."

"That's good. You'll have Thanksgiving with us, won't you?"

"All right, thanks. Mike and Jill invited me, but I know they'll understand. They're having a huge family dinner at their place."

"So ... getting back to the wedding." Charlie pushed her hair back gently and put a kiss just in front of her ear.

"Pick a date," Kate invited, holding out the calendar.

He squinted at it. "How about the eighteenth of December? I have two weeks of vacation left. I can take them after the wedding and before I start my new post. Or I could take the extra money."

"Do you need the extra money?"

He shook his head. "We'll want to take a honeymoon, though. I think we need those two weeks."

"Will we take Alex with us?" Kate asked timidly.

"On the honeymoon? I hadn't thought about it. What do you think?"

"I just—do you think we ought to leave him like that? Everything's changing so fast for him. I'd hate for him to be confused and think we'd abandoned him." She put one hand up to his cheek, looking to him for wisdom where the boy was concerned.

"Maybe Betty would keep him for a few days, and then we could come back for him." He turned suddenly to face her. "Kate, it isn't just Alex for you, is it?"

"No, Charlie. I love you. Very much."

He put his arms around her and kissed her then, and Kate felt the comfort and contentment she had longed for. She knew she would be secure with him. She let her head rest on his shoulder, and they sat for a minute without speaking.

"All right," he said at last. "I'll speak to Betty about it. We'll need some time alone. I'll talk to Alex too. I think he'll understand if I put it to him that people getting married need some time to get acquainted." He clasped her hand in his. "Now, about the ring ..."

"I don't need a ring, Charlie."

"Yes, you do."

"No, well, just a wedding ring. I'd really rather you didn't spend much on that."

Charlie took a deep breath. "Well, Kate, if the thought isn't too repulsive, Joy had my mother's diamond. It isn't fancy, but … well, I don't know. Maybe that's not a good idea." His voice caught a little.

Kate thought about it. "I think I'd like to wear it. I saw the picture of Joy on the mantel, and I thought then, I would have liked her." She sat up and tried to see Charlie's expression, but it was too dark. "She was Alex's mother, and I think she was someone very special. And it was your mother's ring before that."

He was very quiet.

"It might need resizing," she said.

"We can have the stone reset if you want," Charlie offered.

"No. No, I want it the way it is."

"All right. Thank you." He choked a little, and Kate put her arms out to him. He held her for an instant, his cheek against her hair, then said, "Come on, I'll take you home. We have a lot to do tomorrow."

***

Charlie drove slowly, away from the river and past the police station.

"Kate, if you want to take classes toward your degree, we'll work something out."

"Let's see what happens after we things settle down," she said. "It's not as important to me now. And Alex and I will need to adjust to a lot of things. If you think we'll be all right financially, I'd like to just be with you and Alex and get used to being a family."

"That's what I want most," Charlie said. "I think you should put in your notice at both of your jobs."

She smiled, knowing she would miss her coworkers and the patrons at the public library and the academy. "I'll do that Monday. I almost think Heather Wilson's ready to take on the job at school mornings, if she wants to. And I'm sure Marilyn won't have a problem finding someone to replace me in the children's room."

He turned the pickup in at the Palmers' driveway and went to her side of the truck to let her out. The kitchen door was unlocked, and they went in, calling, "Hello!"

"Hello." Dorothy stood in the doorway to the living room. "Come right in."

Charlie glanced behind him toward the driveway before closing the door.

"Still looking for Alex." He shook his head.

Kate smiled. "He's safe at home with Betty."

"Come in and sit for a few minutes, Charlie," Dorothy said, and they went into the living room.

Justin began to rise from his recliner, but Charlie put his hand out. "Don't get up, Mr. Palmer. You look too comfortable there."

They shook hands, and Justin chuckled. "Sit down, son."

Charlie sat with Kate on the sofa and reached for her hand.

"Would it be prying to ask if you've set the date?" Dorothy asked.

"December eighteenth," Charlie said with satisfaction, smiling at Kate.

"Oh, my! Four weeks away!"

"You having it at the church?" Justin asked.

"Yes. I guess we'd better go by the Wilsons' tomorrow and talk to the pastor," Charlie said.

"You know, the church ladies put on a lovely reception for our son Nick and his bride," Dorothy said tentatively. "Have you thought about the refreshments yet?"

"We haven't thought about any of that." Kate's brow furrowed. "I was wondering how I could have everything ready in time. I don't suppose you and Jill would help me with the arrangements?"

"We'd love to," Dorothy assured her.

179

"Great!" Kate leaned toward her and said confidentially, "I'm going to ask Jill to be my matron of honor."

"How exciting!"

"Well, we haven't known each other long, but Jill has been so good to me, and I don't have any sisters."

"I'm sure she'll be thrilled," Dorothy said.

Justin looked expectantly at Charlie. "Who's the best man?"

"Do you think Alex is old enough?"

"I'm not sure," Justin said.

"Would he have to sign the marriage certificate?" Kate asked.

"Guess we'd better check into that. I'd really like to have him be my best man. But if he can't, we'll have him up there with us, anyway."

"Of course," said Kate.

"If Alex is too young, then I guess I'll ask Bob Sorenson. He's probably my best friend. Unless you think your brother would like to do it."

Kate squeezed his hand. "Ask Bob if you want to. Chad and Alex can be your groomsmen."

"Just don't invite any wildlife to the rehearsal, like Nick did," Justin said with a chuckle.

Kate blinked. "What's that?"

"Long story," Dorothy said. "I'll tell you later."

"Oh, I almost forgot." Charlie reached into his jacket pocket and drew out a folded piece of paper. "It's a note from Alex."

Kate unfolded it and looked at wobbly letters that shakily, unmistakably, spelled out, *I love you frum Alex.* Her heart squeezed.

"Should I wait for a reply?" Charlie asked formally.

Kate held the note out to Dorothy.

"Oh, how sweet! Of course you need to send him an answer. Let's see, there's a magnetic note pad on the refrigerator."

Kate hurried into the kitchen, where she found the paper and a pen. She took the pad to the table and wrote, "Dear Alex, Tonight your daddy and I chose the day for the wedding. It will be December 18. I love you both."

She looked up to see Charlie standing in the doorway. "How should I sign it?"

Charlie's brown eyes were fixed on her face. "What do want him to call you? He asked me before I left tonight, and I didn't know what to tell him."

"Do you think he would call me *Mommy*?" she asked anxiously.

Charlie smiled. "I hope he will." He reached out to her and took her into his arms, stroking her hair. When he bent to kiss her, her hands went slowly up around his neck and elation swept over her as she rested in his arms, drawing courage from him.

After a moment, Kate straightened and held up the notepad. Charlie didn't release her, so she propped it against his shoulder and wrote at the bottom of the message, "Your mommy soon, Kate Pierce."

KATE BY THE BOOK

The Mailboat

Chapter 1

Camp Nurse

"Mike! Wait!" Robyn Carver dashed down the slope from her parents' cottage toward the lake.

Mike Borden had put three letters and a flyer in the Carvers' mailbox and was about to shove the boat off when she came running down the dock, her sneakers pounding the boards, a counterpoint to the staccato waves slapping the pilings beneath. He grabbed the edge of the dock, holding the boat in rocking proximity to it.

She ran the last few steps swinging a green duffel bag, her dark ponytail bouncing over one shoulder.

"Have you got room for me, Mike?" she panted as she reached the end of pier.

"Sure. Climb aboard." It was the first time she had ever ventured onto the mailboat with him. He was a little surprised but pleased. Definitely pleased.

Every day when he made his mail run in the boat owned by the marina, he approached the Carvers' dock with anticipation. Would she be there, or wouldn't she? For the last two weeks it had been the high point of his day, the possibility of seeing Robyn for ten seconds.

Usually she was sitting in a deck chair on the dock, reading or writing on a tablet. He looked forward to the moment when she looked up and saw him approaching in the boat, and her brown eyes lit with the pleasure of seeing an old friend. And now she wanted to ride with him.

The young postman extended his hand, and Robyn put the strap of her duffel bag into it. Mike dropped it gently at his feet, then reached out to help her safely onto the pontoon boat. Her eyes sparkled, and she smiled at him.

Mike's heart pounded. He'd had a crush on Robyn Carver all through junior high and high school, but to her he'd been just a shy, brainy kid in her home room—the boy whose family used to own the cottage across the cove.

They were grown up now, and he shouldn't still be flustered every time he saw her. But he hadn't expected to see her ever again, and the mere fact that she was here this summer was part of the allure. She had come back to Belgrade to spend the warm months on Great Pond, just as he had. One last summer on the lake, before he left that part of him behind. It had to be more than symbolic that Robyn had chosen a parallel path.

"Where you headed?" he asked.

"Spruce Island." She pushed back a strand of dark hair that had escaped her ponytail and straightened the striped T-shirt she wore over jeans.

"You going to camp this week?" He grinned. The first crop of campers had arrived at the boys' camp on the island two days earlier and been ferried out from the shore in motorboats owned by the camp.

"No, I'm filling in as their nurse."

"I thought they had a nurse."

"They did, but she got sick last night."

"That's a good one." He smiled, pushing the boat away from the dock.

"The camp director took her to the hospital in Augusta," Robyn said, "and she had her appendix out last night. They're desperate for someone to replace her."

Mike whistled. "So you're going out there? They've got a hundred and fifty campers, I'm told. I thought you were taking the summer off before you start your big new job."

Robyn grimaced. "I was. I am."

He shook his head. "This isn't the way to get rested."

"I told Merton Lipke I'll help him out for a few days while he rounds up someone else. I don't want to live on Spruce Island all summer, and I told him so. But for a week or two ..." She shook her head. "He begged. What could I say?"

Mike laughed.

"Oh, and he said if it works out for you, I can ride out with you every morning and do sick call while you finish your mail run. If you can stop back for me, I'll catch a ride home with you when I'm done. If not, one his staffers will run me home in their motorboat."

Mike pulled his baseball cap off and scratched his head. The mailboat was owned by Jim Doherty, the marina's proprietor. His father, Ben Doherty, had held the mail contract on the lake for decades and made the deliveries himself.

The route only operated in summer, when the owners of the cottages on the pristine Maine lake were in residence. But when Jim Doherty inherited the business, he'd concentrated on expanding the marina. Instead of delivering mail, he'd begun hiring someone every summer to take the postal route and give short cruises around the lake in the pontoon boat after the day's mail run.

"Well, I know what Jim's going to say," Mike told Robyn. "I'll have to charge you, the same as any other passenger."

"I know, Mike. Merton says he'll pay you the seven dollars a day to bring me, and he'll pay me forty dollars every time I come. It'll be less than he pays a full-timer. But I told him he's got to look for somebody to stay over there. I won't stay nights on the island, and I won't do this for eight weeks. I'm on vacation."

"All right, sit down. I'll settle up with Merton when we get there." Mike moved to the steering wheel, just behind the front edge of the canopy. He was hauling passengers today. A family of five had boarded at the marina, and a woman at the bed and breakfast had phoned to make sure he would pick her up there when he stopped with their mail. The tourists made the mail run profitable for the marina.

He started the motor and putt-putted toward the dock at the next cottage, then killed the motor and let the boat glide in under its own momentum. When the hull tapped the dock, he pulled open the mailbox mounted on a post over the water, stuffed the Smiths' mail inside, and flipped the door shut before the boat drifted out of reach.

Each of the cottages on the mail run had a post for him to tie up to if needed, but Mike had perfected his technique of sliding the mail into the boxes smoothly without wasting a second, and without dumping the letters in the water.

As they approached Spruce Island, he kept up a running commentary for the passengers, giving a little of the camp's history. Merton Lipke, the camp director, was waiting for them on the boat dock. Mike cut the engine and drifted in slowly past the float. A war canoe manned by fifteen chanting boys and two counselors flashed past them and down the lake. A beginners' swimming class was under way in the area bounded by buoyed lines.

"We'll be here about five minutes," Mike announced to his passengers, slipping a loop of rope over the mooring post.

Robyn stood ready with her duffel bag. He took it from her and swung it up into Merton's hand.

"Miss Carver! Thank you so much for coming." Merton extended an arm for Robyn to cling to as she scrambled out of the boat and up the ladder, but she ignored it.

"I'm only here for two hours, Mr. Lipke. Mike's agreed to stop in for me at the end of his run."

"Excellent arrangement. Thank you, Mike."

188

"My pleasure." Mike pulled the bin of mail for the camp out from under a tarp and heaved it onto the pier, then mounted the ladder.

"I'll write a check to cover Miss Carver's transportation for the rest of the week, and I'll speak to Jim when I'm at the marina Saturday," Merton said.

"Fine with me." Mike hefted the box and followed Merton and Robyn up the path to the camp office. For a few days, at least, he would have Robyn in his boat for fifteen minutes on the way from her cottage to the island, and again going back two hours later. It was beginning to sink in, and it felt good.

He didn't normally take the boat back past the Carvers' cottage. The return half of his loop took him down the other side of the lake. If he took her home every day, it would add at least fifteen minutes to his mail run. Maybe he wouldn't mention that to Jim.

It would be great having Robyn along for a few more minutes while he cut across the pond to drop her off. If Jim thought of it and complained, Mike would try to make him see it as a public service, so the boys at the camp could have their nurse.

***

Robyn looked around with interest. She and her sister Rebecca had visited Spruce Island many times over the years, after camp was done for the season in August. They had paddled across from the family cottage and beached their canoe on the camp's waterfront, near the docks pulled ashore for the winter, and crept curiously over the grounds, peering into empty cabins. She had never been this close when it was teeming with campers.

Everywhere, there were boys. Pitching horseshoes, chopping wood for campfires, playing soccer, weaving lanyards, climbing rope nets.

When Mike had set down the bin of mail on Merton's desk and accepted a check made out to Doherty's Marina, he touched the bill of his baseball cap and winked at Robyn.

"Think you'll be able to tear yourself away in a couple of hours, Nurse Carver?"

She laughed. "If you're not here on time, I'll scream."

Merton led her out of the office and toward a small cabin nearby. A wood-burned "Infirmary" sign hung over its door. Robyn turned and walked backward for a moment, watching Mike stride down the path to the waterfront, the shade of tall spruce and pine trees dappling his T-shirt. She'd hardly seen him since their high school graduation, and she liked what she saw now.

He'd held the mailboat job summers between his college years, but she had been working elsewhere. The year she graduated from nursing school in Massachusetts, Mike had exited the University of Maine summa cum laude. Someone else had delivered the mail on the lake after that. For the last three years, she hadn't seen him at all. Then, two weeks ago, she'd come to the cottage and the mailboat had carried him back into her life.

Her foot caught on a tree root, and she stumbled. Merton turned and grabbed her elbow, keeping her from splatting on the ground.

"Are you all right?"

"Yes, thank you, Mr. Lipke."

"It's Merton."

"Okay. What do I do?"

In the little infirmary cabin, he showed her the basics—camper records, exam room, first aid supplies, isolation room.

"This is the key to the medication cabinet." He placed a silver key on a blue and red lanyard in her hand. "We've got three diabetics this week, and a boy on antibiotics. You dispense the meds while you're here. I've got a counselor, Uncle Mark, detailed to take care of it the rest of the time, until we get another nurse. Mark and I are the only ones with keys to the med cupboard. I'll give you my key every day when you come."

"All right. What will you do if you have an emergency and I'm not here?"

"We'll call and have an ambulance meet us at the marina. That's what we'd do, anyway, if a nurse was living out here. We don't expect you to handle severe trauma. But then we don't expect to have any." He eyed her hopefully. "You sure you won't stay a few nights?"

"No, but I have a cell phone. If you really need me, you can call me at the cottage. I won't have a motorboat until my dad comes up to camp next week, but I have a canoe."

"That won't help if the lake's rough," Merton said with a sigh.

"True. I don't canoe in whitecaps."

"Well, at least you're helping us meet the bare minimum state requirements while we look for someone else. I appreciate that."

Robyn nodded. "Just get someone as quickly as you can, please. You're right that you ought to have someone here full time. Boys will be boys."

"Right. I'll go announce sick call."

He left her, and Robyn opened her duffel bag, arranging her stethoscope and a box of disposable rubber gloves on the table.

Soon she heard Merton's voice on the loudspeaker, surely loud enough to reach the bed-and-breakfast on the far shore. On a still day, the speaker could even be heard at her family's cottage, nearly a mile away.

"Nurse Carver is now in for sick call. All campers who need medical attention, report to the infirmary."

Pounding feet and the chattering of boys reached her. She went to the door and smiled at the ragged line of a dozen campers. A young man in shorts and a Spruce Island T-shirt stood near them.

"All right, guys, settle down." The counselor pulled apart two boys who were wrestling in the pine needles beside the path.

"Hello," Robyn said.

He glanced toward her, then looked again and smiled. "Hi. I'm Uncle Sean."

"I'm Robyn. How do I do this? First come, first served?"

"Well, Miss Janet did most serious cases first."

"Are there any serious cases this morning?"

"I don't think so." His grin was contagious.

She took the boys inside one at a time and listened to their complaints. An infected mosquito bite, a stomachache, an insulin shot, the antibiotic taker. Sean let them leave for their activities as they emerged from the infirmary. A boy with a cast the length of his forearm reported for a daily check, and Robyn rebandaged a cut sustained the day before. Blisters, sunburn, and a laceration.

Finally, they were all gone but Sean.

"All set?" Robyn asked, eyeing him uncertainly.

He grinned. "Guess so. I have sick call duty this week. I'm supposed to keep the boys in line while you do your work."

"I think it went well." She looked to him for confirmation.

"It went great. So, you live in Belgrade?" He was four or five years younger than her, but Robyn couldn't miss the signals that he'd like to know her better.

"I grew up here, and my family has a summer cottage on the lake. I told Merton I'd come out mornings to fill in until he finds you a replacement nurse."

"You're an R.N. then?"

"Yes." She smiled at his skepticism.

"Sorry. I'm just surprised you have time to do this. Don't you have another job?" He was cute, with sandy hair and freckles and that engaging smile.

192

"Well, I spent the last year working on my master's, and I'm starting a new job in Worcester, Massachusetts this fall. I could have started now, but I wanted the summer here on the lake. Sort of a last family interlude before I settle into the real world, you know?"

He grinned. "Well, I hope you stay with us a while. The boys will behave better for you than they did for Miss Janet."

"Why's that?"

He blushed a little. "Oh, well, she was old, you know? Forty, at least, and ... corpulent. The guys referred to her as Nurse Plenty."

Robyn couldn't hold back a little laugh. "Rude. I can't wait to hear what they nickname me."

"Probably Miss Robyn."

She smiled and began packing her personal equipment. "Is the infirmary locked all the time?"

"No, just the drug cupboard," Sean replied.

She nodded, determining to haul her gear with her every day. Boys had a way of making free with medical supplies, given the chance.

"The mailboat's back," Sean said. "You riding with him?"

"Yes." She picked up the green duffel bag and hurried out the cabin door. She'd have to drop the drug cabinet's key off with Merton before she boarded the boat. "Thanks, Sean. I'll see you tomorrow."

Chapter 2

A Ride Too Short

Mike tied the boat to the Spruce Island dock, looking anxiously up the path for Robyn. His passengers had enjoyed the morning, but he thought they were getting restless.

Good. She was ready. She trotted along the path toward him, the duffel bag slung over her shoulder.

"Hi!" She waved to him as she gained the waterfront.

Mike waved back. He couldn't help smiling. She looked young enough to be a camper herself, but he knew she was twenty-five. Her birthday was three days after his, and in school he had teased her, admonishing her to respect her elders.

She tossed him the duffel bag and scaled the ladder quickly.

"Where do you want me?"

"Sit right there. You want me to take you right back to your place?"

"Oh, I don't know." Robyn looked around at the other occupants of the boat. "Your passengers ..."

"Let me drop them at the marina first, and then I'll run you out?"

"Sure."

Perfect.

She sat quietly on the bench that ran along the side of the boat, and Mike was conscious of her watching him. The 75-horse-power outboard was more than adequate for the pontoon boat, but it wasn't like running a ship. Did she think it was juvenile of him to take back his old summer job this year? But then, she'd come back too. Still, she wasn't babysitting. She was just taking some time off.

She'd told him in snatches, over the daily exchange of mail, that she was about to start a challenging supervisory nursing job. It wasn't so different from his own situation, Mike reflected. A couple of months off, a slower-paced summer, then back into the rat race. He glanced over at her again, and she smiled. He straightened at the wheel, trying to look efficient and seaworthy.

The next cottage they cruised up to was on a small island, with an old wooden dock extending twenty feet over the water. An elderly gentleman and a fluffy collie stood near the mailbox at the end of the pier. When he killed the motor, Mike could hear the collie's bark of welcome.

"You're late," the old man called as Mike brought the boat alongside.

"Sorry, Mr. Foster. I'll be picking up the nurse at the boys' camp for a while, so that will set me back a few minutes."

Mr. Foster scrutinized the passengers. "Which one's the nurse?"

Robyn waved to him and called, "It's me, sir, Robyn Carver. The camp's regular nurse is sick, and Mike's taking me out to fill in for a few days. I'm sorry it upsets your routine."

"Not little Robyn?" Foster said in disbelief, lowering his chin so he could study her through the top of his bifocals. "You can't be all grown up so soon."

"I'm afraid so, sir," she said with a smile.

"No! Is your father at his camp?"

"Not yet. He's coming in July, for a couple of weeks. I decided to spend the whole summer here, so I came first and opened the cottage."

"Tell him to come over and see me when he's settled." Foster reached to accept his mail from Mike.

"I will."

"Have a good day, sir." Mike shoved the boat away from the dock and headed for the next summer home. "Four more stops," he said to Robyn before he gunned the motor.

He eased in at the next cottage and opened the mailbox, retrieved the outgoing mail, and inserted the day's post, then shut the box and flipped the flag down before shoving the boat away from the dock. He could feel Robyn watching him. It was silly, but he wanted to stuff that mailbox with flair, like a gunfighter spinning his revolver before he holstered it.

***

When the passengers had disembarked at the marina, Mike hopped onto the large, U-shaped dock with the bag of outgoing mail and his empty bin.

"Sit tight," he told her. "I'll be back in a minute."

He disappeared into the shop that sold everything from boats to night crawlers, and Robyn took the sunscreen bottle out of her duffel bag and applied it to her arms and face, then leaned against the back of the bench and closed her eyes. Tomorrow she would have to remember her sunglasses.

A short time later, the boat swayed with his weight, and she looked up.

"All set," Mike said. "I told Jim I'm taking you home. He says if I don't have passengers, I can take you straight home with no problem, but it will set me back a little. If I do have riders, you'll have to wait until I'm done with the mail run."

"That's fine. I'm sorry to add to your workload, Mike."

"It's not your fault, and I don't mind. Jim may end up charging Merton more, though."

"But I'm not taking the full cruise," Robyn protested.

"I know. Let Jim and Merton settle it."

She nodded and slid down the bench to where they could talk if the motor wasn't too loud. He started it and smiled at her as they pulled away from the dock, wishing suddenly that she lived at the other end of the lake. The few minutes he'd have alone with her wasn't nearly enough.

***

Robyn's cottage was near the beginning of the mail run, less than half a mile up the shore from the marina. She and Rebecca had walked down for sodas in earlier summers.

Those were idyllic days. Her family lived in an old stone house built in 1856. When she was little, they had nearly frozen in winter. Her father had insulated the house and had a new furnace installed, making it quite comfortable.

But in summer, the Carvers had always moved to camp. "Camp" was the cottage her grandfather had purchased fifty years ago at a trifling price, and the family had lived in it from the last day of school until past Labor Day every year.

"It's not that far, you know," she yelled.

He raised his eyebrows in question and backed the motor off a little.

"I said, it's not that far. I could walk home from the marina."

"No need."

He killed the motor, and they drifted slowly past the Hursts' and the Sibleys'.

"You're not in a hurry?" she asked.

"No. Are you?"

She shook her head.

"I've got a sunset cruise at seven tonight. Nothing till then. Thought it might be nice to have a real conversation with you."

"Can you tie up and come ashore for a soda?" She felt very daring to ask him.

Grinning, he flipped up the seat next to him. Robyn saw that it was a cooler, and he took out two cans of Pepsi with a flourish.

She accepted one with a grin and popped the top.

"So, what shall we talk about?"

He took a long drink from his can. "How about families? How's yours? You always say *fine* when I ask, but how are they really?"

"Good. Dad's working too hard. You know they sold the house?"

"Yeah, I heard."

"They're only going to make it up here for a couple of weeks, I'm afraid."

"And Rebecca?"

"Fine." She smiled sheepishly. "I guess that is kind of a catch-all word. But she is. She got married last year, you know."

"I remember. Living where? Rhode Island?"

"Connecticut. She's working for a title company, and her husband's in construction. He's a nice guy. And Mom and Dad moved down that way too."

Mike nodded. He glanced toward the shore. Robyn swung around saw that they had drifted past her family's cottage.

"Do you mind?" he asked.

She shook her head. "It's nice to have a chance to catch up with you. I'm kind of hungry, though. It's past lunch time."

"I can take you back."

"You don't have anything solid in that cooler?"

He flipped it open again and rummaged. "Let's see. Skittles and a chocolate bar."

"Skittles, please."

He tossed the little red package into her lap. "Good. I'm a chocoholic."

"I never knew that."

"I remember you like red licorice."

Robyn laughed. "Becky and I used to buy long strings of it at the marina and make it last all the way home." She opened the package and took out two purple Skittles. She always ate the purple ones first. "You've heard they're selling the cottage?"

"Who?" He was startled.

"My folks."

"No. That's too bad."

"Well, I know. I thought they might reconsider, but now that they're in Connecticut and Dad can't commute to work from camp anymore in the summer, they decided to sell it and try to buy a vacation home down there."

"Another Belgrade family moves away." He shook his head.

Robyn fought off the depression that descended on her every time she thought about leaving Belgrade for good. First the old house, now the cottage. She might never have reason to return again.

The Bordens had sold their cottage years ago, after Mike's father died. She and Mike were in seventh grade that year. Robyn had missed him that summer. No more swimming and canoeing together.

She and Rebecca had canoed around the cove, feeling depressed when they passed the Bordens' old cottage. The new owners were middle-aged Southerners with no children. The girls water-skied with the Hursts' teenagers and swam with the Sibleys' grandchildren, but Mike's absence put a damper on the fun.

Mike was always a nice boy, if a little studious, and she and Rebecca had liked having him as a summer neighbor. They could always count on him to be doing something interesting, like building a raft or hunting turtles. The summer after fifth grade, they'd built an amphibian zoo on the Bordens' beach.

The rest of the year he'd lived several miles away, but he rode the same school bus they did. Robyn and Mike hadn't been especially close, but she didn't think Mike was tight with anyone. He was a bit of a loner, and she always felt privileged when he let her and Rebecca in on his projects.

After his father died, he was quieter than ever. His mother worked full time after that, and Mike had assorted jobs after school and on weekends. He never tried out for sports or went to after-school activities. The other kids considered him a brain, one of those likely to succeed in college and in life, but he wasn't one of the popular boys.

"How's your mom?" she asked.

"Okay."

"Is she still working at the bank?"

"Yeah."

"How about Pete?" She tipped the package up and poured half a dozen candies into her mouth.

"He's fine. He's working at the Ford garage."

Robyn nodded as she chewed.

Mike looked out across the lake. The local warden had pulled his boat up next to a small motorboat that held two fishermen.

"I guess Jack Porter's out checking licenses today," Robyn ventured.

"Mm." Mike glanced over, then turned his gaze back to rest on her. "So, how about you? Are you fine?"

"Don't I look fine?"

He laughed. "You look terrific."

She felt a blush coming on and turned to trail her left hand over the side. Her fingertips barely reached the water.

"You didn't meet anybody in college?" he asked.

Robyn knew what he meant. "Not really. You?"

"Uh-uh," Mike said, not looking at her. He unwrapped the chocolate bar slowly, as if not tearing the wrapper was crucial.

Robyn sat forward. "I don't want to be nosy, but I heard this high-powered engineering firm you work for is sending you to the back of beyond."

He shrugged. "It's not the first time I've worked out of the country. I spent two months in Mexico, four in Zaire, and all of last winter in Nicaragua."

"And now Bolivia?"

"Yeah."

"Wow. That's a lot of airline miles."

"I've thought about switching to a firm that specializes in domestic jobs."

"You don't like traveling?"

"Traveling is all right, but staying in a foreign country for months on end gets a little tiresome. You're so far from your family, you know?" His blue eyes were serious, a bit wistful.

"So, you think you could find something else?"

He smiled a little. "Well, there's a company in Philadelphia that's approached me. But I'd lose out in other ways if I went with them."

"Like what?"

"Well, while I'm working for Wrenfield, if I'm not abroad, I can live at home and commute from here."

"From your mom's house to Bangor? An hour each way?"

"Just about. It's worth something to be near Mom and Pete when I'm not globetrotting." He took a bite of chocolate.

Robyn brought her hand up out of the water and snapped the droplets at him.

"Hey, you!" He moved threateningly toward her, but the twinkle in his eyes belied his menacing tone.

She laughed. "This is nice. Just drifting along." Closing her eyes, she slouched on the bench.

"I'm just a drifter at heart."

"That so?" she asked lazily. This was the way summer should be: water, sun, companionship. "So you're not serious about switching jobs?"

"I dunno. Philadelphia really wants me, but I'd have to move down there, and that would be almost as bad as going overseas. I've got to let them know right away." He shrugged. "I'll probably say no. The company I'm with has been good to me, extended travel aside."

"You like working for them?"

"Yeah, I do. It's challenging. We've designed two major bridges for the Bolivian government. I have to oversee the prelim work. I told the firm I wanted the summer off first."

"Are they delaying the project for you?"

"Nope. They have summer in winter down there. Well, you know what I mean. The Bolivian construction season follows the rainy season."

She nodded. "So, you took a sabbatical of sorts."

"Yup. To do the mail run one more time."

"Why?" She squinted up at him.

"I dunno. Maybe I'm like you. Don't want to let go of the trouble-free past."

She sat up. "Mike, you had enough trouble for both of us, with your dad dying and you having to work all the time. Your past wasn't exactly carefree."

"I know, but ... somehow Belgrade is still the ideal for me. If I moved to Philly, it would be the same as traipsing off to Bolivia or some other foreign place. It's a world away from here."

"I know what you mean about living in the city. It's a big adjustment, after growing up in such a rural area. You might be happier someplace else."

"Maybe, under the right circumstances. But I'm not sure I'll ever find what I'm looking for."

She sipped her Pepsi. He was right about the nostalgia this summer had brought her. Having Mike back on the mail run was reassuring. So many of the old families had sold their cottages. Here was a bit of the comforting past, and yet it was different. He was different.

"So, what are you looking for?" she asked.

He sighed and stared out over the water. "It's not the job that matters, or even the location, when it comes down to that. I want a family. The way it was before Dad died." He looked at her and chuckled. "Guess I'm asking for a lot."

"No, I don't think so. It's sort of my ideal, too. A family, children, a home."

He took another bite of the chocolate bar. "So why did you go into nursing?"

She smiled. "Figured I'd have to support myself for many years to come. It seemed like a good prospect for steady work. And I like working with people."

"Even rambunctious campers?"

"It's okay. Some of the boys are sweet. Like I told Merton, I don't want to do it all summer, but if I can help out for a few days, that's fine."

Mike looked at his watch. "Guess I'd better take you home."

She nodded with a pang of regret.

He started the motor and swung the boat slowly around.

Robyn watched him, trying not to stare. The mature Mike was worth observing. She had the feeling he knew who he was, unlike some young men. He'd implied that he didn't have a girlfriend. She wondered about that.

He was handsome enough now to cause women to look twice, with his light, wavy hair ruffling in the breeze and blue eyes that held a direct honesty, and somewhere along the way he'd gained a simple charm. In the old days he hadn't shown much interest in girls ... until their senior year. Then he'd agonized through a major crush on Patti Sachs.

Patti was pretty, she was moderately smart, she was a cheerleader, and she paid enough attention to Mike to enslave him. As far as Robyn knew, Patti had never actually gone out with Mike. But she flirted with him between classes, bestowing her winsome smiles on him, and that was sufficient. Mike was won.

Until Patti had accepted Ted Wright's class ring. She had worn the massive ring on a chain around her neck, pulling at it, sliding it along the chain while she sat in class or talked to her friends. Ted wore hers on his little finger.

Mike couldn't afford a class ring. Robyn had one, the delicate, feminine version. She had never gone steady, though, and her ring had stayed boringly on her own finger. Sometimes she'd envied the other girls, but at others she was glad she didn't have a steady boyfriend. The fights in the hall and weeping in the locker room were embarrassing.

Mike apparently had gotten over Patti's defection by graduation. Robyn had seen him a few times during those college year summers, as he came and went in the mailboat, but she'd worked in town to earn money for her tuition, spending less time at the cottage every year. She'd come home the last two years for a couple of weeks' vacation with her family. Mike hadn't been there, and she hadn't expected to see him again.

"He's working for some big construction firm out of Bangor, I think," her father had said.

"That's great. I'm glad he's doing well." And Mike Borden had walked out of her mind.

She was glad he'd turned up again at the lake. He was as quiet as ever, but today she felt the old friendship resurfacing. She wondered if she'd missed out on something fine by not keeping up the contact with him.

Until today she'd only seen him for a few seconds at a time, if she remembered to be on the dock when the mail was due. Their truncated conversations had stoked the embers of her childhood affection for him. Last week he'd handed her the mail and said, "You should come with me on the boat sometime." She'd considered it but hadn't worked up the nerve to take the tour.

The prospect of making the run to Spruce Island with him every day for a week or two didn't displease her. Any fears that it might turn out to be awkward were dispelled by their conversation that afternoon in the boat. It had been in the back of her mind that if she and Mike talked much, they might find that they didn't really like each other anymore.

205

She swallowed hard and braced herself as he killed the engine and let the boat drift toward her dock. The opposite had happened. Mike had opened up to her for a few minutes, and she liked him just fine. He was still serious, but he'd polished his wit over the years, and he still thought about things that mattered.

He looped his painter over the mooring post and turned to her.

"Thanks, Mike." She stood in the swaying boat, hanging on to the gunwale. "It was nice talking to you."

"Yeah. Very nice." His eyes glinted as he reached for her duffel bag.

Chapter 3

Choppy Waters

On Thursday morning, Mike felt his spirits lift as he approached the Carvers' dock and saw Robyn waiting to ride out to the island with him. The sun was already scorching, and she wore khaki shorts, a white sleeveless blouse, and sunglasses. She grinned at him and scrambled quickly into the boat.

He left her off at the island realizing they had barely spoken to each other. At the end of his run, he picked her up again, but he had several passengers, so the conversation between them remained minimal. It's all right, he told himself. It will take Merton a while to find another nurse. You've got tomorrow, at least.

On Friday it poured rain. His bins of mail were secured under blue tarps, and he placed the outgoing mail he collected in a plastic bag. Between the stops he stood shivering, with water streaming down into the bottom of the boat from his rain clothes and soaked sneakers. He had no passengers until Robyn came aboard, and she huddled in a windbreaker under the boat's canopy until they reached Spruce Island.

He disembarked with her and carried the mail to the camp office. Usually a train of boys tagged after him, eager to know if they'd received letters from home, but not today. They were all inside doing crafts, he guessed. Robyn waved and gave him a bedraggled smile, then hurried toward the infirmary.

Mike made the rest of his forty stops alone. He'd bundled each family's delivery together with a rubber band to lessen the chance of dropping the letters in the water. He was practiced enough that he rarely had a mishap, but once in a while he misjudged the speed with which he approached a dock, or the force of the waves on a windy day.

If there was no mail for a particular box, he still had to cruise in close to see if there was outgoing mail. If the flag on the box was down, he'd ease away and head on to the next stop, watching for snags and rocks that might lurk just beneath the surface of the water.

This had to be one of the best summer jobs available. On sunny days, it was perfect. He didn't even mind when the water was rough—he had fewer passengers then and could let his thoughts drift.

But on rainy days it was miserable. He had the canopy and could shelter under it most of the time, but he had to leave it and go to the bow of the boat to place the mail securely in the boxes. Still, even when he was soaking wet and shivering, he was still glad he operated the mailboat.

At last it was time to go back for Robyn. She wouldn't be going to the boys' camp on Saturday, when most of the campers would leave, and he would miss her. Could he work up the courage to ask her to accompany him tomorrow on his route anyway? She was waiting for him under a large pine tree near the beach and scurried out onto the dock as he approached.

"Careful, don't slip." He reached to help her down into the boat.

"Thanks." She hugged herself as she sat shivering on the bench in the cold drizzle. The whitecaps bounced the boat mercilessly, and Mike took her straight home.

"How do you stand it in lousy weather?" she screamed over the engine noise.

"Comes with the job. At least I don't have snow or sleet."

"On days like this, I make a fire in the fireplace and curl up with a book."

"Sounds like fun." He took a deep breath and decided to chance it. He leaned closer. "Make the run with me tomorrow?"

Robyn grimaced. "Not if it's raining."

"But if it's not?"

She wavered. She'd probably been looking forward to a peaceful Saturday. No campers with scraped knees, wasp stings, and poison ivy.

The bow of the boat whacked the edge of her dock, and he quickly fixed the painter to stabilize the craft. As he extended his hand to her, anxiety buffeted him the same way the swells hit the hull of the boat. She climbed out between waves and looked down at him from the dock.

"I'll consider it."

He smiled, content, as he pushed the boat off.

***

Robyn ran up the path to the cottage and stood on the glassed-in porch, watching the pontoon boat grow smaller as Mike headed toward Foster Island. Was it possible that Mike was considering a serious relationship with her? She hadn't come here looking for romance, but she realized the thought wasn't unpleasant.

Mike knew her, and she knew him. She wouldn't have to explain her feelings about the lake and the cottage and the family moving away. Mike understood, just as she understood his past hardships and grief, and the way emerging into the larger world had strengthened him.

When the boat was out of sight, she peeled off her dripping windbreaker and hurried into the living room. She kindled a fire in the fireplace, then went to the kitchen and made herself a grilled cheese sandwich and a cup of hot cocoa.

Wasn't June supposed to be warm? She wasn't asking for a heat wave, just comfortable warmth.

Huddling in front of the hearth with her steaming mug, she began to thaw out. She wrapped a green knit afghan around her and pulled a tall book from the bookcase. The family had gathered books and games over the years, leaving them at the cottage for summer enjoyment.

The book she chose was her high school yearbook. She turned the pages slowly to the senior class portraits. She and Mike faced each other on opposite pages, Borden and Carver. She had always hated her senior picture. Her hair was limp and decidedly unglamorous.

Mike, on the other hand, looked like the studious boy he was then, thin and serious, with a grave outlook. He had always been tall. In adulthood, he had broadened considerably through the shoulders. And he seemed to smile more now.

He was earning good money at the engineering firm, she was sure. He probably didn't have to worry about his mother anymore, although he'd said she was still working. It must comfort him to know he could take care of her now if she needed help.

She smiled as she looked at his picture again. Mike was about the last guy she'd have picked as best looking in her class seven years ago. She paged through the senior section, scrutinizing the faces of the young men who smiled out at her. Funny how your perspective changed.

***

The sky was gray Saturday morning, and the lake was choppy. The boat lunged jerkily over the waves. No passengers. Nobody wanted to be out on the water. It wasn't fun to be tossed from crest to crest. Mike sorted his mail and made his first few stops without much hope of company.

When he rounded the point and could see as far as Carvers', he caught his breath. She was waiting on the dock, wearing corduroy slacks, sneakers, and a sweatshirt under her windbreaker. A UMaine Black Bears baseball cap shaded her brown eyes, but he thought he caught a glint from them as he got closer. Resting on the dock beside her was a canvas tote bag.

He killed the motor at precisely the right moment and let the headway carry the boat to the dock.

"I've got nothing for you today. Any outgoing mail?"

"Just me."

He grinned then. "I was hoping you'd say that. Jump!"

He held out both arms, and she hopped lightly down into the boat.

"Rough today." She leaned on his arm for an instant as she caught her balance.

"Yeah, but it's not raining. You want a lifejacket?"

"No, I'll just hang on to this." She sat firmly on one of the flotation cushions. "I'll warn you, I brought sandwiches today. Cookies too, and a thermos of coffee."

Mike was so happy, he couldn't find a suitable reply but threw the engine into reverse and backed away from the Carvers' dock. She sat watching him with large, solemn eyes. How could he make her smile again? He'd never been a clever conversationalist, and he had to keep the motor running. That made talking hard.

He winked at her, and her bright smile came out. It warmed him all over.

***

When they stopped at Spruce Island, the grounds were quiet. Merton came to the dock and took the box from Mike.

"The boys are all gone today," he told Robyn. "I didn't expect to see you."

211

"She's just killing time with me." Mike was unable to keep a touch of pride from his voice.

Merton nodded.

"Don't you have some boys staying over for next week?" Robyn asked, searching the playground and the waterfront for campers.

"Yes. They've gone on an overnight canoe trip up to the north end of the lake. The new batch of campers will arrive this afternoon."

"Rough weather for canoeing," Mike noted.

"Yeah, but they made it okay. I went up in the motorboat to make sure. It's supposed to be better tomorrow. If it doesn't rain on them tonight, they'll have a good time."

They shoved off, and Robyn looked eagerly ahead. She hadn't been all the way up the lake yet this year, and she was anxious to see how many of the summer residents she knew were at their camps now.

"The Warrens sold their camp," Mike said as he let the motor idle for the next stop.

"Really?"

"Yup. Some folks from New Jersey bought it." He slipped two pieces of mail into the mailbox on the dock.

Their conversation went by fits and starts. Each time he slowed the engine, one of them would pick it up again. Once they'd made the rounds of the north end, Robyn broke out the sandwiches. They ate their picnic between stops, while Mike kept one hand on the wheel. She poured his coffee for him and handed him cookies.

Mike took a large package from beneath the tarp as they approached the dock at a cottage Robyn knew.

"That big box is for the Parkhursts?" she asked.

"Not the Parkhursts. They've rented the place out this summer."

"You're kidding. They wouldn't miss a summer on the lake."

"Nope, it's true. The kids are in college. I guess they wanted the money more than the peace and quiet."

He placed the package carefully on the dock. No one was on hand to retrieve it. Mike picked up an air horn and gave a blast, then shoved off, scanning the shore.

Robyn watched in fascination. Before they moved around the next point, obscuring the cottage, she saw a man in jeans and a black shirt walk onto the Parkhursts' dock and stoop for the package.

"That's the tenant?" she asked.

"Yup."

"Ever met him?"

"Nope. But when he gets a package I blow the horn, and he always comes out to get it after I leave."

"That's weird."

Mike shrugged. "I think he's an artist or a writer. Wants his solitude. And he leaves packages for me to take sometimes, and money for the postage. They all go to –" He broke off suddenly. "I'm not supposed to talk about it. Sorry. Confidentiality and all that."

"No problem." Robyn didn't imagine Mike was tempted to blab very often. But he talked easily with her, and she was glad.

They had no need to return to the boys' camp on the home stretch, and with a shock Robyn realized they were approaching Foster Island and were nearly done with the route.

"Funny, he's not down there." Mike nodded toward the empty wharf.

"It's cold today," Robyn ventured.

"Yeah, but he was out yesterday, even in the rain."

She nodded, remembering the elderly man and his collie standing motionless on the dock, waiting when Mike pulled up each day.

"It's windy today. I guess he's staying inside," she said.

Mike scanned the shore, frowning as he studied the cottage.

"He's always there. Every day since I started." He killed the motor.

The bow bumped the dock, and Mike slipped a loop of the painter over a protruding post.

"I'm going up and have a look."

Surprised, Robyn stood and watched him climb onto the dock and trot up the path. Foster's cottage had a little gazebo entry near the water, then half a dozen steps up to the porch proper. Mike didn't pause in the gazebo but went right up onto the porch and knocked on the door.

Inside the cottage, the dog began to bark. Robyn could see the frenzied collie jumping and snapping at the window. Mike looked toward her. She gave an exaggerated shrug. He put his hand on the doorknob and turned it, and the door swung open.

Suddenly apprehensive, Robyn scrambled out of the boat and ran along the dock. Mike had disappeared inside the cottage, leaving the door open.

"Mike?" She paused on the threshold. The dog barked.

"In here. Come quick."

Chapter 4

Ripping Up Roots

Robyn followed his voice through the rough kitchen and a board-paneled sitting room. The door of a tiny bedroom was open, and she went as far as the doorway.

"Must have fallen and bumped his head," Mike said.

He was kneeling beside the old gentleman. The brown and white collie stood beside them, whining. Robyn hurried forward. Foster's face was pale, but he was breathing. She felt his pulse. It was fast, and none too strong.

"Better get some help," she advised.

The old man moaned.

"Mr. Foster," she said distinctly, "can you hear me?"

His eyes fluttered open.

"Huh—who—"

Robyn bent forward, watching the man's eyes until they focused on her.

"Mr. Foster, it's Robyn Carver. I'm a nurse. I think you've hurt yourself, sir. Are you in pain?"

He struggled to sit up. Mike put one gentle hand on his shoulder.

"Better take it easy, sir."

"Just lie down," Robyn agreed. "Let me check you out."

"My head," Foster said.

Robyn felt the back of his head, her tender fingers probing beneath the gray hair.

"You have quite a bump there. I think you should see a doctor."

Mike stood and brought a pillow from the bed, easing it under Foster's head. "There aren't any electric or phone lines out here, but I've got a radio in the boat."

"I have my cell phone in my bag," Robyn said. "I might not be able to get a signal out here in this weather, though. This is the only cottage on the island, isn't it?"

"Yes."

"Doesn't seem as though an old man should be this isolated." She counted Foster's respirations.

"Well, his grandson, Gerald, lives in Oakland. I think he comes out some and stays in the summer."

"Jerry's still around?" Robyn asked. He'd been two years ahead of her and Mike in school.

"Yes, and his sister Meg and her husband. They check on him, I'm sure."

Robyn turned back to Mr. Foster. "Sir, we want to see about having a doctor look at you, to make sure you're all right, and we can call your grandson to let him know you've had an accident."

"All right," he said feebly.

"Does anything hurt, other than your head?"

"My elbow."

She unbuttoned the cuff and turned his sleeve up, exposing a spreading bruise. "Mike, would you go down to the boat and call for help? My phone's in my bag."

"Sure." Mike left her with the old man.

Robyn pulled a comforter off the bed, laid it over Mr. Foster, then sat beside him, talking quietly. Mike came back, his face somber.

"They said if there aren't any broken bones, we'd better take him in the boat. It will be a lot faster than bringing the EMTs out here. The ambulance will meet us at the marina."

"Can you carry him? I don't think anything's broken. There's a lump on the back of his head, and a little blood. I suspect he tripped and fell back against the corner of the dresser. He probably hurt his arm on the way down. But a doctor ought to examine him thoroughly, to make sure it's not serious."

Mike stooped over the elderly man. "Mr. Foster, do you think you can get up, sir?"

He strained to sit, and Mike pulled him up.

"I ... I don't know," Foster murmured. I'm a little shaky.

"I can carry you to the boat, if you don't mind."

"Well, I guess so."

Mike leaned over him, bending his knees. He tucked the quilt securely around the man, then stood, lifting him without obvious strain.

"Why, Michael Granville Borden! You were so skinny in high school. What happened?" Robyn was only half teasing.

"Guess I grew up." Mike tossed her a grin and headed for the door.

"What about the dog?" She picked up the pillow.

"Better bring him, too," Mike said. "Can't leave him out here alone."

The wind had picked up. Robyn pulled her jacket closer around her as she closed the cottage door and followed them down to the dock. The collie danced fretfully at Mike's heels.

In the boat, he laid Mr. Foster on the deck. Robyn sat down beside the old man and replaced the pillow, then checked his pulse again. He lay back with his eyes closed, and the collie sat whining at his head.

"Is he conscious?" Mike asked.

"I think so, but he may be a little shocky. Let's not waste any time. We don't want him to get chilled."

Mike started the motor, and Robyn pulled the comforter snugly up to Mr. Foster's chin. With the engine pushed to its highest speed, and the ride to the marina took only ten minutes.

217

The ambulance was there, lights flashing, when the pontoon boat hit the dock.

The two EMTs had a stretcher waiting on the wharf. They jumped into the boat and did a quick assessment.

"His name's Robert Foster," Mike supplied.

"Any family?"

"Not on the island. His grandson, Gerald, lives in Oakland."

"We'll call him."

"Tell him we've got his father's dog at the marina."

"Will do."

Mike stood leaning on a piling, watching while they loaded Mr. Foster in the ambulance and drove away, its siren fading. Robyn felt terribly let down. Their part of the adventure was over, but there was no resolution yet.

"Did you finish the run?" Jim Doherty was standing in the side door of the marina.

"Four more stops, between here and Foster Island." Mike jerked his head toward the lake.

"You've gotta finish," Jim said.

"I know. Can you tie the dog up until someone comes for him?" Jim came out and took the collie by the collar, pulling him gently toward the building.

Mike turned toward Robyn. "You ready to see this thing through?"

She nodded, shivering and rubbing her upper arms.

"Let's go." Mike put his arm around her and they walked out the dock together. He climbed into the boat and help up his arms. This time, when she hopped down, he stood holding her by the shoulders for a moment, looking into her face as though looking for something particular there.

Without a word, he went to his seat before the steering wheel and started the motor. Robyn sat down on her cushion in the seat nearest Mike. Finding the old man and taking him off the island together had bound her and Mike closer with a new thread. She wanted to be near to him.

He took the boat out slowly and turned toward the next cottage on his route. When he looked down at her, Robyn couldn't read his face, but he reached out deliberately and took her hand, squeezed it, and held on.

When all the mail was delivered, he headed across to her cottage and cut the motor, drifted in to her dock, and tossed the loop over the post.

She was at his side, ready to climb out.

"Thanks for lunch," he said.

"No problem, but I think I owe you seven dollars."

"It's on me this time." His look was intense and his voice quiet, now that the engine was silent.

Robyn caught her breath and shifted her weight. She didn't mind him looking at her, but his unrelenting gaze rattled her a little. She put one hand up to her temple and realized the futility of attempting to straighten her windblown hair.

"You remembered my middle name."

The blood rushed into her cheeks, and she looked down at their sneakers, almost toe to toe on the deck.

"I had the old yearbook out last night," she confessed. "Michael Granville Borden, National Honor Society. No other extracurricular activities."

"I didn't have time." His voice was hoarse.

"I know. I'm sorry. We were all so thoughtless. Mike, I could have done more to help you through that time."

He shrugged. "It was a necessary part of my life, I've found."

"How do you mean?"

"It made me what I am now." He paused as though deciding what mood to take, then he smiled. "Whatever that is."

She smiled back.

"Do you have plans for tomorrow?"

219

It was unexpected, and Robyn wasn't sure how to answer.
"I ..."

"I was thinking maybe lunch at the restaurant?" He nodded
in the direction of the village.

"I'd like that."

The satisfaction that crossed his face sent a surge of
anticipation through her, and she was glad she'd said yes.

"Can you stand a late lunch? Pick me up around one?" she
asked.

"Sure."

She nodded. That would give her time to visit her old
church in the morning and get reacquainted with the members
there. But afterward ... She couldn't think of anything she'd
rather do on Sunday afternoon than be with Mike.

***

The lake was so flat on Sunday afternoon that Robyn almost
convinced herself she could skate on it. The sun shone fiercely,
as though determined to make up for the two gray days it had
permitted on Great Pond.

When she got home from church, she sat on the dock
sipping coffee and enjoying the quiet as she waited for Mike. A
long canoe full of boys glided down the lake toward Spruce
Island. The overnight campers were back. With no wind to
battle, the canoe sliced through the still water. The surface
healed as soon as the craft passed, once more an unbroken
expanse of gleaming blue.

So far, the summer was hardly the peaceful interlude she'd
expected. So many things had unsettled her: Mr. Foster's
accident; Mike's presence; the crisis at Spruce Island Camp;
her parents' decision to sell the cottage; Mike's vacillation
toward his job; and her own discontent as she faced the new
position at the medical center in Worcester.

That last one was the main source of her uneasiness. It was true that Mike stirred her emotions, but that was a good sort of edginess. Her new job was another story.

She would be in charge of one shift of nurses in the surgical wing. It was a huge responsibility. She had wanted the job very much and had worked to exhaustion all winter to gain the needed credentials. Why?

Being back here made the city seem very unappealing. The fantastic job took a poor second when held up against life in Belgrade, Maine. Especially when her city life, while exciting and professionally fulfilling, was lonely, and life here on the lake was slow-paced and satisfying. And it had Mike.

Silly woman! Mike's only here for a few weeks, then he's off to the ends of the earth. The lake will never be the same again, even if you come back—which you won't.

She heard a small outboard and turned toward the dam and the marina. An aluminum power boat was humming toward her, and Mike sat at the tiller. She would recognize him anywhere now. He returned her wave and brought the small boat in, right up to the shore, instead of to the end of the dock as he did the mailboat.

"Whose boat?" She asked.

"Jim's. He'll be taking the pontoon out for a cruise later."

Robyn hopped off the shoreward end of the dock and down the path to the tiny gravel beach.

"Want me to shove off?"

"In a dress? I don't think so." Mike grinned and came forward, climbing carefully over the seats. He stepped out of the bow onto a rock that was half out of the water. "Let me help you."

He put his hand under her elbow and boosted a little as Robyn stepped awkwardly over the prow, lifting her calf-length skirt slightly.

"Guess I'm overdressed." She laughed and then stumbled a little and grabbed the gunwale. She sat down on the middle seat, facing the motor in the stern.

"There are times when it doesn't hurt to relax the dress code," Mike agreed. He rested his hand on her shoulder as he passed her to get to his station. "Better let me help you make a modest exit when we get to the marina."

Robyn laughed. "I wasn't sure if you'd come by land or by sea. But I ought to have worn pants. I don't want to give the patrons of the restaurant something to write home about."

"I can see the postcards now," Mike said. *"Dear folks, Wish you were here for all the excitement. The nurse from down the shore fell off the dock at the marina, and the mailman got to rescue her."*

She grinned but took extra care when they docked and managed to make it onto the wharf without having a mishap or exposing her lingerie.

The lunch crowd was thinning, and they got a table on the restaurant's deck over the water. A large umbrella kept the direct sun off them.

"I never ate here before," Robyn confessed as Mike seated her. "We couldn't afford it."

He laughed. "Me either."

She studied the menu. The prices weren't too bad. She guessed out-of-staters would find them more than reasonable.

"What are we having?" she asked. There were too many choices, and she wasn't sure what Mike liked, other than chocolate.

"Get what you want."

"Clams?"

"Sure."

It was fun sitting opposite him. They chattered away almost as if they were in high school together again and making up for all the silly conversations they'd never had. They discussed which classmates they'd seen in the past seven

years, how many of their former teachers had retired, and the new shops that had opened in the village.

"So, your folks are really selling out?" Mike asked at last.

Robyn sighed and sipped her iced tea. "You would have to bring that up."

"You don't want them to?"

"No. Would you?"

He winced. "It was tough when my mom sold our cottage, but I knew she had to."

"My parents don't have to. Just like they didn't have to move to Connecticut."

"But you girls are grown up. They wanted to be near Rebecca and any possible grandchildren, I assume?"

"Something like that." Robyn picked the last French fry off her plate and pushed it around in a puddle of ketchup. "I won't even get into how I, as elder daughter, have fallen down on the job of supplying grandchildren."

"Do I sense an underlying resentment? You didn't want them to sell the big house either, did you?"

She eyed him and decided to be frank. "You know, I just assumed my home would always be there. When they sold the house last fall, my mother actually said to me, 'But, Robyn, you're an adult. You have your own life now. You'll probably never be at home much anymore. What difference does it make?'" She grimaced.

"That hurt," Mike said.

"Well, yes. Am I immature? I know my folks have their own life too, but it seemed sudden and … Hey, Dad was a seventh-generation resident of this town. I felt like he ripped up the roots of the family."

Chapter 5

For the Boys

Mike thought about Robyn and what she was feeling. She was definitely a woman who valued roots and traditions. She was young, and she hated to lose the only home she had known.

The old stone house was sold. He'd been by it many times, on his way from his mother's house to the marina every morning. He'd seen the cars that still had Virginia plates parked in the driveway, seen strangers coming out of the house. And now she was losing the summer home too, where so many cherished memories lay. He knew what it felt like.

"Your family was an important part of this town's history, for sure. But you'll make new memories in other places, Rob."

She smiled at his use of her nickname. "Thanks. I know you're right. I'm being unreasonable."

"No, but … some things are out of our hands."

She nodded, regarding him with sober brown eyes. "I guess I am a little put out with my folks. I mean, if I'm an adult, why am I still powerless to help make the decisions in the family? Don't say it," she added quickly.

"Say what?"

"Those aren't my decisions to make."

"Your time will come." He smiled at her. "Let's go back to your place."

"You want to?"

"Sure, if you think it's okay. I'd like to see that fireplace you were telling me about."

She nodded, and he paid for the meal. She was becoming expert at boarding the boat in her skirt and sandals, and this time the craft barely swayed.

At the little beach beside the Carver dock, the bow ran up on the gravel, and she climbed out carefully. Mike got out and pulled the boat halfway onto the shore, then followed her up the path.

It was odd going inside. All those years he'd known the family, and he'd never been in the cottage.

The kitchen was spacious, if simple. Open shelves above a Formica-topped counter, a steel sink, an old gas range, an ancient refrigerator. It was a lot like the cottage his family used to own.

"Shall we have a fire?" Robyn asked a bit formally.

He turned toward her. She was nervous, he could see.

"If you want." He wondered if she was having second thoughts about inviting a man in. It was silly. They were twenty-five. The neighbors couldn't care less. Still, if it bothered her …

Robyn went into the next room, and he followed. The fireplace was fieldstone, nicely shaped, with the rocks artistically balanced. She knelt on the hearth and began snapping small sticks and piling them in the grate.

"Let me do that."

"All right." She moved aside, and he took her place, building the foundation of the fire.

"Matches?" he asked.

She stood and retrieved the little rectangular box from the mantle. In a moment the kindling was ablaze. She handed him a couple of small birch logs, then she sank into an armchair. Mike stayed where he was until the fire took hold of the fuel, then sat down opposite her. The room felt cozy. Her parents must have sat in these chairs hundreds of evenings.

He wasn't sure she wanted to talk about real estate anymore. Maybe best forget about the impending sale of the property. But Robyn brought it up a moment later.

"You know, this place has its own septic system."

"Really?" he asked.

"Yes. We could have winterized it and lived here year round."

"Your folks didn't want to?"

"No. I'd have loved it, though." She stared into the fire. "It's too small, I guess, but still ... to be on the lake all the time!"

"It wouldn't be so nice in winter."

"Oh, come on! Skating, snowmobiling ... I'd love it. Wouldn't you?"

"I suppose I would." He hesitated. "When the Warrens' cottage came up for sale in the spring, I asked my mother if she thought I ought to buy it." Her glance flashed to his face. "I could have," he said. "Well, not bought it outright, but I could have made a down payment."

"What did she say?"

"She told me not to on her account. Said she's comfortable where she is, and I hadn't ought to sink a lot of money into something unless it was what I really wanted." He paused, but she said nothing. She sat watching the flames. "See, parents don't always think the way we do."

"You're telling me!" Her brown eyes had lost the hurt look, but she still seemed baffled by her parents' betrayal.

"So maybe, when we're older, we'll look at things differently. Something we cling to now might not be so dear then."

"Do you really believe that?"

He shrugged. "My mom changed a lot after Dad died. It's hard to say how different she would be if he had lived. I'm just saying, don't be too hard on your folks."

"I've always loved the lake," she said fiercely. "I really, truly think I'll still love it when I'm fifty. Or sixty. Or a hundred."

He nodded. "I understand. But we can't see the whole picture from this vantage point."

She sighed and looked into the blaze. "You may be right. I just wish I could keep this place. If I had enough money … well, that's silly."

Mike felt a compassion for her that went beyond the problem of the cottage. "Robyn … "

When she turned her gaze on him again, there was a softness about her that caught at his heart. He wanted to know her deepest, dearest thoughts.

"Robyn, are you happy?"

"In general?" She nodded, her eyes wide, her lips in a straight line. "At this moment, yes. And lately …" She turned back toward the fireplace. He waited, trying not to be impatient. "Lately, I've done a lot of thinking about my future." She chuckled. "My present, too."

"How?"

"It's not just this cottage. I'm wondering about my new job, and if I'll like it. Is it what I really want to do?" She turned to look at him, almost eager now. "I love nursing, but I hate living in the city. Coming here has made me consider options I never thought about before."

"Such as?"

"I could come back here and rent a place. It would probably be a cut in pay, but I'm sure I could find work at the one of the hospitals in this area."

He smiled. "But you'd be away from your family then."

"I won't be close to them in Worcester, either. Oh, I'd be a few hours closer, but … it's quality of life, Mike."

"Would you be lonely so far from them?"

"I … don't know. Probably. I get lonely sometimes as it is. But I think I'd be more content here." She smiled at him.

"Thanks for listening. I'm sorry I pouted and tantrummed on you."

He wished he was near enough to touch her, but as soon as the thought came to him, he chased it away. Had their relationship progressed that far yet? He felt entirely too much at home here. The very comfort of her presence made him uncomfortable.

"I guess it's time for me to go."

"Do you have to?" Robyn seemed genuinely sorry, but not bereft.

Mike smiled. "There are things I should do at home. Let's do this again next Sunday."

"Let's. If it doesn't rain."

"I'll order sunshine again."

"All right. And I think I'll wear slacks."

He hesitated, then said, "I told Merton I'd come next Sunday afternoon and play ball with the boys who stay over the weekend."

"That's brave of you."

Mike laughed. "Well, it will give a couple of the counselors the afternoon off. I don't suppose …"

Her eyes were wide with expectation.

"…you'd want to tag along?"

She was silent for a moment, and he regretted asking.

"I guess you see enough of the little monsters all week."

"No, I … think I might enjoy that. I'm starting to know some of the boys, and a few of them have decided they're my special friends. Wesley's told me he's staying all summer, and I think he's a bit homesick."

Mike grinned. "You'd really do it? For the boys?"

She stood up. "Yeah, why not? Some of those little guys are endearing, and it will give them something different to think about for a little while. But I'm holding you to the sunshine."

Mike backed toward the door. "Guaranteed."

***

All week Mike took her to Spruce Island in the morning with his tourist passengers. As soon as she mounted the camp's dock, she became the center of a cluster of adoring boys.

"Have you found another nurse yet?" she asked Merton on Wednesday morning.

"Not yet." Robyn wasn't sure whether he had exhausted all options or was deliberately dragging his feet. She heard Mike speak to him about it, rather sharply, on Thursday.

"I know, I know, Mike. It's just been so hectic here," Merton said.

"Well, Miss Carver won't stay on much longer."

"I'll see what I can do this weekend," Merton promised.

Robyn enjoyed being on the boat with Mike each day, although they had no chance to talk privately. She treated an assortment of minor ailments at the camp and doled out prescription medicine. The daily routine began to tire her. By Friday, she was restless and ready to be finished with sick call, although a few of the smaller boys had wriggled their way into her heart.

"Miss Robyn," cried eight-year-old Wesley, one of the diabetic boys, as she disembarked Friday morning. "Let me carry your bag."

"No, me," shouted Teddy, who had suffered a twisted ankle on Monday and came back to sick call each day for sympathy.

Uncle Mark, the counselor who had sick call duty for the week, chatted amiably with her while she treated the boys. Uncle Sean managed to drop by during infirmary hours as well, and Robyn wondered if he was manufacturing excuses to see her.

When Mike took her home near noon each day, he didn't linger. Some days Robyn wished he would, but he always had to get the boat back for a cruise or tend to other business for Jim. June drifted into July, and the golden days were slipping away.

Mike dropped her off at her parents' place with obvious regret on Friday.

"It's supposed to be nice tomorrow."

"That's good," Robyn said absently, watching her footing as she climbed onto the dock.

"No, that's bad."

She laughed and looked at him then. "Okay, why is that bad?"

"I'll have passengers. I was kind of hoping you'd go on the mail run with me again."

"Ah."

"What are you going to do all day?"

She looked up at the sky. "Laundry, grocery shopping, take a swim, and read a big fat book."

He smiled. "I guess you deserve a day off. Enjoy. I'll see you when I bring the mail, if you're here."

Mike looked so wistful, she almost gave in and told him she'd go with him. But, no. She needed a rest. "I'll see you," she said, and walked up the dock toward the cottage.

***

On Saturday morning, Robyn puttered restlessly around the cottage. She took her swim, made her grocery list, and put her dirty laundry in the car. Somehow she couldn't drive away until the mail came.

Of course, it wasn't the mail she was waiting for. It was Mike. She wasn't one hundred percent sure she liked that. Why should she kill half the morning waiting to see a man for an instant? She almost got in the car and headed for town. Almost.

She sat down and scrawled a note to her mother. *See you next week! Please bring my blue jacket.* As she put it in an envelope, she sneered at herself. Who was she kidding? The note wasn't for her mom, it was a prop. Something to hand Mike at the dock.

She went down and slipped the envelope in the mailbox, then tipped the red flag up. She would leave it and go off to town.

The distinctive whine of the pontoon boat's motor reached her from the distance.

Move it, girl, she told herself. You don't have to see him.

She turned her back to the lake and resolutely walked the length of the dock.

She couldn't help looking down toward the Hursts', two cottage lots away. Yes, the boat was there now. Maybe he'd seen her already.

All right, I want to see him. Is that so bad?

She went back to the mailbox and took the letter out.

"Hey!" Mike grinned as the boat nosed up to the dock. He reached for the letter, and she handed it to him.

Robyn looked over his riders. The boat was so full, she'd have had a hard time getting a seat.

"You're full up."

"Yeah, capacity crowd today," he said ruefully.

"Well, I'm heading for town."

"Do we still have a date for the ball game tomorrow?" He passed her a postcard from Rebecca.

She smiled. "I'll be ready."

He threw the motor into reverse and backed out, grinning. She waved.

There! You've had your five seconds of camaraderie. Get a life!

232

Chapter 6

Cooling Off?

When they joined the campers on Sunday afternoon for their ball game, Robyn and Mike wound up coaching opposite teams. The campers loved it, and little boys clustered around Robyn wherever she went, but she didn't get to spend much time with Mike.

In the end, Mike's team won. However, they showed good sportsmanship, prompted by Mike, by inviting Robyn's team to join them in eating ice cream cones, provided by the camp.

"Miss Robyn," Wesley said, snuggling up to Robyn on a bench outside the dining hall, "Can you come stay at camp all the time?"

She smiled at him. "I'm afraid not, Wesley. But I had a lot of fun with you and the other boys today."

Merton came out of the building carrying two ice cream cones in a cardboard holder. "Here we go. No sugar added."

"Thank you so much." Robyn took them from the holder and handed one cone to Wesley. She'd asked Merton to give her a cone like the diabetic boy's, so that Wesley wouldn't feel left out or "different."

Mike and his team were already halfway done with their cones. Teddy, who sat on Robyn's other side, had his and was licking it with fierce concentration.

Robyn licked her cone. "Mm, that's good."

Wesley shrugged. "Not as good as with sugar."

"Well, maybe, but after a while you'll get used to this and the sugary stuff will taste too sweet." She ought to eat less sugar herself and get over the sweet tooth.

"I miss candy," Wesley said. "The sugar-free stuff gives me the trots."

She smiled. "Yeah, sometimes things like that happen when our bodies don't like what we put in them. But you know, if you eat regular candy, your body will react even worse."

His face drooped. "I know."

"Hey, your ice cream's melting! Lick right there before it splatters on you." Robyn pointed to a drizzle rolling down the outside of his cone. Wesley gave it a quick lick and then took a bite from the scoop at the top.

Mike came over and stood by them. "Looks like rain. Can we head out soon?"

Robyn scanned the sky. Sure enough, it was full of lowering gray clouds. "I'll get my stuff." She quickly finished her cone, gave Wesley and Teddy quick hugs, and grabbed her duffel bag. "See you tomorrow, guys," she yelled to the other boys.

They answered with shouts as she and Mike headed for the boat.

By the time he stopped at her dock, it was pouring. He gave her a hand up.

"Don't get out," Robyn shouted. She snatched her bag from his hand and ran up the dock with the downpour pelting her.

***

All week, Robyn rode across the lake with Mike, back and forth. They had a few words each day, but there were always other people aboard. The tourist season was in full swing, and Jim pushed Mike to get the boat back as soon as possible every day. No idyllic moments of drifting along together. Mike was friendly, but he seemed a little guarded, and he and Robyn didn't delve into personal concerns again.

She realized she was brooding. On Tuesday Mike brought her a letter from the hospital administrator in Worcester, urging her to start her job in early August if possible. For several days she put off replying. Earlier she had arranged to begin work the Tuesday after Labor Day, and she didn't want to change that. Still, if things were cooling off with Mike, she might not want to stay here after all.

Cooling off? she chided herself. Things were never hot.

Mike steered for her dock on Friday. He cut the motor, and they waited in silence until the prow bumped the dock. He came to give her a hand up.

She scrambled out awkwardly and slipped. Avoiding tumbling into the water, she landed in an undignified heap on the edge of the dock. Mike gritted his teeth and passed her the duffel bag.

"Go with me tomorrow?" He said it softly, and her heart lurched. "Please, Rob?"

"You'll have a million passengers for the Saturday run."

"Come anyway."

She saw something in his face that told her it mattered a lot to him. If she said no this time, would he ever ask her again?

"What if there's no room?" she asked doubtfully.

"I'll stow you in the locker."

She smiled. "Let's see what happens."

Chapter 7

Torture by Decibels

Robyn woke early the next day and tried to go back to sleep, but as soon as Mike Borden's shadow crossed her mind, it was hopeless. She took an early swim, staying in the shallows near the dock, then dressed and drove to the Laundromat in town with another week's worth of dirty clothes. While they cycled, she bought a few groceries.

She was back at the cottage by nine, hoping Mike hadn't been there yet. Glancing out the porch window, toward the dock she could see that the red flag was still up on the mailbox. He hadn't yet removed the letter to Rebecca that she had put in the box early that morning.

Passengers or no passengers, she wanted to spend the morning with him. The decision was made, and she grabbed her sunglasses, two cans of Pepsi, a hat, and a book. If the boat was full, she would read. But she would sit close to Mike and let him know, if only by her presence, that she cared for him.

Sitting on the end of the dock, she dangled her bare feet in the water. She ought to have put on long pants. She would sunburn in shorts. She heard the boat. Too late to change. She ran up to the porch and retrieved her tote bag and bottle of sunscreen. She was back on the dock shoving her things into the bag when Mike pulled up, her packet of mail in his hand.

"Hey, gorgeous," he called.

Robyn laughed. She stared past him at the empty boat as the pontoons bumped the dock. "What did you do with all your Saturday passengers?"

"Tossed them over the side so you'd come."

"No, really."

His blue eyes were dancing. "I have ways of arranging things."

"You didn't!"

"Didn't what?"

"You bought the whole boat out?"

"Not exactly. There were only two ladies wanting to come this morning, and Jim had scheduled a sunset cruise tonight anyway. I suggested they might want to join the beautiful sunset cruise instead of my boring mail run."

"Does Jim know?"

"No, and you'd better not tell him."

"I won't breathe a word." She took his hand and swung down into the bottom of the boat. "Oops, my tote bag! And my sandals."

Mike managed to grab her gear off the dock then pushed off. Passing her to return to the helm, he tugged a lock of her hair. "It's gratifying to know I won out over the dirty laundry."

"I rose at dawn and vanquished it." She tried to keep a straight face, but when he laughed, she joined him.

"Get over here." He nodded toward the bench beside him.

She smiled. His bossiness was unconvincing. She slid onto the bench, sitting on an orange floatation cushion. Mike ran the boat out away from shore toward Spruce Island without looking at her, but he was smiling.

They delivered the camp mail then made their way slowly up the east side of the lake. Three cottages, out around Squire point, seven cottages in a row, then Ballard Cove. Robyn thought he was concentrating on getting the mail out quickly. He checked his watch often.

They eased up to the dock at Parkhursts'. A package lay waiting in a plastic bag. Mike placed it in the carton of outgoing mail and put the money that was with it in a zippered bag. The red flag was up on the mailbox too, and he extracted a letter from there. Robyn saw him frown as he tucked the letter into his outgoing bin.

"Seen the mystery man lately?" she asked. Then, quickly, "Don't answer that, if you're not allowed to."

"No, it's okay. I haven't seen him for a couple of days. He got the mail Thursday, I think it was, before I was around the point. That's the last time I actually eyeballed him."

Robyn looked back, hoping to glimpse him, but there was no movement on shore before they rounded the rocky point.

When the mail run was finished, Mike took the outgoing mail into the marina. He returned carrying a paper bag and jumped down into the boat.

"Does Jim care if you take me home?"

"Nope. I'm paying for the gas. He says just have the boat back here by five."

"Five o'clock? It's barely noon." Robyn was a little taken aback.

"You got a picnic in that tote bag today?"

"No, just Pepsi."

"Good. I got sandwiches." He handed her the bag and started the motor. Robyn peeked in the bag. Seafood salad and pastries. Jim's seafood salad was famous in the area. She opened the seat that hid the cooler and stuck the bag in on top of the cans of soda, adding her own contribution of cans.

Mike held out his hand, and when she took it he pulled her over closer to his seat. She sat, holding his hand while he ran the boat up the lake again without stopping. At the widest point of the channel, he slowed then stopped the engine.

Robyn looked all around. Far away, near the west shore, she could see a rowboat with two people in it. To the north, a

239

boat was pulling a novice water skier, but they didn't venture this far down the lake.

Mike released her hand and walked to the stern of the boat. He opened a locker, took out a weight tied to a rope, and heaved it over the side.

He came back to her beneath the canopy, taking his sunglasses off and folding them carefully into the pocket of his green T-shirt. He sat, not in the driver's seat, but on the bench beside her, his right arm sliding around her shoulders. With his left hand, he lifted his baseball cap and dropped it to the floor of the boat.

She looked into his pensive face and saw his longing. I am way past ready for this, she thought.

It was still a shock when his lips touched hers. She felt she had slipped beneath the surface of the placid waters that were Mike Borden and was drowning in that kiss. But it wasn't her past that flashed before her eyes. It was her future. And in every scene, Mike played a prominent role.

He pulled her close when it ended, and she collapsed against the front of his T-shirt. He smelled faintly of sunscreen and soap, with a dash of motor oil. His cheek rested for a moment on the top of her head, then he kissed her hair.

"Your part's sunburned," he said.

Robyn pushed away from him, the way Mike shoved the boat away from the dock, and looked into his clear blue eyes. He met her gaze steadily, soberly, and stroked a strand of hair away from her cheek. She wondered what he saw in her eyes. She felt a bit stupid, unable to speak.

She wasn't at all ready for the intense feelings that closed over her as he bent and kissed her again. The waters weren't calm anymore. Waves of emotion crashed over her.

I love him. It was unexpected knowledge, and she examined it as carefully as her muddled mind would allow. She wanted to be with him for the rest of her life, and she wanted only good things to happen to him. She longed to do anything, everything, that would help him succeed and bring him happiness.

She broke the embrace, gasping a little, and hid her face in his shoulder. He held her close and lightly stroked her back. *How does one know if the kisser feels the same way the kissee does?* She'd never known this depth of feeling before. If she found out Mike's feelings were less profound, she would be crushed.

There was an ancient rule, she knew, having learned it in junior high—never say you love him before he says it. But she had to know. Deep inside, something told her this wasn't the cliché summer romance. Even so, he was going off to Bolivia, and she to Massachusetts, in a matter of weeks. Yes, she had to know.

"Mike—"

"Hm?" Suddenly he stiffened, and she could feel him lift his head.

She sat up.

"What is it?"

He sighed and leaned back against the side rail.

"Kids."

Robyn turned her head and looked down the lake toward Spruce Island. Three war canoes bristling with paddles and boys were pulling toward them. Over the water, the whoops and laughter came to her.

"Boys," she acknowledged.

"Time to pull up anchor." Mike gently pulled her arm down from around his neck, smiling. He dropped a kiss on the tip of her nose and stood, going quickly to the stern to retrieve the anchor.

"Why don't we just eat lunch?" Robyn suggested.

He stopped with the anchor line half coiled and let the wet rope slide through his hands. "Good idea."

She opened the cooler and got out the sandwiches and drinks. As the yelping boys paddled toward the pontoon boat, she spread a beach towel on the deck and set out their sandwiches.

The frenzied yells increased in volume, and soon the three canoes were circling them.

"Looks like we're surrounded," Mike deadpanned.

Robyn rolled her eyes and opened the Pepsi.

"Hey, Uncle Mike," one of the older boys shouted, "got any Grey Poupon?"

Uncle Sean was acting as guide in the longest canoe, and he coached the boys into pulling it alongside the pontoon boat.

"Hey, don't you let those savages board me," Mike warned.

"Miss Robyn! Ricky hit me with a canoe paddle, and I think my finger's broken," one of the campers called.

The boys began an ear-splitting war cry, punctuated by Sean's sporadic, "Pipe down, you hooligans!"

Robyn took a look at the injured boy's hand and determined nothing was broken. After five minutes of torture by decibels, the counselors commanded the boys to move on, and the canoes plowed through the water toward the head of the lake.

Mike sat still, staring after them, then turned to look at Robyn. "Could have been worse. They might have splashed us or raided our lunch."

She nodded. "They'll be back in a few minutes, though."

"Right. We'd better eat fast."

Robyn laughed and handed him a sandwich. It was a sloppy lunch, and they wound up using towels in place of napkins.

"I should have worn my swimsuit, and we could jump into the water to clean up," she said.

"It's tempting, but the Little Rascals are coming back."

She looked northward, and sure enough, the boys were returning. This time they passed the mailboat without stopping.

They exchanged waves and taunts, but the boys went on toward their island.

"Maybe we should find us a quieter lake," Mike proposed. "Hop over to Messalonskee or Long Pond."

Robyn laughed. "Actually, there's not much traffic out here today, not counting them."

Mike held her gaze with his serious blue eyes. "We need to talk."

THE MAILBOAT

Chapter 8

Before I Kissed You

"So, you want to start?" Mike asked.

"Not really."

"Not?"

She shook her head.

"How come?"

Robyn looked out over the water. Gentle waves rocked them. "I guess I'm not sure what direction you're thinking of talking in, and I don't want to take off on something completely different from what you were thinking of."

"Well, what I was thinking of was …" He stopped, as though he couldn't bring himself to say it.

He's still shy, she thought. But he's trying.

"About … kissing me?" she offered tentatively.

"Thank you."

She smiled at his evident relief.

Mike said with a nod, "I, uh, thought it was okay."

Okay? her brain screamed. Okay as opposed to what?

"Guess I said the wrong thing." He peered at her anxiously, and she knew her expression had betrayed her dismay.

"No, I just—" *I have to know.* Robyn steeled herself. "Look, if it was just okay for you, then I guess for me it was awful."

His eyes widened, then he dropped his gaze, flushing. "Oh. Because … you didn't look like you thought it was awful at the time."

"Of course not. It was wonderful!"

Mike stared at her, clearly baffled.

Robyn shook her head in impatience. "Look, if what you felt was … *okay* … well, that was the most thrilling moment of my life, and if it was only *okay* on your scale of enrapturement, then I just think maybe we're on different wavelengths."

"Is that a word?"

"What?"

"Enrapturement."

"Who cares?"

"I do."

She glared at him. This wasn't going at all the way she had intended.

Mike said, "Well, I mean, if I thought I could make you feel enraptured, I'd be a pretty happy guy."

She breathed out slowly, staring at her toenails. She couldn't trust herself to speak. This was a serious thing, and she refused to take it lightly.

"Mike," she whispered.

It was a long moment before he answered. "What?"

"I was serious."

"So am I. About you, I mean." He raised one hand with an air of futility. "Man, I'm supposed to be a smart guy. I mean, well, you know. In school. But when it comes to –" He sighed heavily. "My bosses are talking about bringing in some consultant to teach all the employees about interpersonal relationships. I thought it was a crock at first, but now I'm starting to think I *do* need sensitivity training."

Robyn looked at him from the corner of her eye. "What are you talking about?"

"How do you feel right now?"

"Bewildered."

246

"Me, too. But, besides that?"

"I ... don't want to say." It was too scary. She couldn't bear it if she said *I love you,* and he laughed.

"Why not? I won't be upset, I won't make fun of you, I won't deep six you. I just want to know what you're thinking. It's important, Robyn. Very important."

She bit her top lip. It was what she wanted, too, but did he want to know her feelings based on the knowledge of his own, or was he still trying to define what he felt? The ancient rule was firmly entrenched. She knew, she just knew, that if she said it first he would tell her it was all a great misunderstanding. The kiss was *okay,* but it wasn't the life-changing moment she had thought it was. Women just read more into these things than men did.

"Did you ever kiss anyone else like that?" she asked at last.

"Like what?"

"Oh, come on! Like what? You know like what!" She felt she was dangerously close to crying, and she didn't want to use the towel-slash-napkin for a tissue, too.

Mike swallowed hard. "You mean, like what happened before the three canoes full of little terrors came?"

"Yes."

"Uh-uh. I mean ... well, no."

"You want to qualify that, or is it a no?"

He reached out and touched her hand, and Robyn looked at him. There was some pain in his eyes, and some wariness, with a smidgen of hope.

"Rob, I never kissed a woman like that. Seriously, I mean."

She sat thinking it over.

"What about ... Patti Sachs?"

He guffawed, looking out over the lake. "Not the same. Not at all the same. We are talking puppy love. Worse than that. Foolish boy's first kiss. Cynical girl's five hundredth." He had hold of both her hands, and he edged closer to her. "Robyn, come on, you know that wasn't serious."

"I thought it was at the time. You'd never had a girlfriend before."

"I didn't then. Patti was never my girlfriend. I liked her, and she paid me a little attention, then she moved on. You don't think I've mourned her all these years?"

Robyn shifted uneasily, but he wouldn't let her pull her hands away. "Well, I don't know," she muttered. "I didn't know what to think."

"I'm surprised you thought about it at all."

"Of course I did. I always liked you. I cared what happened to you. I could have, *should* have done more, reached out to you. I guess we were both shy."

"But we're over that now."

"Are we?" She smiled and made herself look him in the eye. "I didn't know how to act around you in high school. We weren't the same kids anymore. Your father had died. What could I say? I felt totally helpless, so I more or less ignored you. It was wrong, and stupid."

"Aw, Rob." It shocked her to see tears in his eyes. "Maybe if I'd known you cared a little it would have helped, but I'm okay now."

"I see that."

"How about you? No serious boyfriends?"

"Not really."

"No dashing doctors in Worcester?"

"Ha! The doctors there are all very cynical and liberal-minded."

"Never thought about getting married?"

"Well, sure." She felt the blush coming on. "Every girl thinks about getting married."

"I mean with a particular man."

"Not seriously. A couple of times I had vague thoughts about it, but … " She shook her head. "It never panned out. It may seem incredible to you, but … I've never really been in love before. I don't think I've ever been *loved* in that way." She clamped her lips together and wondered whether she should ease her hands away from his.

"Well, I love you," Mike said.

She sat very still. He was looking down at their hands and holding her fingers tightly.

"It's your turn," he said shakily.

"Could you … define that, please."

"How do I love thee?" he smiled. "I think it's the real thing."

"So, you're saying the kiss was technically better than okay?"

He gave a short laugh. "Robyn, that's the way guys talk. We don't go around saying, 'I kissed her, and it was absolutely fantastic.'"

"Oh."

"But it was."

"Oh."

She felt him leaning toward her, and she lowered her eyelashes, unable to meet his gaze.

"And another thing," he said, his voice low. "The kiss is only indirectly related to how I feel. I loved you before I kissed you. I kissed you because I loved you. You see?"

She nodded, and he was so close to her that her cheek brushed his nose.

"So, do you hate me?" he whispered, close to her ear.

"No, but I think you'd better take me home."

"It's not five o'clock yet."

"If you want to keep me out another three hours, I think you need to talk to my father."

He laughed and leaned back, facing her. "When's your dad coming?"

"Tomorrow."

"All right. I'll be ready."

"I love you." She swallowed hard and raised her eyes to his.

He looked long and deeply at her, then took a deep breath. "Do you have a passport?"

"A passport?" She pulled away and stared at him, then dropped her eyes. "Yes."

"You do?" Surprise and joy leaped into his eyes. Robyn's stomach fluttered, just seeing it in his face.

"Yes, I do."

"Where've you been?"

"Nowhere," she said with dignity.

"Nowhere? You just have a contingency passport?"

"I was going to go on one of those student culture exchanges a few years ago, but I couldn't scrape up the money, and then I decided I'd better stay home and work anyway. But I'd got my passport. I take it out sometimes and look at it and sigh over all the blank pages. The picture is awful."

"I don't believe it." He bent toward her and their lips touched gently.

"Take me home, Mike." It was a whisper.

"Really?"

"I think you should."

"What time do you look for your folks tomorrow?"

"Late afternoon. Are you going out to Spruce Island in the afternoon?"

"No, not this week." He hesitated. "So, it's all right for me to come by and see them tomorrow night?"

She swallowed hard. "Sure."

He stood and went to pull up anchor.

***

Mike tied up the boat at her family's cottage and climbed up onto the dock with Robyn.

"Can I take you to lunch tomorrow?" he asked.

She winced. "I'd like to, but I've got a lot of things I need to do to get ready for my parents' arrival. And Becky's husband managed a week off, and they're coming too. I need to make up an extra bedroom for them, and I wanted to have supper all ready. I'm not used to cooking for five." Her eyes pleaded for understanding. "I want it to be nice."

He decided she wasn't just making excuses. "Can I help you?" He gave her his hangdog look.

She melted a little. "Just show up around four or four thirty. We'll put you to work."

"You don't mind?"

"No, that would be fine. Great, actually. Have supper with us."

"Can you cook for six, or is that one-too-hard?"

She smiled, and he couldn't resist touching her, sliding his hand up her arm to her shoulder.

"It's okay, if I keep the menu simple."

"Does your family know I've been hanging around shamelessly?"

"I've mentioned it. You must have read my outgoing postcards."

"No, mailmen aren't allowed to do that anymore."

He pulled her close to him and hugged her. She slipped her arms around him and laid her head on his shoulder. He shut his eyes and savored the moment, standing on the dock with Robyn in his arms. Mild surprise hit him. She didn't keep looking around, checking on who else could see them. Gentle waves slapped the shore, and the light breeze rippled his hair.

"My mom keeps asking when I'm going to bring you out to the house." He kissed her temple, where her hair was pulled back.

"Soon."

"Great. She's really happy. About us, I mean."

"You told her?"

"Couldn't help it. Do you mind?" He hoped he hadn't spoken too soon. He would do anything in his power to keep Robyn from feeling uneasy.

"No. I'm glad," she whispered. "Now, go."

"Is that an order?"

"Yes. But come back tomorrow."

He wanted badly to kiss her again, the way he had in the boat, but she wouldn't look up at him. He released her and climbed down off the dock. She stood there waving until he turned toward the marina. Mike smiled all the way back to Dohertys' dock.

***

Robyn spent the rest of the afternoon making beds and cooking. By sundown, she was played out. She grabbed a peanut butter sandwich and a glass of almond milk and made herself eat.

She built a blaze in the fireplace and sat for a long time before the fire that night, staring into the flames. She thought about Mike and the different sides of his character she'd seen during the past month. His patience with the boys at the camp. His kindness with Mr. Foster. His steady reliability on the mail run. His lack of jealousy over the people who kept their cottages when the Bordens lost theirs. His modesty, his lack of pretension.

Thankfulness flooded her. She might have missed meeting Mike again, so easily. She'd almost stayed at her nursing job, to put away a little extra money.

And now Mike was inquiring about her passport. Could he really mean it? He'd meant it when he told her he loved her, of that she was sure. Was it possible he was thinking of a future together that included passports and other documents?

She let the fire burn down to embers and sat a little longer. A joyful anticipation began deep in her chest and bubbled up inside her.

Chapter 9

A Suitor Underfoot

"Becky! I'm so glad you came." Robyn launched herself into her sister's arms. They hadn't seen each other since Christmas, and it seemed an eternity.

They had been close, very close. Rebecca was only eighteen months younger than Robyn, and they had always shared secrets.

"Hey, Robbie." Rebecca kissed her cheek and stood back to look at her. "You look fantastic. Love the hairdo."

Robyn put one hand up to the sleek updo she was experimenting with. "Thanks. Hi, Eric." She embraced her brother-in-law. "How was the traffic?"

"Not bad."

Their parents had pulled into the gravel parking area behind Eric and were climbing out of their car. Robyn rushed to her father.

"Daddy!"

He laughed and threw his arms around her. "How you doing, Sweet Pea?"

She kissed her mother and scrambled to help with the luggage while her father unhitched the boat trailer.

"You and Eric get our old room," she told Rebecca.

"Where are you going to sleep?" The cottage had only two bedrooms upstairs.

"I'm having the cot on the porch," Robyn replied.

"Are you sure?"

"Of course." She had moved her things down that afternoon, after Mike left, and arranged her suitcase and boxes in a corner of the glassed-in veranda, near the daybed.

She dragged a heavy duffel bag up the stairs for Rebecca, while her sister and Eric carried the rest of their things.

"It's great to be back." Rebecca looked out the bedroom window, toward the dock. "Hey, the float isn't in yet."

"No, I couldn't do it by myself. We can put it in tonight, if Daddy and Eric help us."

"Great. I can't wait to get into that water!"

"It's pretty warm," Robyn said. "I haven't swum much, really. I've been so busy, with the camp nurse thing and all."

Rebecca opened her suitcase and began shifting her clothes from it to the dresser. "What are these cryptic notes you've been sending me about Mike Borden?"

Robyn threw a glance toward Eric. "Well, you know. He's been around."

"Girl talk?" Eric asked. "I'm out of here." He pulled his swim trunks from his suitcase and went out the door.

"So, do you like him?" Rebecca asked.

Robyn sat down on the edge of the bed and watched her sister unpack.

"I've always liked him."

"Well, yeah, he was a good kid, but you never seemed to be too enamored."

"It's different now. He's different. Or maybe I'm different."

Rebecca laughed. "We're all different, Robbie. It's been a while. We've matured."

"And how."

Rebecca smiled. "I take it Mike Borden's matured nicely?"

"This is yours, Becka," Mr. Carver said from the doorway, swinging a tote bag toward Rebecca.

"Thanks, Dad."

"What were you saying about Mike Borden? He's on the mailboat again?"

"Yes, he wanted to spend the summer on the lake, so his bosses let him take some time off, and Jim Doherty gave him the mail run again."

"I thought he was an architect," Rebecca said.

"He's an engineer. This is just a hiatus."

"I'd like to see Mike again," Mr. Carver said. "Smart fellow."

"Well, you'll probably get to see him soon." Robyn felt her blush coming on. "I mean, *real* soon, Daddy."

"How's that?"

"He's having supper with us."

Rebecca and her father stared at her.

"I knew there was something more to those notes," said Rebecca.

"I'd better go start the chicken." Robyn pushed hastily past her father, toward the stairs.

Her mother was peering into the refrigerator.

"Heavens, Robyn, you're fully stocked. I don't know as there's room for all the food we brought."

"Well, I'm taking that chicken out right now. That will give you some space."

She reached past her mother and pulled out the chicken and a container of sour cream.

"Is there something I should know, young lady?"

She swung around, balancing the packages. Her father had followed her into the kitchen.

"What do you mean, Dad?"

She knew what he meant, but she wasn't ready to just blurt it out.

"Michael Borden is coming to supper the first night we're here. Doesn't that seem a little significant to you?"

Her mother's jaw dropped. "Mike Borden? Whatever for?"

257

Robyn looked from one to the other but couldn't say anything. It was almost amusing, to see her parents so shocked at the prospect of their twenty-five-year-old daughter having a suitor underfoot at last. She turned to the counter and set down the chicken and sour cream, then opened a cupboard, not seeing the dishes inside.

"Oh," said her mother.

"Yes," said her father.

"Well, you've mentioned Michael a few times in your letters," Mrs. Carver ventured. "You said he's been taking you out to the island and back."

"He has."

"Is there more to it?"

She turned to face them, wishing she had told them more, prepared them better. Or that she had told Mike to come tomorrow, not tonight. "I'm sorry. I guess I ought to have told you, but I didn't know until yesterday, really. We just … I think a lot of him. I asked him to eat with us tonight."

"Fine. I'll be down at the beach. Rebecca tells me she has to have the float in the water tonight." Her father walked out the door.

Robyn took a deep breath and turned to her mother. "Mom …?"

Her mother's arms went around her. "I think it's wonderful, dear. Mike's a nice boy."

"He's grown up, Mom. You haven't seen him for a while." She felt some comfort in her father's casual acceptance and her mother's emotional display. It was a unique situation for their family, but her parents had responded in character, after the first shock.

Tires crunched on the gravel outside, and Robyn looked out the window, startled. It was the first time he had come by land.

***

Rebecca bounced into the kitchen in her swimsuit. "Someone's here."

"It's Mike," Robyn told her.

"Great. He can help with the float." Rebecca turned back toward the living room and yelled, "Come on, Eric!"

Eric followed her onto the porch and out the door facing the waterfront. As they disappeared down the path, Mike knocked on the kitchen door.

Robyn glanced at her mother. Mrs. Carver smiled in encouragement.

"Hi!" She pushed the screen open and Mike stepped inside.

"Hi." He smiled at her, and his eyes went beyond, to her mother. "Hello, Mrs. Carver. Glad you had a safe trip."

"Nice to see you again, Michael. Robyn, why don't you take him down to the shore? I can put the chicken in the oven."

"Oh, no, Mom, you're tired. It will only take me a second."

After a short debate, her mother went upstairs to change, and Mike leaned on the counter, watching Robyn as she quickly put the boneless chicken in a pan and covered it with sour cream and cracker crumbs.

"Dad and Becky and Eric are down at the dock," she said. "You can go down if you like."

"I'll wait for you."

She pushed the pan into the oven and slammed the door. "Done."

"Great." He reached for her, and she went slowly into his arms, peering over his shoulder toward the doors that led to the living room and the porch.

"Listen, I'm a little nervous, okay?" Her voice quavered.

Mike let go of her immediately. "I'm sorry. I guess I'm nervous, too, and wanted a little support."

Her breath was choppy. "I still ... feel the same way, but I don't want to shock my folks too badly. They're still reeling from hearing that you're on the guest list for supper."

"You didn't tell them anything?"

"What was there to tell? Until yesterday, I mean." She looked down at the battered green linoleum.

"So, what's the plan for tonight?"

"I think we're going to put the float in, then supper will be ready. After that, I don't know. They brought ice cream. We'll swim, maybe. I should have told you to bring your suit."

"Well, I've got a suit in the car. That's not a problem. Are they working on the float now?"

"I think Becky's trying to get Daddy in gear. She and Eric are dressed for it. You want to go down there now?"

Her father met them at the beach with a broad smile and extended his hand to Mike.

"Good to see you, Mike."

"Hi, Mr. Carver. Robyn says you're putting the float in tonight."

"Well, Becky thinks she can't swim unless the float's out there."

"Hey, Mike!" Rebecca was wading in the shallows, but she ran up onto the shore. "You haven't met my husband, have you? Eric Kelvin, this is Mike Borden."

After a few minutes of small talk, Robyn went back to the cottage with her father and Mike to change clothes. When she got back to the waterfront, Mike was there already, chatting easily with Eric about the latest construction project Eric's firm had undertaken. Mr. Carver appeared in his swimsuit, and Mike peeled off his T-shirt.

"All right, kids, I think we can do this," Mr. Carver said.

He put Rebecca and Robyn together on one side with Eric, and he and Mike took the other. They lifted the anchors on top and inched the square float into the water. When the water lifted it, they all swam, pushing it out to diving depth. Mr. Carver asked for Mike's advice on positioning it.

"Trust an engineer for a job like this," her dad said.

Robyn ducked underwater to cool her flaming cheeks. Eric and Mike dropped the anchors, and Becky gleefully climbed the ladder and ran to the opposite side of the float, arcing gracefully through the air and into the lake with hardly a splash.

Mike jumped off the float and surfaced beside Robyn.

"Hey! Quit splashing!" She pushed a spurt of water at him.

He ducked and laughed. "Happy?"

"Yes."

It was true. She had the lake, her family, and Mike. The moment was perfect, and she couldn't think of another thing she would ask for, given the chance.

A few minutes later, she went ashore to change and help set up for the meal.

"We'll need the chair from the porch, dear," her mother said, as Robyn put the silverware around.

Becky and Eric came in clutching towels around them, dripping water across the floor.

"Hang those wet things right on the clothesline," Mrs. Carver ordered.

"Where's Mike?" Robyn asked her sister, keeping her voice low.

"Yonder with Daddy. Don't fret. They're getting along." Becky smiled knowingly, and Robyn's stomach flipped.

She stood gripping the edge of the pine table, wondering if she'd be able to eat a bite. He's just getting to know Dad, she told herself.

"Are you all right, dear?" Anne Carver looked at her daughter with concern.

"I'm fine, Mom."

"Do you want to go down and talk to Michael? I can finish up here."

"No, that's okay." She took a deep breath. Maybe she should go and stop that conversation. *Silly! They're discussing the Bolivian bridges.* But she knew they weren't.

When she went to the porch for the extra chair, she sneaked a look toward the dock. They were sitting in deck chairs, and Mike had his T-shirt on again. His back was to her, but her father's face was grave.

He's not smiling. He ought to be smiling.

Maybe they really were talking about Bolivia.

She sucked in a breath. The passport. He had asked her about it. But you couldn't just pack up and go to Bolivia at the drop of a hat. People going to Bolivia needed a visa, at least. If Mike were really, truly thinking of taking her to Bolivia, he would have to act fast, or she wouldn't get the paperwork done in time.

She was horrified at her thoughts. He hadn't said a word about taking her to Bolivia. He'd said he loved her. That was all. Except for asking about the passport. What else could he mean?

Until that moment she had kept the idea in a box in her mind, waiting for Mike to take the lid off, but now the enormity of it came over her. She would have to resign her job in Worcester. She had worked so hard for it. And she hadn't even told her supervisor yet that she didn't want to start in August!

Was she willing to give up not only the job, but her career? If she followed Mike hither and yon, she might never practice her profession again. Her last job as a nurse might be as Spruce Island Camp's substitute.

Chapter 10

Not Too Mad

Mike's heart was pounding, but he kept his voice even as he exchanged small talk with Wayne Carver.

"Yes, the Warrens sold their cottage. Robyn says you're selling out too, sir."

"Well, yes, I think we will. Anne and I have talked it over. The girls are grown up now. Last year, Robyn only got up here for two weeks, and Rebecca got married in May, so she didn't come to the cottage at all."

"Robyn seems really happy to be here this summer."

"That's true, but from now on she'll only have two or three weeks' vacation. And since we've moved, I can only get away for a couple of weeks a year. It doesn't seem worth maintaining it and paying the taxes."

Mike said cautiously, "She told me it meets the building code for winterization."

Wayne nodded. "It would take a lot of work, but, yes, it could be winterized. The septic's up to spec."

"I know the town's really strict about building and renovating on the lakes."

"This was approved in my father's time." Wayne turned and looked out across the lake. The sun was lowering toward the trees beyond the cottage, and it threw a brilliant orange light out over the water, touching the tips of the tall trees on

Spruce Island. "Pretty place," he murmured. "We've had a lot of good times here."

"You have a wonderful location, sir. If you don't mind my asking, what's the price?"

Wayne turned toward him in surprise. "I thought it was my daughter you had designs on. You're interested in this property?"

Nonplused, Mike tried to gauge his seriousness. "Well, sir, is it either-or?"

"No, I guess not." Wayne smiled. "I always liked you, Mike."

***

Robyn's hands shook all through supper. She tried to avoid passing dishes so no one would see how nervous she was. Mike sat next to her, so close her shoulder touched his sleeve. That in itself was disquieting, but knowing her family was watching made it worse.

The discussion leaned toward jobs and relatives, along with Eric's plans to buy a new truck and Anne's decorating woes in the Connecticut house. Robyn heard it as though from very far away.

"So, you like this company you're with, Mike?" Wayne asked, helping himself to a third biscuit.

"Yes, sir. I thought about going with Harper Associates, in Philadelphia, but I told them this week I'm staying with Wrenfield."

"Better pay here?"

Robyn felt her cheeks flame, embarrassed that her father was questioning Mike about his salary.

"Not really, but I think the prospects are better, and I know what I'm dealing with at Wrenfield. It's always hard to start out with a new organization."

"Yes," Wayne agreed. "I did that this year, and it was no picnic."

"Do you like it, sir?"

"I think so, now that I've made the adjustment. For the first few months, I was wishing I was back here in Maine."

"We drove by the old house," Rebecca said. "It looks good."

"Yes, the new people are keeping the grounds up," Anne agreed.

"Have you seen it, Rob?" Rebecca asked.

"Yes, but I try not to."

"Oh, honey." Her mother's eyes shone with sadness as she frowned at Robyn.

"It's just a house, Sweet Pea," Wayne said gently.

"I know, Daddy."

"Still mad at me for selling?"

She smiled and shook her head. "Not too mad. I miss it, though."

"Are you really going to sell the cottage, too?" Rebecca asked.

"Thinking seriously about it," her father said.

"Well, there are cottage lots available in Connecticut," Eric said. "You could build on one of the lakes there and commute to work summers, like you did here."

"Yes, we're looking into that," Wayne acknowledged.

Robyn realized the tears hadn't swamped her this time. She was getting used to the idea that the cottage was going out of the family, and this was her last visit to Great Pond.

"I've had an offer on this place," Wayne added.

Robyn's eyes snapped to her father's face. "You haven't even listed it, have you?"

"No."

"You didn't tell me, dear," Anne said, frowning.

"Well, I told the fellow I'd consider it and let him know." Wayne pushed his plate back a little and sighed. "Good meal, Robbie."

"Thanks, Daddy," she choked out.

"Do you want your ice cream now or later?" Anne asked.

"Later, I think," Wayne said.

"I couldn't eat another bite, and I want to go swimming again," Rebecca moaned.

"Let's clean up. That'll shake it down some," Eric suggested.

"All right, I'll wash, you dry." Rebecca rose and began stacking the plates.

"I'll help," Robyn said.

"Nope, you cooked. Eric and I are taking over."

Wayne stood and looked out through the porch doorway and the windows beyond. "The lake's calm. Nice night for a canoe ride."

"I think I'll pass," Anne said. "I want to settle in a bit."

"You want to go, Daddy?" Robyn asked. She glanced at Mike, and he smiled a little.

"Oh, no, I meant you and Mike."

"That's okay. We're in the boat every day. We don't need to go canoeing." Blushing, she looked quickly at Mike. His smile was broader, and he gave her a surreptitious wink.

Robyn wasn't sure how to take the signal and stammered. "I—we—well, I don't know. What do you want to do, Mike?"

He shrugged. "I saw some games in the other room."

Robyn seized on it with relief. "Sure. Let's play Jeopardy. If we bring it out here, Becky and Eric can answer questions while they do dishes."

***

It was a nice evening, Mike thought. Robyn was extremely nervous about his introduction to the family circle, but things

266

had gone well. He thought she declined the canoe ride to avoid being paired with him while the rest of the family talked about them.

Or maybe there were vestiges of her initial shyness with him, and she just didn't want to spend too much time alone with him yet. He didn't think it was coincidental that she had made him leave every time things got too intense.

The Jeopardy game was competitive, and he learned a lot about Robyn's family. Her brother-in-law, Eric, was sharp and wound up the winner by a small margin. Mike could envision lots of board game tournaments with him at future family events.

After the game, Robyn opted out of the moonlight swim, and Mike sat with her on the dock, content to hold her hand and watch Eric and Becky splash each other. Mr. Carver strolled along the shore, then went up to the cottage, returning with his wife.

"Here, Robyn, I brought you a sweater." Her mother held out her cream cardigan.

"Thanks, Mom, I'm not cold." Robyn took it and laid it on the dock.

"Clouding up," Wayne observed.

"It's so peaceful here." Anne sank into her lawn chair.

Wayne looked over at Mike. "I s'pose you have to work early, Mike?"

"Yup, I'd better get going pretty soon."

"I didn't mean that as a hint. Just thinking about you sorting the mail."

"Yeah, I go to the post office around seven thirty."

"What time do you leave for the island, Robyn?" Anne asked.

"Whenever Mike comes. Nine fifteen or so."

"Merton promised he'd find another nurse, but I haven't heard anything on that score yet," Mike said.

"I'll have to ask him again tomorrow. He was supposed to post an ad at the hospital in Waterville." Robyn determined to make Merton listen to her and take action, if he hadn't already done so.

"Well, I'd better go." Mike stood and folded his deck chair. "Walk me to the car?"

Robyn extended her hand and let him pull her up out of her chair. He took his key ring from his pocket as they approached his vehicle.

"I like your family."

"They seem to like you." She stopped beside the car and faced him in the twilight.

"Rob, it's been a crazy day, but I don't want to leave without saying I love you."

She melted into his arms, and he knew he'd said the right thing. He was happy. Very happy. And beneath her jitters, Robyn exuded quiet passion.

"You didn't tell me about the Philadelphia company," she said softly. "You're really going to Bolivia, aren't you?"

"Yes. I'm sorry—I guess I should have told you. I just told them no and put it out of my mind. I didn't realize you were wondering about it."

"It's okay."

"Really?" He leaned back and tipped her chin up, so he could see her eyes. "Rob, you weren't hoping I'd go with Harper so I wouldn't have to go to Bolivia, were you?"

"I ... no. I didn't hope anything, exactly."

She tried to look down, but he forced her chin up again.

"Maybe I should have asked you before I decided for sure."

"Asked me about working in Philadelphia?"

"No, asked you to marry me."

She caught her breath.

"Will you, Robyn? I don't want to go off to Bolivia for six months alone. Or anywhere, for that matter."

"I ... this job ... the one in Worcester—"

"Did you sign your life away?" he asked with apprehension. Maybe she had an ironclad contract and would have to stay in Massachusetts for months.

"Not quite. I'm sure they can get someone, but I wasn't expecting ... Oh, Mike, this is moving so fast."

"Really?" It seemed turtle-slow to him. For weeks, the high point of his day had been spotting Robyn on the dock at Carvers'. He had worked on her slowly, convincing her to take the Saturday run with him, then catapulted into spending Sundays with her. Maybe it was sudden, since the attraction had come into the open. It didn't seem that way to him.

"Do you think we really know each other well enough?" Her voice shook.

"I've known you all my life. You've grown up, but you're still the same in a lot of ways."

Robyn rested her head against his arm. "I'm sorry. I was thinking today that, if something like this happened ... well, you'd have to get me a visa, and I don't know if you can get them that fast. Oh, Mike, Bolivia?"

He swallowed the lump in his throat. "Afraid so. I'm committed to it now."

"You're not just asking me so you won't be lonely down there?"

"No. I thought I was doing the right thing when I turned down Harper Associates. I'm sorry, sweetheart." He thought she jerked a little when he said that. "I should have discussed it all with you. I could have taken the other job. That would have given us more time to sort things out, I guess." Real regret was overtaking him. If he'd messed this up, he would never forgive himself.

Robyn took a deep, shuddering breath. Her hands went slowly around him, under his arms, to his back, and she squeezed him.

In a very small voice, she said, "What does one wear in Bolivia in fall? Or is it spring there?"

"It will be spring. They say it's beautiful." He put one hand up to her hair. It was still up in the sophisticated knot, sleek and shiny in the half light. He'd never seen her wear it that way before. She usually had the girl-next-door ponytail, or let her locks fall loose about her shoulders. "How do you do that?" he asked.

"What?"

"Make your hair stay like that?" Not hair spray. It wasn't stiff.

She laughed and put both hands up to the knot and began manipulating it. "An engineer can't figure it out? A few hair pins and an elastic band." She was pulling the pins out. Her dark hair fell down in a ponytail, and she slid the band off. She shook her head a little, and it cascaded over his hands.

"Magic," he breathed, caressing the silky tresses. "So you were hoping I'd take the Philly job?"

"No, I never really thought you would."

"So, will you marry me? Please?"

She looked very young with her huge, solemn brown eyes and her gleaming hair fluttering in the slight breeze.

"You'll take me with you, won't you? Because I won't marry a man who's going to go off and leave me for six months."

"Aw, Rob." He gathered her in close to him. His car keys fell to the ground, but he didn't care. "Of course I'm taking you. I thought that went without saying. I love you so much!"

"Yes, then. But you'll have to handle the paperwork, Mike. I'll have my hands full getting out of my job, and I'll have to go to Worcester for my things and close my apartment and—well, a lot of things."

She stopped for breath.

He didn't say anything. She looked up at him, and he tried to fix the way she looked at him forever in his mind.

"I don't know what Daddy will say," she breathed.

"That's easy. He'll say, *Mike, if she'll have you, I've got no objections. Just take care of her, son. She thinks she can take care of herself, but I think she needs a strong shoulder now and again.*"

She stared at him. "He said that."

"Yes."

"When? Before supper?"

"Yes, on the dock."

"My face is red."

"I can't tell. It's too dark. Are you embarrassed?" He put both hands on her cheeks. They were warm.

"Yes. I wasn't sure you and Daddy had progressed that far."

"You told me yesterday I needed to speak to him."

"I know what I said. I wasn't sure you took me seriously." She put her hand out and touched his lips with her fingertips. "Thank you, Mike. That means a lot. The more I learn about you, the more I love you."

He bent toward her, and her nervousness seemed to dissipate. Her hands were gentle on his shoulders, and he folded her in his arms, kissing her softly.

"It's official, then?" he whispered in her ear.

"Yes."

"I'll call my boss in Bangor before I go to the post office in the morning."

"You need to get their approval?"

"Well, they'll need to know because of the travel arrangements. Is your passport here?"

"Yes, in my purse."

"Can you give it to me tomorrow?"

"Sure."

"Good. I'll take care of the other documents. You may need some shots."

"For you, anything."

He laughed. "Do you want to set a date now?"

"When do you leave?"

"You mean, when do *we* leave."

"Right."

"I'm not precisely sure. After Labor Day. I told them I'd stay here through the holiday, and they agreed. Maybe I'll have a better idea after I call tomorrow."

"Let's talk about it then."

"Okay." He kissed her again, and her response thrilled him. He was finally starting to believe she was going to marry him.

"Mike," she gasped. "I love you. Go home."

He laughed and opened the car door.

***

"Where's Mike?" Rebecca was dishing out ice cream in the kitchen when Robyn went in by the screen door.

"I sent him home."

"What did you do that for? He didn't get any ice cream." Her sister seemed slightly annoyed.

"Any developments, Sweet Pea?" her father asked, watching Robyn keenly.

She walked slowly toward him. "Yes, Daddy. We're getting married."

"What?" Rebecca shrieked.

Her father grinned and stood up to hug her. "I thought maybe."

Robyn ignored Rebecca. Her father's warm approval enveloped her like a hand-stitched quilt. "Thanks for being so good to him, Daddy."

"It wasn't difficult."

Robyn turned to embrace her mother.

"Your father tells me to have no qualms about this."

"Mom, he's terrific."

Her mother smiled. "I'm very happy for you, dear."

"You didn't tell me it was so serious," Rebecca pouted. She moved in for a hug, then Eric pulled Robyn into an embrace.

"Congratulations, sister-in-law."

"Thanks."

"Did you grill him thoroughly, Dad, the way you did Eric?" Rebecca asked.

Eric laughed. "Yes, can Mike support her in the manner to which she's accustomed?"

"I didn't ask him directly, but I don't think there's any worry there," Wayne said.

"What *did* you talk about all that time?" Rebecca persisted.

"I asked him a few pointed questions about his plans and his feelings for my daughter." He put his arm around Robyn's shoulders and drew her close again. "He's solid all the way through, honey. Don't play games with that young man."

"I won't, Daddy."

THE MAILBOAT

Chapter 11

Is It True?

Robyn hopped into the mailboat the next morning, leaving
Rebecca, Eric, and her parents waving on the dock. Somehow,
getting the mail had become a big production for the Carver
family.

Mike kissed her on the cheek and settled her, blushing, on
the side bench next to his seat. The eight passengers smiled and
greeted her like an old friend.

"Congratulations, dear," said one grandmotherly woman.

"Best wishes," said another.

Robyn's face was scarlet by then. She wanted to be furious
with Mike. He had obviously told the world.

But she couldn't hold it against him. He looked so
apologetic, but at the same time so proud, that she caught the
joy from him and smiled at the well-wishing passengers.

He handed her out at the island and climbed up the ladder
to take the mail to the office.

"Lots of packages today," he said, picking up the bin. "All
the campers are getting care packages from home."

"Did you call your boss?" she asked. It was the first
private moment they'd had, and even so, it wasn't private. A
score of boys ran up the path ahead of them, behind them, and
alongside them, vying for their attention.

"Yes. They want me to send more data right away. You
need a visa, since we'll be staying more than ninety days. They

need your passport and a copy of your birth certificate. Can you get that?"

She went with him into the camp director's office, where Merton sat at his desk.

"My passport's here." She lifted her duffel bag to the desktop and unzipped it. "I'll ask Mom about the birth certificate. If she can't help me, I can probably run to Augusta this afternoon and get a copy."

"What's going on?" Merton asked.

Robyn and Mike looked at each other and smiled.

"We're going to Bolivia," Mike said.

"Bolivia! What on earth?"

"We're getting married first." Robyn knew she was wearing a silly grin, but she couldn't help it.

"Well, now." Merton stood up. "I guess congratulations are in order." He pumped Mike's hand and turned to kiss Robyn.

"Oh, no you don't." She smiled but held him off firmly. "Unless you've got a new nurse, you don't come near me."

"I have. She'll be here late Wednesday."

"Hooray!" Robyn permitted a peck on the cheek.

"She's only an LPN," Merton said. "Still, she'll be here full time, and that's what we really need."

"I've got to run," Mike said reluctantly. "See you soon. We need to talk over about five thousand things later."

"Lunch at our house?" Robyn asked.

"Absolutely." Mike jogged off toward the dock.

She smiled all morning, cajoling the bruised little boys out of tears, checking weekend injuries, and doling out medication.

"Miss Robyn, will you marry me when I'm grown up?" Wesley asked when she'd given him his insulin shot.

She smiled and squeezed his hand. "No, Wes, I'm afraid not. Uncle Mike has asked me to marry him."

"Nobody gives shots as good as you," he said wistfully.

SUSAN PAGE DAVIS

With a hug, she said, "Thank you. Now, go on to your woodcraft class."

Uncle Sean limped into the infirmary after all the boys had left.

"What happened to you?" Robyn asked.

"Oh, we were water skiing yesterday, and I hit the dock."

"Ouch." Robyn could see that his left ankle was bruised and swollen. "Sit up here, please."

She examined his ankle carefully. "Very colorful." The skin ranged from deep purple to yellow. "Wiggle your toes."

He winced as he complied.

"Does it hurt when I do this?" She pushed his toes back toward him.

"Yes."

"But you didn't scream."

He grinned and shrugged. "I guess it's not that bad."

"I don't think anything's broken. If you want to get an X-ray to make sure, I'll tell Merton, but I think acetaminophen and rest will take care of it. Don't go water-skiing for a few weeks."

"Don't worry, I won't." He eyed her sharply. "Is it true you and Mike are getting married?"

"Yes."

"Man!" He shook his head. "And I was hoping I was making some headway."

She laughed. "I guess this isn't the best spot for romance."

"You're telling me. If I ever work at a camp again, it will be a co-ed camp, no mistake about that."

She finished her tasks before the mailboat returned, and when Mike came back she was sitting on the dock amid a throng of boys. They shouted and waved as the boat pulled away, and Robyn settled with a sigh onto the bench beneath the canopy.

"Only two more days," Mike yelled over the engine noise.

She nodded.

At the marina, the passengers left the boat with more good wishes and questions Robyn couldn't answer.

"When is the wedding?"

"Do you have an engagement ring yet?"

"Are you getting married on the mailboat?"

The last query startled her, and she looked quickly toward Mike.

He laughed. "Couldn't fit many witnesses on here."

When he'd taken the outgoing mail inside, he came back and helped her into Jim's small motorboat. He pushed off and moved toward the stern, climbing nimbly over the seats. When he passed Robyn amidships, he dropped a kiss on her forehead.

"We could moor the boat at the marina for the wedding, and set up chairs on the dock," he said and started the engine.

Robyn sat watching him, not sure if he was serious. He looked straight ahead, up the shoreline. She leaned forward and removed his sunglasses carefully.

He gave her a wink.

"Just checking," she screamed in his ear above the roar of the motor.

"We could, you know."

She didn't say any more until they climbed out at the Carvers' beach.

"Where *do* you want to get married?" she asked as he beached the boat.

He shrugged and hauled the boat farther ashore. "Maybe the mailboat's not such a bad idea. It will be a small wedding, won't it?"

Robyn considered. "Well, my folks, Rebecca and Eric, your mom and Pete. Who else?"

"A minister, I hope."

She laughed. "Half the people on the lake seem to think they have an interest in our wedding. Should we invite Jim and Merton?"

"How about Mr. Foster and the boys from Spruce Island?" Mike chortled.

"And the mystery man from Parkhursts'. What a coup that would be!"

Mike frowned.

"What is it?" Robyn asked. "Did I say something wrong?"

He shook his head. "No, I just wonder about that guy. We'll probably never know who he is or why he came here for the summer."

***

On Tuesday it rained, but Robyn didn't care. There were no other passengers, and she and Mike held hands all the way to Spruce Island and back. When the mail run was done, he ate lunch at the cottage, then they took the boat to the marina, where he had left his car.

"I phoned Worcester yesterday afternoon," she told him.

Mike turned on the windshield wipers and headlights, then looked over at her.

"And?"

"They weren't happy at the hospital, but it's official. I gave up my position."

He nodded. "Better to tell them right away, so they can start looking for a replacement, I guess." He bent toward her and kissed her. "Robyn, thanks for doing that for me. I hope it wasn't too stressful."

She shook her head with a smile. "It wasn't too bad. I dreaded telling my new supervisor, but she was decent about it. Still, I don't want to get a reputation as a quitter."

"You're not quitting. You're just moving your hard work to different place."

They sloshed around in the rain all afternoon, from one errand to another. First they went to the town office, to start the paperwork on the marriage license. Next was a brief visit to

279

Robyn's former pastor, to schedule the wedding at the church her family had attended when they lived in Belgrade.

Augusta, the state's capital and the nearest town of any size, was the next stop. They walked into a jewelry store. Robyn came out a bit starry-eyed, knowing that in two days Mike would have her engagement ring in his pocket.

To humor Robyn, Mike drove to the public library. She checked out three children's books on Bolivia.

"Do you always do your research in the children's room?" he asked in amusement.

"Preliminary research, yes. Kids' books are simple and direct, and they're quick to read. They give you the major facts in small bites."

"I'll have to remember that next time I'm researching a project."

As he drove to the bank, she regaled him with facts she pulled from the books.

"Bolivia's a major exporter of tin, and they have some oil and silver, too, and lots of other good stuff."

"No kidding." Mike tried to keep a straight face.

"I guess you knew that. Did you know it's the only South American country with no seacoast?"

"Well, yes, actually."

"Capital?"

"Trick question," Mike said accusingly.

"Yes, it is. Are you stumped?"

"No. Bolivia has two capitals: Sucre and La Paz."

"You've done your homework. Where will we be going?"

"La Paz, at first, anyway."

She squinted at a map in one of books. "Goody! It's near Lake Titicaca."

"Yes, fairly close."

"Ever been there?"

"They flew me down for a week when I left Nicaragua in April," he confessed. "They wanted me to view the bridge sites in person."

"No fair. You could have told me."

"Maybe I should ask the partners if we can have a houseboat on Lake Titicaca, instead of an apartment. That might suit you."

"Brilliant! We should always live on water."

He threw back his head and laughed.

The rain had stopped when they arrived at his mother's house in time for supper. Robyn felt a tad guilty. Jane Borden had worked in the bank all day, then come home to cook for her and Mike and Pete.

"She wants to do this," Mike assured her as he pulled into the driveway. "She's really excited about me getting engaged, and she's happy that it's you."

"Does she even remember me?"

"Of course. And once she knows you better, she'll know you're perfect for me."

He got out and went around to open the door, and Robyn took a deep breath. Mike's mother looked just as she remembered, except that her sandy hair was liberally sprinkled with gray.

"Robyn, dear, I'm so glad!" Jane Borden held out her arms, and Robyn embraced her with tears in her eyes.

The meal was nearly ready. Robyn insisted on helping, and Jane brought her an apron. By the time the food was on the table, Pete had arrived.

"Hey, Robyn," he said as he came in the back door.

"Well, hi, Pete."

"Welcome to the family." He kissed her on the cheek, and Robyn smiled at him. She remembered him as a little pest Wesley's size, who could swim like a fish. He'd coaxed her and Rebecca for pennies one summer, so he could lay them on the railroad track, to be smashed by trains. She still had one of those squashed pennies somewhere.

When they left two hours later, Robyn was content. Mike's mother hugged her again, holding her close for an instant.

"I always hoped for a daughter, dear."

Robyn smiled. "That's really nice. I hope we'll be around some, after Bolivia, and we can do things together."

Jane eyed her with satisfaction. "Yes, that would be wonderful."

Mike and Pete had drifted toward the car. Robyn said quietly to Jane, "I've been wanting to see you. I needed a chance to say thank you."

"What for?"

"For bringing Mike up the way you did. I think you're a very special mother." She kissed Mrs. Borden, who blushed a becoming rose.

"You keep me up to date on the wedding plans."

"We will. And I wondered if you would like to go to town with me one day next week, when I talk to the florist."

"I'd love to," Jane said.

Mike drove back to the cottage in companionable silence.

"Tired?" he asked as he parked in the gravel clearing.

"A little."

"Tomorrow's your last day as camp nurse."

"I'm looking forward to it. Oh, I suppose I'll miss it a little."

"I'll be here at the usual time."

He kissed her tenderly and left her at the door.

Chapter 12

Company on the Mail Run

Thursday Mike drove with his mail from the post office to the marina in a drizzle. No passengers. His heart leaped. Robyn was done at Spruce Island, and she had promised to take the mail run if he had no passengers.

He checked in with Jim and carried the bins to the pontoon boat. He was just about to cast off when two men in business suits came swiftly down the wharf, black umbrellas shielding them.

"Borden, wait!"

He looked closely at them and swallowed hard. His bosses were at the top of the ladder.

"Mr. Fields," he stammered, "Mr. Wren. What brings you here?"

"A couple of things, Borden. May we come aboard?"

"Of course." He moved the mail bins a little and stepped forward to help the men embark safely.

"How did you find me?" he asked, when they stood under the canopy. All sorts of thoughts were surging through his mind, and none of them was good.

Had they tracked him down because he had announced his impending marriage? Did they see that as an impediment to his work? Did they want to check Robyn out to see if she was worthy of representing the firm in Bolivia? Or had they changed their minds about sending him to South America?

"We went to the address you gave us, and your mother said if we hurried we might catch you at the marina." Mr. Fields looked around the boat in bewilderment. "We had no idea—"

"You could have told us you'd taken a second job," Wren said with an injured tone.

"Oh, this is just temporary," Mike assured them.

"You needed money?"

"No, no. See, this was my old summer job when I was in college. After Nicaragua, I was so tired, I just wanted to come spend one more summer on the lake."

"Yes," the gray-haired Mr. Fields interrupted. "You told me you'd be on the lake. I assumed you meant in comfort, not as a laborer."

"It's not hard work," Mike said with a smile. "I enjoy it. And my family doesn't own shorefront property anymore. It seemed like a good way to get out on the water."

"Borden—Michael," Fields said, trying to adopt a fatherly tone. "You are happy working at Wrenfield, aren't you?"

"Yes, sir."

"Not thinking of jumping ship, are you?" Wren asked, eyeing him pointedly.

Mike smiled. He felt like jumping over the side just then, to escape their sharp stares. His casual clothes made him feel out of place. He'd certainly never showed up for work at Wrenfield in cut-off shorts and a sweatshirt before. But he reminded himself that the two engineering partners were the ones who were out of context, and he could see they were worried.

"I was approached," he began.

"We heard," Wren admitted, shaking his head. "You might have told us."

"I turned them down, sir. Didn't see any reason to go into it with you."

"Hmm," said Fields. "Is there someplace we can converse?"

"Well, sir, actually, I have to make the mail run now." Mike glanced at his watch. "I'm a few minutes late starting already."

"When will you be free?"

"Around noon."

Fields sat down experimentally on one of the benches. "Do you take passengers?"

Hastily, Mike said, "Well, occasionally, but it's wet out today, sir. It will be chilly on the water." He had brought along his raincoat, unsure of how the weather would turn out, but Fields and Wren had no outerwear to keep them warm and protect their three-piece suits.

"We have other business in town," Fields said. "Perhaps we should tend to that this morning while you go about your … job. We need to find a man named Blankenship. Ever hear of him?"

Mike gulped. "Yes, sir."

"Do you know him?" Wren stood up eagerly.

"No, sir. I've never actually met him, but …" he paused, realizing he would breach confidentiality if he told them Blankenship was on his route.

"Well, his agent let slip that he lives on this pond, and his address is Box 32, Star Route, Belgrade. What does that mean?" Wren folded up his umbrella and parked it on a bench.

"It … it means he's on a special, contracted mail route."

"Like this one?"

Mike opened his mouth, then closed it. He nodded, wishing they would just leave.

"Well, then," Mr. Fields smiled. "What are we waiting for? Proceed with your route, Borden, and when we reach Box 32, we'll get off."

Mike hesitated.

"Is there any reason we shouldn't go with you?" Wren asked, watching him intently.

"N-no, sir." Mike had worked at Wrenfield for three years, and he knew the partners wouldn't be easily dissuaded. He loosed the painter and shoved off, then went to the helm.

"We've been trying to get Blankenship to come to Wrenfield for months," Fields said.

"He's an engineer?" Mike couldn't hold the question back. That might explain some things that had troubled him.

"No, no, a psychologist. He's the one we've been wanting for the sensitivity training. We've written three or four times, trying to negotiate, but he's very elusive."

Mike turned that over in his mind as he made the first few deliveries.

"Box seven," Fields muttered as Mike placed a packet of letters in the Sibleys' mailbox.

Before he gunned the motor, Wren said, "When you're done with this, Borden, we'll go to lunch somewhere and discuss the Bolivia trip."

"Yes, sir. That would be fine."

Mike's stomach was churning. He could see Robyn standing alone on the Carvers' dock. She was wearing jeans and a red turtleneck, topped by a gray zipped sweatshirt. Her UMaine baseball cap was perched roguishly on her head. She waved and smiled, and he waved back.

What on earth do I do now? he asked himself. *I did ask her to go along.* The prospect of turning his daily job into a pleasant outing with a little sweet talk and hand holding thrown in had capsized long ago. He killed the engine and stepped into the bow to help her.

She jumped down lightly, her hands on his shoulders. "I couldn't stay away. Are we—" She stopped abruptly as she looked over his shoulder and saw the two men.

***

"Passengers on a day like this?" she whispered.

"Afraid so."

She looked into his face, trying to read the worry lines there.

"What's going on? Those aren't typical tourists."

"I ... it's ... I guess I need to introduce you to Mr. Wren and Mr. Fields."

She threw another furtive glance toward them. "Of Wrenfield, Inc.?"

He nodded.

"Why are they here?" Panic seized her.

Mike shrugged helplessly. "They wanted to talk to me about something, and they also want to meet with another man who's living on the lake."

He hitched the painter to the mooring post, took her hand, and drew her under the canopy. The two men stood.

"Mr. Fields, Mr. Wren, it gives me great honor to introduce you to my fiancée, Miss Robyn Carver."

Astonishment registered on the men's faces.

"Well, good day," Fields said, shaking her hand.

"A pleasant surprise," Wren murmured.

Of all the days to wear my grubbies! Robyn moaned inwardly. She put on her best smile. "How do you do, sir? Nice to meet you."

"Next stop, Spruce Island," Mike said brightly. He started the motor.

Robyn sat down on the bench opposite the two men. Suits, expensive suits, on the mailboat. Was that how Mike dressed for work? What was she getting into? Maybe they would think she was too unsophisticated. Would they tell Mike his choice of brides was inappropriate?

"We'll be here about five minutes," Mike said automatically as he pulled up to the camp dock.

Robyn stared at him. It was what he told his passengers every day, when he carried the bin to the camp office. Should she scramble up the ladder after him? She didn't want to stay on the boat with his bosses.

"What is this place?" Fields asked, looking about with interest.

"It's a boys' camp, sir. Would you like to get out and see it?"

"No need, Borden. We don't want to hold you up. I'll just chat with this young lady while you're gone."

Robyn had started to rise, but she sank back onto the bench. Mike's look seemed to be measuring her mettle, and she determined that she would hold her own with the partners.

"Go ahead, Mike," she said, smiling.

Mike put the bin on the edge of the dock and climbed the ladder.

"So, Miss Carver, you and Borden are tying the knot." Fields sat back with a jovial air and smiled.

"Yes, sir."

"How do you feel about going to South America?"

"I'm looking forward to it. I hope it hasn't caused too many complications for the firm."

"No, no," Fields said. "We frequently send married men out. It adds a few details to the paperwork, but overall I think the men work better if they take their families with them."

She nodded. "I'm glad to hear it."

Wren spoke up. "It was rather unexpected with Borden. We'd gotten used to him batching it."

"He kept you under wraps, all right," Fields agreed.

She smiled, uncertain of how to respond.

Wren said, "Borden's overseeing this project. We expect our managers to sort of look out for the crew and entertain the local dignitaries. City officials, government inspectors, and so on. You might be quite a help to him in that department."

Robyn swallowed. "You mean, give dinner parties and things like that?"

"Well, as a single man, Mike would just take them out to dinner. As a married man, he might want to do some entertaining in his home."

"Yes, you see, we usually put the bachelors up at a hotel when they're on foreign soil," Fields explained. "But married men get an apartment, or a house. It all depends on the area and what's available."

Robyn thought fleetingly of the houseboat Mike had suggested and decided this was not the time to bring it up.

"I expect Mike is paying the extra expense of taking me along?" she asked.

"He's paying for the visa and incidental expenses, but actually we've found it's sometimes cheaper to send a married couple out than it is a single fellow. A rental house is often less than a hotel room, and they do apply themselves harder. They drink less, and so forth."

Robyn stared at Mr. Fields, but he was serious. "I don't think you have to worry about that with Mike."

"Oh, no, not Borden. I was speaking generally."

She nodded and looked toward the shore, glad to see Mike hurrying down the path.

The men practiced patience until they came to the upper end of the lake.

"Box 30," Wren said as Mike collected outgoing mail at a wooden pier. "We're nearly there."

Robyn eyed Mike curiously. Surely they couldn't be calling on the mystery man?

THE MAILBOAT

Chapter 13

We'll Swamp Your Boat

When he eased the pontoon boat up to the Parkhursts' dock, Mike threw the painter over the mooring post without saying anything.

"This is it," Wren said. "Will you wait?"

"He might not be home," Fields said, surveying the Parkhursts' cottage. As usual, there was no sign of life.

"I'll wait," Mike said.

"Have you ever met Mr. Blankenship?" Wren asked.

"No, sir. We've never spoken."

Mike helped the two men out of the boat, then sank into his pilot's seat.

Robyn stood up and put her hand on his shoulder.

"Mike, they're really here to see the mystery tenant?"

"That's correct."

"But why?"

"Turns out he's a hotshot psychologist." She thought Mike's eyes looked slightly glazed as he turned to look at her. "Remember I told you they wanted someone to come in for a month and give seminars on interpersonal relationships?"

Robyn gasped. "Inter—you've got to be joking. The man hides in his cottage until the mailman's gone! How could he ever teach people how to get along?"

"Don't ask me. All I know is, the partners saw that his address had the same zip code mine did and decided to kill two birds with one stone." He squeezed her hand and looked anxiously at her. "One unannounced stone. I'm sorry, baby. They just turned up on the marina dock as I was about to shove off. If I could have warned you they were coming, I would have."

"So I could wear a designer dress and put my hair up?"

He smiled. "I love you. You're perfect the way you are. If they can't see that—"

"What?" she asked. "What if they don't think I'm an asset to the company?"

"Don't worry. Anyone can see what a wonderful fiancée I've got. And I'm marrying you, no matter what they think."

"But you were committed to Bolivia before you were committed to me." Fear began rising in her. Somehow, it had been too good to be true. Out of the blue, a wrecking ball was crashing down on their wedding, their trip to South America, and their future together.

"Robyn, don't worry. You hear me?" He stroked her hand.

She stared into his blue eyes and saw his love there, firm and solid. She nodded. "I hear you."

"Good." Mike glanced toward the cottage. Fields and Wren stood on the porch, knocking. Mike leaned toward her and gave her a brief kiss.

"Did they want you to go back to work soon?" she asked.

He sighed. "I don't know. Somehow they'd heard about the offer Harper made me. Maybe they were afraid I was checking out a new employer this summer and would leave them. Anyway, I hadn't told them I was delivering mail, see, and it shocked them to find out I had another job this summer. They thought I'd be water skiing and sunbathing, I guess."

She heard voices, and they turned to look toward the cottage once more. "They're coming back." She sat demurely on the bench beside Mike's seat, and he went forward to help the partners back into the boat.

"I don't understand that fellow," Fields scolded. "I never saw anything so rude."

"He could have been civil," Wren agreed. "If he doesn't want to earn a good sum, all he has to do is say, *No, thank you.*"

"That's right," Fields agreed. "He didn't have to yell insults out the window."

Mike's lips twitched. "He yelled at you?"

Wren nodded. "After we'd knocked several times he opened the side window a crack and shouted to go away and leave him in peace. Said he didn't want anyone coming around and bothering him while he was working on his next book."

Fields glared toward the cottage. "Then he said if we didn't leave immediately, he'd call the police. Wouldn't even listen to why we were there."

"Look at it this way," Mike said. "Is that really the man you want teaching your employees how to treat other people?"

Fields stared at him. "Absolutely right, Borden."

Wren shook his head. "His books are so lucid. And that last article of his ... No, I don't understand it."

"His books are best sellers," Fields agreed. "I thought if we could get him as instructor for our employees, we'd have the best."

"Some writers are lousy speakers," Mike offered.

"Hmm."

"Look, why don't Robyn and I take you to lunch?" Mike said.

He looked quickly at Robyn, and she smiled. She'd always known he was brilliant.

"There's an excellent restaurant on the lake," she said.

"Sounds good, but this is on us," Fields insisted. "We came all this way to see Blankenship, but I think we've put Mike out a little in the process. Lunch is definitely on Wrenfield."

The sun came out, and the bosses were soon removing their suit jackets and loosening their ties. Mike and Robyn peeled off their sweatshirts.

At Foster Island, Robyn was surprised to see the old man and his dog standing on the dock.

"Mr. Foster! You're feeling better?" she called.

"Is that you, Robyn Carver?"

"Yes, sir."

"I certainly am better! My grandson and his wife brought me back out here yesterday. They're going to stay a while with me." He studied the two men on the other side of the boat. "These two saved my life," he called.

"Is that so?" Wren asked.

"Yes, it's so. They rescued me in good order."

"Take care, Mr. Foster," Mike said, handing him his insurance bill and a catalog from L.L. Bean.

***

Robyn asked Mike to drop her off at her parents' cottage after the last mail stop, so she could change her clothes and meet them at the restaurant. With Mike heading toward the marina at a moderate pace, she tore up the path and into the cottage.

"What's your hurry?" Becky stood at the kitchen counter, mixing tuna salad for lunch.

"Mike's bosses from Bangor are here. They're taking us to lunch."

She ran to the porch, picked out the dressiest outfit she had, then scurried to the bathroom to change. She quickly pulled her hair into a high ponytail, then twisted and pinned it. Five minutes later she was in her car, driving as fast as she dared to the restaurant.

Mike and the bosses were sitting at a table on the deck, glasses in hand, staring out over the water. Mike looked decidedly casual in his shorts and polo shirt, or maybe the other two just looked a bit stuffy in their suits.

All three stood when she came out through the restaurant door.

"Miss Carver, you look lovely," old Mr. Fields said with a debonair bow.

"Care for a drink?" asked Wren.

Robyn hesitated. "Whatever Mike's having." She hoped she sounded gracious. Mr. Fields held her chair for her.

"Well, Mike's been telling us about life on Great Pond," Wren said with a smile. He swirled the liquid in his glass and took a sip.

Robyn looked toward Mike. He shrugged and winked at her.

"Here you are, ma'am," said the waitress. "Diet Pepsi."

Robyn beamed at Mike and lifted the glass to her lips.

"It's a lovely little town," Fields said. "Picturesque."

"And you'll be living here after Mike wraps up the job in Bolivia." Wren scanned the panoramic view of the lake as he spoke.

"Well ..." Robyn glanced at Mike. They'd agreed they wanted to live in the Belgrade area if they could find housing, but nothing was settled yet. Mike just smiled at her with a half shrug.

"So nice the two of you have found a cottage for sale," Fields murmured.

Robyn choked on her Pepsi and made a dive for her napkin.

Mike leaned hastily toward her. "You all right, Rob?"

She nodded, coughing.

"Charming location," Fields said.

"And Mike tells us it has its own septic system," Wren added.

She turned wide-eyed to Mike.

"Engineers always ask about the septic." His voice was matter-of-fact, but his eyes were pleading.

She gulped in a deep breath.

After consulting them, Mr. Fields ordered lobster all around.

"You know, we like to send a medical liaison out with our crews," he said to Robyn. "They can deal with minor ailments the men have and work with the national doctors when needed. Would you be interested in that position, Miss Carver? As Mrs. Borden, of course."

Robyn turned toward Mike.

"A step up from Spruce Island," Mike said with a smile.

"Oh, my Spanish is very poor. I only had two years in high school."

"We'll get you some tapes." Wren signaled for the waitress to refill his glass. "And you've got Mike. He's fluent."

Her head was whirling. They were offering her a job on the Bolivia project.

"There would be a stipend, of course," Fields said with a smile. "Your credentials seem to meet our criteria, and it would give you something to do while Mike's working."

"Why don't you think about it for a week or so, Robyn?" Mike suggested.

"I ... " She swallowed hard. She did like her profession, and time would be heavy on her hands while Mike was at work. "All right, I'll consider it."

The lobster was delicious, and Robyn set aside her nerves, deciding to enjoy the moment. She watched Mr. Wren downing martinis, and she hoped Mr. Fields was driving home.

"Mike says you like living on the water," Fields said over coffee. "I've spoken to the real estate agent in La Paz about it. She'll have several places for you to look at when you arrive."

Mike's sheepish smile spoke volumes. He cleared his throat. "The firm is hoping we can leave soon after Labor Day."

"Can we?" she asked.

"I guess it's up to you. We need to set the date, and then they'll buy our plane tickets."

"Labor Day is September fifth," Fields said, consulting a pocket calendar.

"Well, I …" Robyn paused, going over the dates they'd discussed with the pastor for holding the wedding ceremony. "I don't see a problem with us leaving that week."

"We'll let you know," Mike promised. "Soon."

They walked the two partners out to their car. Fields got behind the wheel, and Wren fumbled with his seat belt, strapping himself into the passenger seat.

"So glad we had a chance to meet you, Miss Carver," Fields said.

The car rolled out, and Robyn exhaled slowly.

"Come on," Mike said, grasping her hand.

"Where to?"

"Out in the boat."

"My car—"

"I'll drive it up later. Come on. Please? I need to talk to you. It has to be in the boat."

"All right."

They walked over to the dock, and she saw that he had moored the mailboat there. He ran it out away from shore, up to the widest point of the lake, killed the engine, and dropped anchor.

"So, what are we here for?" Robyn asked. It was warmer than it had been in the gray morning, but the wind whipped her long cotton skirt around her legs. Far down the lake, a war canoe full of boys moved out from the camp dock.

"This." Mike opened the locker and brought out a small box.

"My ring?"

"Yup. Picked it up last night."

He opened the box and took the ring out, kneeling beside her on the deck.

"Robyn, I love you."

"Aw, Mike, you're buying my folks' cottage, aren't you?"

"We are."

She blinked back tears. "You didn't need to. I'd reconciled myself to losing it. I'd be happy with you anywhere."

He slipped the band onto her finger. "I know, Sweetheart, but this way, when we come back from Bolivia, we'll have someplace to come to, and it will be ours. Next summer we can work on weatherizing it, and then we can stay there year round if we want to, whenever we're in the area."

She looked down at the sparkling diamond on her finger, then settled into his arms, her head comfortable on his shoulder. "Mike, you won't ever go off on one of these trips without me, will you?"

"No chance. While we were waiting for you at the restaurant, Fields and Wren made it clear that I can pretty well write my own ticket, so long as I stay with them. Your ticket, too."

He kissed her, and she thought nothing could go wrong now. He lifted her left hand and looked at the diamond, glittering in the brilliant sun. "Happy?"

"Very." She looked up into his eyes. "They're pretty anxious for us to set the date."

"How about next Saturday?" Mike asked.

"That's too soon. Don't you have to do the mail run until Labor Day?"

"Lots of people would kill for this job. I'm sure I can get out of it. Jim might even do it himself the last week or two of the season."

He kissed her again. Robyn let herself visualize their future together, and she was very thankful.

"All right, August … whatever is a week before Labor Day weekend," she said breathlessly. "The twenty-seventh."

"Sooner."

"The twentieth?"

"Done." He held her for a long minute. The boat swayed gently.

"Mike … "

"Time to take you home?"

"I think so."

"Okay." He let go of her reluctantly and turned to start the engine. Fifteen boys were grinning at them from a war canoe that had silently glided up beside the mailboat.

"I can't believe it," Mike yelled to Sean, amidships. "You finally taught them to be quiet."

Wesley said solemnly, "We came to invite you both to a solemn powwow. Tonight. Spruce Island. You be there."

"What if we don't come?" Mike asked.

"We'll swamp your boat," Teddy said with a gruesome smile.

The boys let loose in a blood-curdling whoop.

"Sounds like you're having a bridal shower tonight," Mike said to Robyn. He turned the key and pulled her over close beside him. As he steered for her cottage, she waved at the boys. They raised their paddles in salute.

About the author

Susan Page Davis is the author of more than one hundred published novels. She's a winner of the Carol Award, two Faith, Hope and Love Reader's Choice Awards, and three Will Rogers Medallions, and a finalist in the WILLA Literary Awards and Selah Awards. A Maine native, she now lives in Kentucky. Visit her website at: https://susanpagedavis.com, where you can see all her books, sign up for her occasional newsletter, and read fun features on her "Freebies" tab. If you liked this book, please consider writing a review and posting it on Amazon, Goodreads, or the venue of your choice.

Find Susan at:

Website: https://susanpagedavis.com
Amazon:
https://www.amazon.com/Susan-Page-Davis/e/B001IR1CGA
BookBub:
https://www.bookbub.com/authors/susan-page-davis
Twitter: @SusanPageDavis
Facebook:
https://www.facebook.com/susanpagedavisauthor
BookCave:
https://mybookcave.com/profile/susan-page-davis/
Goodreads:
https://www.goodreads.com/author/show/255473.Susan_Page_Davis

And subscribe to her newsletter to receive a free short story:
https://madmimi.com/signups/118177/join

Did you read the rest of the Mainely Romance series?

In Book 1, *She Gets July*, Rebecca and Rob bought a cottage together when they were engaged, but they haven't seen each other in more than three years. Since they broke up, they've been alternating the warmer months at the cottage in beautiful Belgrade, Maine, and are careful never to cross each other's path. It would take a crisis or two to start them speaking to each other again.

Book 2, *Off the Record*, finds Rebecca's younger sister Wynne wrestling with her new job as a news reporter. She went to central Maine to start a long-term, exciting career, but now she's having doubts. Andrew Cook never wanted to work his family's farm. He's a pilot at heart, but circumstances placed him here, with his grandparents and his four-year-old twins. Can he and Wynne get past their personal differences and their career problems to form something true and enduring together?

Just Be Here is Book 3, featuring Libby Sharpe, who has accepted a job teaching at a small private school in Waterville. She lives with Kim Richardson, a fellow teacher who is widowed and has a young daughter. The local game warden, Nick Palmer, helps rid their property of poachers. Nick is interested in Libby, but she's still recovering from a failed relationship. Aiden jilted her in a very painful manner. Can she really depend on Nick? A hunting accident tests them both.

More of Susan's Novels you might enjoy

Contemporary Romances:

Mainely Romance series:
  She Gets July
  Off the Record
  Just Be Here
  Kate by the Book
  The Mailboat
The Charm Bracelet
Trail To Justice
Alaska Weddings Series:
  Always Ready
  Fire and Ice
  Polar Opposites
Love Comes to the Castle
Revolution at Barncastle Inn
Short and Sweet: 13 Sweet, Romantic Stories

Mystery and Romantic Suspense:

True Blue Mysteries:
  Blue Plate Special
  Ice Cold Blue
  Persian Blue Puzzle
  Scream Blue Murder
  True Blue Christmas
Skirmish Cove Mysteries:
  Cliffhanger
  The Plot Thickens
  Backstory
The Maine Justice series:
  The Priority Unit
  Fort Point

Found Art
Heartbreaker Hero
The House Next Door
The Labor Day Challenge
Ransom of the Heart
The Saboteur
The Frasier Island Series:
  Frasier Island
  Finding Marie
  Inside Story
Breaking News
Just Cause
You Shouldn't Have
Hearts in the Crosshairs
What a Picture's Worth
The Mainely Mysteries Series (coauthored by Susan's daughter, Megan Elaine Davis):
  Homicide at Blue Heron Lake
  Treasure at Blue Heron Lake
  Impostors at Blue Heron Lake
Tearoom Mysteries (from Guideposts, books written by several authors):
  Tearoom for Two
  Trouble Brewing
  Steeped in Secrets
  Beneath the Surface
  Tea and Promises
  Tea Leaves and Legacies

Also from Guideposts, selected books by Susan appear in the Patchwork Mysteries, Mysteries of Mary's Bookshop, Miracles of Marble Cove, Secrets of the Blue Hill Library, and Mysteries of Silver Peak series.

Historical novels:

1880s Christmas Mystery Series:
   The Spinsters Next Door
   The Gunslinger Next Door
Homeward Trails Series:
   The Rancher's Legacy
   The Corporal's Codebook
   The Sister's Search
The Outlaw Takes a Bride (western)
Counterfeit Captive
Almost Arizona
River Rest (set in 1918)
The Crimson Cipher (set in 1915)
Mrs. Mayberry Meets Her Match
Hearts of Oak Series (Co-authored with Susan's son James S. Davis, set in the 1850s):
   The Seafaring Women of the Vera B.
   The Scottish Lass
The Ladies' Shooting Club Series (westerns):
   The Sheriff's Surrender
   The Gunsmith's Gallantry
   The Blacksmith's Bravery
Captive Trail (western)
Cowgirl Trail (western)
Hearts in Pursuit (western novella)
Christmas Next Door
Echo Canyon
The Prairie Dreams series (set in the 1850s):
   The Lady's Maid
   Lady Anne's Quest
   A Lady in the Making
Maine Brides series (set in 1720, 1820, and 1895):
   The Prisoner's Wife
   The Castaway's Bride

The Lumberjack's Lady
Seven Brides for Seven Texans
Seven Brides for Seven Texas Rangers
White Mountain Brides series (set in the 1690's in New Hampshire)
Wyoming Brides series (set in 1850s):
  Protecting Amy
  The Oregon Escort
  Wyoming Hoofbeats
The Island Bride (set in the 1850s)

And many more. **See all of her books** at
https://susanpagedavis.com.

Sign up for Susan's occasional newsletter and receive a free short story at
https://madmimi.com/signups/118177/join